Stan Rogers

Northwest Passage

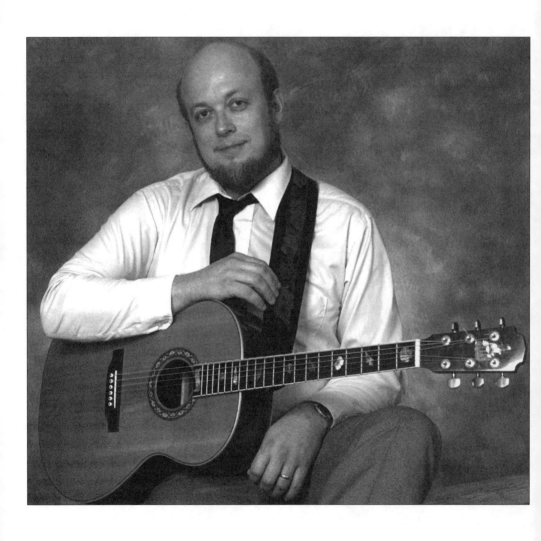

Stan **R**ogers

Northwest Passage

Chris Gudgeon

Foreword by Sylvia Tyson

F O X
MUSIC
BOOKS

Lyrics by Stan Rogers are quoted by permission of Ariel Rogers and Fogarty's Cove Music. All rights reserved.

Lyrics to *Garnet's Home-Made Beer* quoted by permission of Ian Robb.

The publisher acknowledges the support of the Department of Canadian Heritage, Book Publishing Industry Development Program.

A previous edition of this book was released by Penguin Books Canada Ltd in 1993 as *An Unfinished Conversation: The Life and Music of Stan Rogers*. This special commemorative edition has been substantially updated, expanded, and annotated.

ISBN 1-894997-01-8

Photographs courtesy of Ariel Rogers and David Woodhead.
Edited by Bob Hilderley.
Design by Gordon Robertson.
Typeset by Laura Brady.

Printed and bound in Canada.

Published by Fox Music Books, PO Box 1061,
Kingston, Ontario K7L 4Y5 Canada.

Contents

Song Lyrics (Released and Unreleased)

Writings (Published and Unpublished)

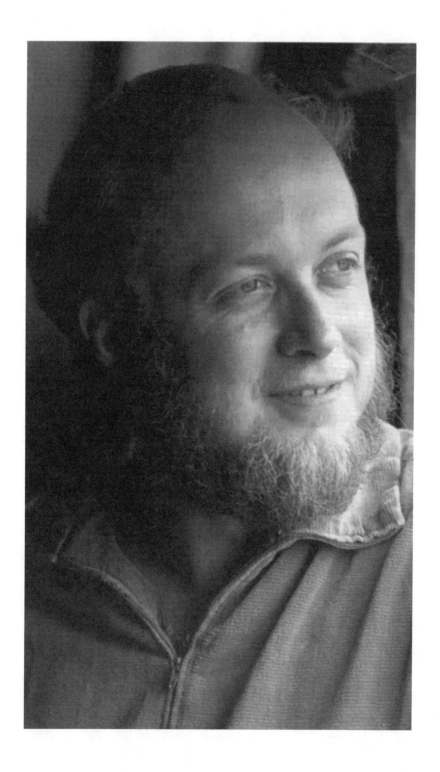

Foreword

Songwriting is a solitary art.

Once songwriters absorb their early influences, a funny thing often happens: their listening becomes more academic, and they tend to stop looking outside themselves for long periods of time in order to get about the business of writing. This can lead to stagnation, but I have found that whenever I reach this point of introversion, something happens to push me right back into the middle of things — to make me start listening again.

One of these points came in 1974 when I was approached by Paul Mills to host a weekly CBC Radio show called *Touch the Earth*. Initially the concept was to do a folk music show, but since my own definition of folk is a rather narrow one, I suggested that we expand the concept and play live and recorded traditional and roots music, along with those contemporary artists whose roots were apparent in their music — a real mouthful, but it turned out to be a fairly sound policy.

Of course, one of the first performers we featured was Stan Rogers. Stan and Paul were pals from way back, but at the time I hadn't even heard of him. Not that this was particularly surprising: I hadn't heard of half of the songwriters we had on the show that first year. Five and a half years later, I knew them all.

I took an immediate liking to Stan's music. He had a great bass-baritone voice and an imposing presence. Stan's songs were always interesting; a bit over-traditional for my tastes, but very good nonetheless. That was Stan-the-performer.

My first meeting with Stan-the-person was at a party at Paul's home. Stan had made a fairly pompous speech about the integrity of the artist, and how if you were good enough — even if you only ever sang songs on your own back porch — you would inevitably be discovered and appreciated. I immediately saw red; there was no way I was going to let him get away with that kind of naïve pronouncement. So I went for the jugular. I was of a generation of songwriters even earlier than Joni Mitchell and Neil Young, and as an artist who had struggled to establish myself in the United States in order to survive, I did not take kindly to Stan's suggestions that one could write only Canadian songs for a Canadian audience, now that there finally *was* one.

This pretty well summed up our relationship for the next few years. We didn't have the same friends or work in the same places, so we didn't actually see each other that often. Needless to say, Stan's views changed as his audience broadened and he himself achieved success south of the border. But he never compromised his music. And I must have mellowed a bit myself, because by the end of the now famous Alberta bus tour of 1980, Stan and I were friends.

When I heard the news of Stan's death, I was stunned; I simply did not believe it. With some people, it's not exactly that you expect them to die, but that you are somehow not surprised — maybe it's something in the aura or the lifestyle. Stan should not have died in that accident. It just wasn't his time. As good as he was, he was getting better still. I realized that what I felt was terrible anger. The grief came later.

In the aftermath of the fire that claimed Stan's life, I was asked to give a deposition to the insurance company. Giving my deposition to the two southern airline lawyers — dark-suited, bow-tied, sus-pendered — is not an experience I'd care to repeat. Their ques-tions were pushing me to sum up a creative life in dollars and cents. I knew it was important to his family, but I resented the hell out of the approach.

"How successful would you say Stan Rogers was?"

(As compared to whom, I wondered?)

"We have a poster here of one of his last shows that puts him last on the bill," they say.

("I think that you will finds the names are listed alphabeti-cally," I reply.)

"Would he ever become as successful as, say, the Beatles?"

("Stan was not that kind of performer," I answer. "He would have had the kind of long, solid career of, say, Roger Wittaker or Nana Mouskouri, but enhanced by the strength of his songwrit-ing.")

"Did he ever talk to you about how much he was earning?"

(I've finally had enough. "No, no, you don't understand. Canadians don't talk about money, especially when they're doing well. They think it's in bad taste.")

The essence of Stan's life, with all its contradictions, is captured in this book. And in the end, it's the contradictions that make Stan Rogers so fascinating to so many people. You can see it in the attitude towards women. Stan Rogers took great delight in his own particular brand of male chauvinism, and yet the two women in his life whom I knew — his mother and his wife — are extraordinarily strong. His persona was tough, but his songs could be tender and poetic.

Those of you who knew Stan will discover in these pages an abundance of memories to rejoice in. Those of you who never had the pleasure during his too-brief life will meet him now, warts and all: Stan-the-performer and Stan-the-man.

— *Sylvia Tyson*

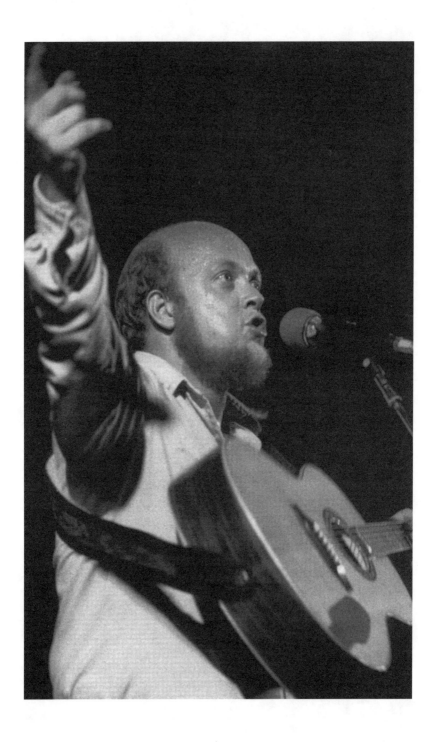

Introducing

Stan **R**ogers...

I had a dream last night. A giant, bald-headed man danced across a sawdusty barroom floor. He wore a denim work shirt, with yellow Texas roses embroidered on the front and back. His budding gut was hogtied in his jeans by a leather belt, the buckle — a silver bull's skull with ruby eyes. The man rested his hands on his hips, like a champion log roller, and performed a kind of decelerated step dance in perfect time with two dozen otherwise unlikely hoofers. It was a Texas Line Dance.

The man was Stan Rogers.

In reality, Rogers never had to suffer the indignity of doing the Achy Breaky. He died over 20 years ago in an airplane fire. A tireless performer, Rogers was en route from a special Canada Celebration in Texas to his home in Dundas, Ontario. The plane's emergency landing in Cincinnati was the top story on every television news show for days to follow — the dramatic footage made sure of that — and for a little while, Stan Rogers was a celebrity. He certainly deserved attention. Although only 33, Rogers had earned an international reputation for his songwriting and performing genius — Pete Seeger himself hailed Rogers as one of the best songwriters of the age. But outside folk circles, and pockets of popularity in Alberta, the Maritimes, and America's eastern seaboard, most people had never heard of him.

Until the fire, that is. In death, Rogers found the fame that eluded him in life. He was nominated for a Juno award by the Canadian Academy of Recording Arts and Sciences — a move that appalled some of Stan's friends. The Canadian music establishment had ignored Stan before; the nomination seemed a little late, if not downright cynical. In any case, Rogers didn't win. The Juno for Best Male Vocalist of 1984 went to Bryan Adams. Rogers did win the Diplome d'Honneur, though. This little-known award was in fact the highest arts honor in the land — until the Governor General's various arts awards supplanted it — presented annually to a Canadian who "made a sustained contribution to the cultural life of the country." It's one award, believe or not, Bryan Adams has never won.

Stan Rogers, Maritime Folksinger. To many it was as simple as that. Stan, the hearty, jovial seafarer who hailed from some fishing community on Nova Scotia's eastern shore, was an evocative symbol. To fans around the world, he embodied the popular image of Canada: vast and weathered, a wilderness tempered with a touch of British civility, a country of sensible, hard-working, working class people with middle-class sensibilities.

But behind the straightforward public image — his friends called this image "Maritime Stan" — was a complex man. He wasn't even from the Maritimes. His parents both came from Nova Scotia, but Stan was a Hamilton boy, born and raised in Ontario. Stan spent his career chronicling the struggles of the working class, making their simple struggles seem heroic, but he never joined their ranks. Stan could be difficult. Thoughtful and compassionate in song, in life he could be brash, loud, stubborn, and outspoken. He was confident, egotistical, brilliant, and original; he was at times a braggart, brash, insensitive, intolerant, ill-tempered. His everyday relationships were complicated and intense, which may explain why he thrived on the clearly defined relationship between artist and audience.

Stan Rogers' status as a 'media event' did not last. He did not become a household name, let alone a music celebrity. I'm not saying his music didn't sell; but his family-run record business, Fogarty's Cove Music, has sold upwards to a million copies of his various albums, tapes, and CDs. Meanwhile, songs like *The Mary Ellen Carter, Barrett's Privateers*, and *Northwest Passage* are pub-band and folk-fest staples throughout the English-speaking world. No one who's ever joined in on the hypnotic chorus of *Barrett's Privateers* can ever forget it.

> God damn them all!
> I was told we'd cruise the seas for American gold
> We'd fire no guns, shed no tears
> Now I'm a broken man on a Halifax pier
> The last of Barrett's Privateers

While few people may have heard his name, Stan Rogers' songs are instantly recognizable. "He wrote that?" friends typically ask when I play *Barrett's Privateers* or *Northwest Passage* for them. "I thought that song was a hundred years old!"

So, what does all this have to do with my dream? Maybe nothing. But Rogers always had a way of imposing himself on people; maybe he decided to impose himself on me. Maybe he's trying to tell me something, tell me that he's ready — he's tired of waiting in the wings. Maybe this time, his time has come. I only know that my dream ended when Stan uttered a single phrase.

"Yippee-ky-yi-a!"

Stan Rogers, singing cowboy? Right up there with Roy and Kenny?

My dream may not be as crazy as it sounds. Although Stan called himself a "folksinger" — and sometimes made fun of country and western music from the stage — he had a strong country edge. It's something Canadian musical artists can't seem to avoid. Murray McLauchlan has that edge. So do Joni Mitchell and Gordon Lightfoot. And what about Blue Rodeo? Neil Young? That black-suited bard Leonard Cohen, of all people, started out in a band called The Buckskin Boys.

In Rogers' case, the country influences run deep. Just listen to a song like *Front Runner* or *Night Guard*. *Make And Break Harbour* is about the decline of the East Coast fishing industry, but with its country waltz rhythms (Stan always favored that rolling 3/4s time when writing songs about the sea), it's just another somebody-done-somebody-wrong song.

> In make and break harbour
> The boats are so few
> Too many are pulled up and rotten
> Most houses stand empty
> Old nets hung to dry
> Are blown away, lost, and forgotten . . .

Stan Rogers liked to say that he grew up on a diet of Mozart and Hank Williams. When he was a kid in a rural area outside of Hamilton, he listened to classical music, largely at his mother's insistence, and to country and western, the music his father and uncles preferred. As an adult, Stan's music was a curious — and unprecedented — hybrid, blending the drama and scope of classical music with the melodrama and raw emotion of C&W. It creates a wondrous tension. Listening to a Stan Rogers album, you wouldn't be surprised if he all of a sudden began yodeling Beethoven's Fifth Symphony.

In his style and delivery, the folksinger Stan Rogers was a lot closer to country than classical — and in a lot of ways, he was closer to contemporary country music than pure folk. What he hated, though, was the trappings of country music. A boy from Southern Ontario has no business dressing up in cowboy duds and singing through his nose like he just rolled out of the Grand Ole Opry. There's a determined nationalism at work here. Stan was fiercely protective of Canadian culture, and he rightly perceived of country music as a Romantic art, harkening back to a mythical America Golden Age. Rogers was instinctively a Romantic artist, but if he was going to revel in a Golden Age, it should be at least one of his own.

So Rogers turned to the traditional music of Canada's Anglo-Celtic settlers for his inspiration and became, almost by default, a "folk" artist (the various terms become meaningless after a point anyway: what we call "country" was originally defined as "folk" music). What Rogers did was take a popular American music form and reinvent it in a Canadian context: the themes and characters and musical antecedents are from one country, the musical sense, from another. This is perhaps his greatest, and most overlooked, achievement. He virtually created a new musical genre — I call it Can Trad, after its Anglo model, Brit Trad — that laid the foundation for a generation of Canadian recording artists: The Rankin Family, Great Big Sea, Loreena McKennitt, Crash Test Dummies, Spirit of the West, and on and on and on. Don't get me wrong. I'm not saying that Stan started the whole East Coast music thing: other artists having been playing traditional fiddle tunes and reels and laments for generations. What Stan did was to take this music and make it consciously Canadian.

Despite his importance as an artist, or perhaps because of it, Rogers has yet to achieve widespread fame. Today, his music has a curious bookend appeal. At one end is the rural and working class audience, who supported Rogers from the start. At the other is the educated, urban, 40-something crowd, who discovered Rogers only after his death. Guys like me, for example. What's missing — and what keeps Stan from being a truly popular artist — is the middle class. Stan Rogers is not the opiate of the masses. Part of the problem is exposure. You never hear a Stan Rogers' song on the radio, outside of the Maritimes or CBC. But I suspect a much bigger problem is Stan himself. In almost everything he did, Rogers defied the conventional collective self-concept of Canadians. Now, that's a problem.

Stan Rogers' death was a triumph of irony. It was ironic that he died just on the verge of wider success. It's ironic that he died in a plane fire, because he hated to fly; he only did it on this occasion because he was pressed . . . for time. It's ironic that Stan was even on the ill-fated Flight 797; his two band mates, including brother Garnet, changed their travel plans on the spur of the moment and took earlier flights. It's ironic that in death Stan finally found — well. You get the picture.

But what I call irony, Stan might have called something else. Fate? Destiny? Poor planning? You see, Stan Rogers the artist lacked a well-developed sense of irony. Like many artists of his stature, he was aware of his own importance and, despite his insecurities, accepted it wholeheartedly. Writer Rick Salutin has called Rogers a "passionist," to distinguish Rogers from that particularly Canadian brand of artist, the "ironist." Ironists set themselves apart from their subject, observing at a distance (insert name here of any wry CBC commentator). But Stan never stood apart from the people and places he wrote about. Ask anyone: Stan Rogers was involved.

In fact, his level of involvement is legendary. The folk music world is full of Stan Rogers' stories, most of them concerning his quick temper. He had a hard time with audiences. Always the egalitarian, he was never quite able to separate himself from the people who came to see him play. Rogers was a big hambone who loved to be the center of attention. But he just couldn't check his passions at the door. He hated hecklers and, even more, people who wouldn't shut up when he was playing. It was just plain bad manners — to Rogers' way of thinking. He got into more than one shouting match with noisy patrons, and, in one famous incident at Rocky Mountain House, hurled his mike stand javelin-like at some guy who pushed his patience too far.

The last studio album Stan Rogers recorded was also his most passionate musical statement. FROM FRESH WATER was recorded a few months before his death, and not released until a few months after. It was a homecoming for Rogers, artistically. After four albums about other parts of the country, mostly the Maritimes, with a good dose of the North and Alberta, Stan turned to his home province for inspiration. All of the songs are set in the Great Lakes region of Ontario and, if you'll excuse one more irony, all of them were about death and failure. The song *Flying* repeats the chilling line: "Going up flying, going home dying."

Stan Rogers' decision to write about Ontario was a deliberate attempt to gain popularity in that huge market. He was sick-and-tired of standing on the verge of success, and knew that if he could break in Ontario, the rest of the country would follow suit. Success and struggle were foremost in Stan's mind when he recorded FROM FRESH WATER, as the song *MacDonnell On The Heights* shows. It's about an actual soldier, John MacDonnell, who died along with General Brock trying to take back Queenston Heights from the Americans in the War of 1812. But Rogers was also consciously writing about himself, only persuaded at the eleventh hour by his wife to change the narrative point of view of the song from "I" to "you." In its original version, the song went a little bit like this.

> . . . I know what it is to scale the Heights
> and fall just short of fame
> And have not one in ten thousand know my name . . .

But I still wonder. What about my strange dream? What meaning, if any, does it hold?

There's the obvious. Stan hasn't changed, but the music business has. Now there's a market called Adult Contemporary that didn't exist in Stan's day. Record companies have discovered that, among other things, adults like to buy music. What adults don't buy, though, is a lot of noise. They like pleasant melodies, thoughtful lyrics, accessible arrangements. In other words, Stan Rogers.

Then there is the whole country thing. Having barely survived the rootless, soulless 1980s, the middle class of the 1990s turned to country music in a big way. Two country music specialty channels took to the air in Canada alone. Of course, it's sanitized, video-friendly country music (can you say "Shania," "Garth," or "Faith"), with a dance orientation, which kind of makes it the disco music of our age (for middle-aged heterosexuals). But it's still country, and that's pretty close to Stan Rogers' folk music. Imagine how Stan would fare in this market if he were he alive today. Now that *would* be something — Stan Rogers, King of the Texas Line Dancers.

"Oh, the year was 1718 . . ."
(step two three kick)
"How I wish I was in Sherbrooke now . . ."
(step two step and turn)

But maybe there's another side to my dream. A darker side. A passionate side. A Stan Rogers' side. As trade barriers fall and culture is thrown on the table for the examination of bureaucrats and emissaries and undersecretaries and drawling Members of Parliament and Congressmen — maybe my dream-world Stan isn't learning the Achy Breaky?

No. Maybe he's not learning it at all. Maybe he's taking it over, making it is own? Maybe he's reinventing it for us, a little bit country, a little bit Celtic, and little bit Toronto downtown. That'd be like Stan. Not quite happy with the way things are, not quite happy even with the way things were, building something new for Canadians to call their own. He took the old-fangled ballad form and raised it to unparalleled heights in this century, in the process making Canadian history seem exciting. The thing is, Stan Rogers might just be the greatest songwriter Canada has ever produced. He is certainly one of the most influential folk musicians of the past 20 years. He changed the way all of us — not just folk music fans — appreciate traditional music. While other artists blasted their way into the collective unconscious, Stan quietly slipped in through the back door.

Yippee-ky-yi-eh.

During the past few years, quietly, almost unnoticed, Stan Rogers has moved from being a forgotten folk hero — a modern day MacDonnell, lost on the fields of Canadian culture — to something approaching a national icon. True, while not one in ten thousand know his name, Stan's fan base is growing.

The first version of this book became a bestseller in 1993, reaching number three on the national lists. Later that year, the great HOME IN HALIFAX concert recording saw strong sales and received Stan's second posthumous Juno Award nomination — this one for Best Roots and Traditional Album. Up for the same award was brother Garnet, whose album AT A HIGH WINDOW, with its stunning title song, was also nominated. Both men came out on the short end when James Keelaghan — Stan's musical and spiritual descendant — took home the trophy for his MY SKIES album.

Stan's wife Ariel followed up in 1996 with the release of POETIC JUSTICE offering two CBC radio plays, one based on the song *Harris and the Mare* and the other Silver Donald Cameron's maritime fantasy *The Sisters*. Both plays were produced by Stan's friend and frequent collaborator Bill Howell, who now oversees the popular Mystery Project series for CBC Radio. Three years later, Fogarty's Cove Music put out FROM COFFEE HOUSE TO CONCERT HALL, a collection of rare and previously unreleased tracks. Fifteen of the songs were Rogers' originals. A number of them — like *Day by Day, Your Laker's Back in Town*, and, in particular, *The Puddler's Tale* rank among his best work.

Other artists got into the act as well. While Stan's songs started turning up on a wide range of albums by others, his songs received star treatment on STAN ROGERS: AN EAST COAST TRIBUTE. Members of the Rankin family, Rawlins Cross, the Irish Descendants, and a range of other Maritime performers gave their take on classics like *The Mary Ellen Carter, Lock-keeper,* and *Northwest Passage*. Recorded in Stan's favorite venue, the Rebecca Cohn Theatre at Dalhousie University, the album was taken from a concert originally recorded for a CBC Halifax TV special.

In the late 1990s, the music fans in Stan's spiritual home Canso, Nova Scotia, began running the Stan Rogers Folk Festival, an annual tribute (usually held the first weekend of July) that has quickly grown into one of the top summer music festivals in the country, attracting artists and fans from around the world. In 1999, Stan's stock reached new heights as recently appointed Governor General Adrienne Clarkson borrowed his oft-quoted line from *Northwest Passage* about "tracing one warm line, through a land so wide and savage" for her first official public speech.

Then in 2003, an online petition was directed at the Canadian Academy of Recordings Arts and Sciences to induct Stan Rogers into the Canadian Music Hall of Fame. Sponsored by Vancouver cultural magazine *Geist*, it was supported by a who's who of Canadian musical talent, including Colin James, Barney Bentall, Great Big Sea, Bill Henderson and Chilliwack, Shari Ulrich, Sylvia Tyson, Prairie Oyster, Spirit of the West, and Bill Wallace of The Guess Who. The campaign became front-page news and garnered its goal of 10,000 signatures in less than four weeks. Even the politicians got into the act. Sackville-Musquodoboit Valley-Eastern Shore MP Peter Stoffer stood up in parliament and commented, "It is hard to imagine how Rogers' enormous contribution to the music and mythology of the country have been overlooked for 20 years." Time will tell if the campaign is a success, but one day I'm sure we will see Stan Rogers become a member of the Canadian Music Hall of Fame, and take his place beside such artists as Joni Mitchell, Neil Young, Leonard Cohen, Gordon Lightfoot, and Ian and Sylvia Tyson.

Stan Rogers' impact is now clearly understood. He popularized traditional Celtic music, paving the way for the Celtic renaissance in the 1990s. He was a music industry pioneer, an independent artist who contributed to the development of Canada's thriving indie music scene. His talents and presence personified an entire country and lifted the abstract notion of "Canadian culture" to the highest levels of art.

But Stan Rogers' greatest impact has been as a songwriter. Dozens of artists around the world have now recorded his music. Songs like *Barrett's Privateers, The Mary Ellen Carter,* and *Northwest Passage* are modern folk classics.

Stan Rogers packed a lot of living into his 33 years; it's only fair that this book strive to be as spirited and entertaining as the man himself. But there are a couple things to know right from the start. First. This book is a collection of stories. They might be true stories or they might be made up. It's hard to know. Maybe it doesn't matter much anyway. Stan was a man who loved to tell stories. Tall and short. The ones included here have been told to me by people who knew Stan — neighbors, friends, family, fellow folk musicians, fans, and blood enemies. Second. This book offers a generous sample of Stan's lyrics, some of them previously unreleased and unpublished. Some have stories to go with them. Third. For the first time, Stan's talents as a playwright are presented in the reprinting of his radio play *The Greenway Curse*. The potential was there for so much more.

Finally. Stan Rogers loved to argue. To him, it was better than drinking coffee. That's what got him going. That's how he related to people, how he connected. Those who never argued with Stan could not count themselves among his friends. He loved to argue and he loved the people with whom he argued.

That's why Stan's sudden death in a fire on board Air Canada Flight 797 stung so many. He was a young man — and no one expects a young man to die. Besides, he left too many people in mid-argument. Those who knew him and loved him were still mulling over the things-they-should-have-said-the-last-time and the things-they're-going-to-say-the-next-time. They all knew that Stan never really finished a conversation; he just picked up where he left off.

> An unfinished conversation
> In a picture of the past
> Like the one that I just found of you
> Out of the many that I had
> I remember I saw you laughing

With my camera close at my hand
We were minutes from a quarrel
And forever from understanding . . .
— *An Unfinished Conversation (It All Fades Away)*

This is where Stan left off. There are lots of good stories here, and, I hope, an argument or two. I don't think Stan Rogers would have wanted it any other way.

And so, without further ado:

Ladies and gentlemen, Stan Rogers . . .

One Hour of **H**ome

But that anchor chain's a fetter
And with it you are tethered to the foam,
And I wouldn't trade your life for one hour of home.

— Lock-keeper

Sunday, 29 May 1983. Stan Rogers and his band left the stage without a word. When a show went poorly, there was nothing to say. In part, it was their own fault: the band had drunk too much before they went on. In part, it was the sound system. The feedback on stage was incredible, and at times they could barely hear themselves. But there was something strange in the air. The instruments picked up on it: the guitar, the bass, the fiddle kept falling out of tune, as weary as the men who played them. When the Kerrville Folk Festival workers saw him coming, they made themselves scarce. It was almost three o'clock in the morning and the last thing they needed was an earful of Stan Rogers.

After one month on the road, Kerrville was Stan's last show. He'd been as far afield as Bermuda, then made his way across North America down to Texas. Normally Stan and his band traveled in an old Chevy van. None of them liked to fly, and, besides, they could carry more gear in the truck. But, on this leg of the tour, there wasn't a lot of time. Within 10 days, they had hit Calgary, Vancouver, Victoria, Seattle, San Francisco, and finally Los Angeles, where they played four sold-out shows at McCabe's folk club.

They had taken the plane from Los Angeles that morning and were picked up by a festival volunteer in San Antonio, three hours northeast of Kerrville. Kerrville wasn't the best-paying gig but it was worth the effort. Kerrville had prestige; it was a songwriter's festival that had launched the careers of some of the best musicians in Texas. The band members were bone tired when they arrived at Kerrville. They were scheduled to go on at 10 o'clock, but things just dragged on. The boys started with just one beer at 10:00 to loosen up, aware that they might be called to the stage at any moment. One beer led to another, and they didn't hit the stage until after one o'clock in the morning.

In folk circles, it was called Stan Rogers' Big Band. They didn't just take the stage; they took it over. At six-foot-four and 235 pounds, Stan was the smallest of the bunch. Garnet Rogers — Stan's accompanist, onstage foil, and younger brother — and bass player Jim Morison completed the lineup. They were three superb musicians with a presence unlike anything folk fans had seen before. The band marched onto the stage that night and launched into the *a cappella* ballad *Northwest Passage* and something clicked.

> Ah, for just one time, I would take the Northwest Passage
> To find the hand of Franklin reaching for the Beaufort Sea
> Tracing one warm line through a land so wide and savage
> And make a Northwest Passage to the sea

Al Simmons watched Stan's show from backstage. Al was a comedian and musician from Winnipeg, who, along with Stan and singer Connie Kaldor, made up the Canadian contingent at the festival. Al had met Stan before, but this was the first time he'd seen Stan in concert.

"Stan later said it was the worst show he'd done in years," Al remembers. "But I was absolutely blown away, and they had the audience absolutely hypnotized. I'd never seen anything like it before. When he sang and when he performed, the power coming off the stage was incredible."

Stan Rogers was the kind of man who stood out in a crowd, even in a crowd like this, full of long, tall Texans. He was a giant man, already bald at 33, with a thick beard and a slight moustache. He had a vaguely scholarly look, a little like a half-crazed history professor. But it wasn't just his physical attributes that caught people's attention. Stan had presence, energy. Musicians called him the "Mount St. Helens of folk music," poking fun at the way steam rose off Stan's bald head when he performed, but also a backhanded tribute to a man who was both explosive and powerful.

Stan Rogers was a man of vision, and his kind were in short supply in the early 1980s. The Canadian economy had been declining steadily as bankruptcies, unemployment, and interest rates all reached record highs, while the political climate was unstable. In barely five years, Canada would have four different prime ministers. Pierre Trudeau — who, 12 years earlier, had embodied a new sense of Canadian identity — now played out his last days as a transitional figure, and an unattractive one at that. It was the era of the "patriated constitution" and "six-and-five restraint." To many, Trudeau seemed conceited, sour, gaunt. This was what Canada had become.

Maybe that's why Stan Rogers stood out. At a time when every Canadian was looking for answers, Stan seemed sure of himself and confident about his future. He'd built an international reputation in folk music circles, counting among his many fans such legends as Tom Paxton, Pete Seeger, Sylvia Tyson, and Peter Yarrow of Peter, Paul and Mary fame, who once called Stan "the best young songwriter alive today." This recognition meant that, for the first time in his life, Stan had some financial stability. He commanded top dollar in many concert halls throughout North America, and the sales of his four independently released records were building steadily. In 1981, he sold fewer than 13,000 albums. The following year, he sold more than 16,000, and only halfway through 1983 Stan had surpassed the previous year's total. Not bad for a record company that operated out of his mother's dining room.

Still, Stan was struggling for recognition in his homeland. Canadians are notoriously fickle, always the last to acknowledge homegrown talent. Talent, especially an obvious talent like Stan's, is considered somehow impolite. To become a success in Canada, Stan often joked, you have two choices: you can either move to the States or you can die.

At the end of the set, the Kerrville crowd demanded an encore. Stan obliged with *The Mary Ellen Carter*, his most inspirational song. The story was simple: some sailors salvage a sunken boat. The song paid tribute to those who go against the grain and still find success — people just like Stan Rogers. And as the band rolled into the final chorus, the audience was on its feet, singing along.

> Rise again, rise again — though your heart it be broken
> And life about to end
> No matter what you've lost, be it a home, a love, a friend
> Like the *Mary Ellen Carter*, rise again

As the house lights went on, there was a wave of applause and a disappointed buzz as the audience realized the show they hoped would never end was now over. That was the thing about audiences: the more Stan gave them, the more they wanted.

White **S**quall

But I told that kid a hundred times "Don't take the Lakes
    for granted.
They go from calm to a hundred knots so fast they seem
    enchanted."
But tonight some red-eyed Wiarton girl lies staring at
    the wall,
And her lover's gone into a white squall.

— *White Squall*

Stan Rogers was out of breath as he took his seat on Air Canada
Flight 797. He'd just made his connecting flight and had run from
one end of the Dallas airport to the other. Stan was on his way
home from Kerrville to Dundas, a small town at the western edge
of Hamilton, Ontario. One night's rest at home, then another
show the next day at the Fiddler's Green Folk Club in Toronto.
Stan was cursing Air Canada for the benefit of anyone who'd listen. He'd never been a fan of the national airline, which seemed to
make a habit of crushing his guitars. A *Toronto Sun* story from 21
October 1980 tells of how Stan once made the mistake of sticking
his head into the handling area to see what actually happened to

his precious cargo. "He got to watch in horror as the guitar case went cart-wheeling end-over-end down a ramp past a bemused airline baggage employee," the *Sun* reporter wrote. "Rogers let out a loud shout and was immediately apprehended by the local airport Mountie." In any case, Stan was in a cantankerous mood as he took his seat, suffering from the effects of too much travel and too little sleep.

It was a sultry, calm evening in Dallas, more summer than spring. As the pilot warmed up the engine on the runway, some of the passengers skimmed through the Canadian papers for news of home. There was a lot of speculation about the upcoming Progressive Conservative leadership convention. The smart money was on incumbent Joe Clark, although Newfoundland's John Crosbie was expected to make a good showing. Few pundits gave a relative unknown from Quebec, Brian Mulroney, much of a chance.

At 4:25 central daylight time, Flight 797 took off with 41 passengers — less than half capacity — and five crew. Its final destination was Montreal, with a brief stop in Toronto. By seven o'clock that evening, halfway through the five-hour flight to Toronto, many of the passengers were drifting off to sleep. Senior Flight Attendant Sergio Bennetti had just brought the captain dinner when a passenger reported smoke coming from one of the washrooms. Bennetti's first thought was that someone had thrown a cigarette into the trash bin. Since the bins are mounted in fire-resistant casing, this kind of problem would be easy to contain. But when Bennetti opened the washroom door, he didn't see any flames. Instead, black smoke curled out of the seams of the back wall panel above the sink. He flooded the bathroom with foam from the fire extinguisher, closed the door and returned to the cockpit.

No one on board knew the danger they were in. An electrical fire had been burning for 15 minutes before the first signs of smoke were detected. The flames had already melted the wires on the flush pump, causing the breakers to trip, and by the time the first smoke was detected, the fire had spread through the ceiling.

Once he was aware that there was a problem, Captain Donald Cameron quickly decided what to do. At exactly 7:08, he radioed to anyone who could hear.

"Mayday," he said. "Mayday! Mayday! . . . We're going down. We have a fire."

In the cabin, the flight attendants were moving the passengers forward, away from the smoke. Stan Rogers moved forward with the rest of them. As he passed the flight attendant, she handed him a wet towel to put over his nose and mouth — a makeshift mask to filter the smoke and fumes. The emergency descent to the Cincinnati airport lasted eight minutes. By the time the plane broke through the clouds, chunks of plastic were falling on the passengers as the ceiling melted away. One of the survivors told me that the smoke was so thick he couldn't see his hand in front of his face. And yet there was reportedly no panic; the passengers quietly prepared for what was bound to be a rough landing.

By the time Cameron made his final approach, the cockpit was so full of smoke he had to crouch to see the runway. As soon as the jet touched down, he slammed on the brakes. Like everything else, the antiskid system was out; the four main tires blew on landing. Cameron stuck his head out the window and gasped for air. His first officer Claude Ouimet tried to exit through the cabin, but was pushed back by the smoke and had to escape through the cockpit window. When he saw Cameron unconscious in his chair, Ouimet alerted a fireman who blasted the captain with water. It was enough to rouse Cameron, and he too squeezed through the cockpit window, dropping 15 feet to the tarmac.

Inside the cabin, there was no time for organized evacuation. Bennetti sent an ailing passenger down the slide, then called out to anyone who could hear, although he could barely draw enough air to speak. He waited at the doorway, until the heat became too intense.

No one on board Flight 797 saw flames during the emergency descent, but as the plane made its final approach, witnesses on the ground saw flames spew from two holes on top of the fuselage. Thirteen firefighters were at the ready. They flooded the top of the plane with foam and sprayed the ground beneath it to protect against a fuel leak. Two firefighters attempted to enter the plane from the middle emergency exit. But, just as they were about to go inside, all hell broke loose. Barely one minute after the plane had landed, the cabin exploded in a ball of fire.

The end came quickly; the worst was over in seconds. Twenty-three people died in the flames. Eighteen passengers and all five crew members survived.

———

At her home in Dundas, Ontario, Stan Rogers' wife, Ariel, watched the news in horror. There was Flight 797, flames twisting through two giant holes in the roof, while a grim reporter speculated on the number of dead. Ariel tried to get through to Air Canada's office in Toronto, but all they would do was confirm that Stan had been on the flight. They offered no further information.

Ariel was still watching the TV news at four o'clock in morning when she heard a knock at the door. She opened the door. It was a pair of plain-clothes policemen who had come to confirm what she already knew in her heart.

A Dozen **G**enerations

Well, the track of my beginnings
Has been buried 'neath the years
For a dozen generations,
We have toiled the land here.

— *Pocketful Of Gold* (unreleased)

Stan Rogers, dead at 33, an age when most artists are just establishing their careers. Suddenly the country, the world, was taking stock of his legacy. Very quickly, everyone realized that Stan's strongest characteristic was his profound sense of history. The history of the music he loved, the history of his country, the history of his family, the personal histories of people he met along the way — Stan was fascinated with it all.

Stan Rogers had a rich family history of his own. According to legend, the paterfamilias of the Rogers clan was John the Martyr, the first Protestant executed during the reign of Bloody Queen Mary in the 16th century. James Rogers, thought to be the martyr's grandson, immigrated to New England in 1635 and became a wealthy plantation owner.

A tradition of religious dissent followed the Rogers family to the New World. James's son John was a notorious religious radical who formed his own breakaway church in 1674. It was a political act, a defiance of the state-supported Congregationalist Church. Even so, with discretion, John and his followers might have continued with little trouble — religious dissent was a popular recreational activity in pre-baseball America. But true to his family name, John Rogers was conspicuous and provocative. He encouraged his congregation to defy the state, and he took great delight in disrupting Congregationalist Church services. Stan apparently came by his combative nature honestly.

Stan's Maritime connection dates back to 1760, when Rolen Rogers, old John's great-nephew, moved to Horton Township, on and around the Gaspereaux Mountain in Nova Scotia. There were practical reasons for the move: land was growing scarce in Connecticut, while Nova Scotia was largely unsettled. And the Rogerenes, as old John's followers called themselves, were becoming more disruptive and were often publicly flogged or tarred and feathered for their actions. Rolen Rogers didn't relish the role of human target; he wanted to get while the getting was good.

Stan's Nova Scotia roots were neither Scottish nor particularly Maritime, but remarkable nonetheless. His paternal grandfather and namesake was born in Stellarton, Nova Scotia, on February 26, 1889. Stanley Edward Rogers was a lumberman, who in 1934 moved to Pictou County and bought a large farm with a water mill. Stanley was a remarkable man. He served overseas in both World Wars. He was almost 50 when World War II broke out and he had to lie about his age to enlist. He was gentle and industrious, and built a prosperous business with the help of his wife Jaunita Mae — a not-too-distant cousin of Sir Charles Tupper, a Father of Confederation — and their eight children.

Stan's Uncle Prescott, Stanley and Jaunita's son, has fond memories of childhood on the Pictou farm. "We just thought of ourselves as a typical country family," he recalls. "We did the usual things. We often had a singsong around the piano on a weekend. Sometimes we sang hymns, but our music wasn't

restricted to hymns because we sang a lot of the songs popular at
the time. Mother played the piano, as did my two sisters. My oldest brother Emerson was something of a fiddle player. And if we
were going to have a little dance music, Dad would get out the
mouth organ."

Stan's mother Valerie Bushell grew up just outside of Canso,
Nova Scotia, in a place called Hazel Hill. The locals say that the
area is the most easterly point on the continent, "as close as you
can get to Ireland without getting your feet wet." Stan liked to
claim that this town might just have been the site of one of the
oldest European settlements in the New World. There was evi-
dence, Stan said, that Portuguese fishermen lived in the area
before Columbus's era.

Canso is one of the most beautiful spots on the coast. It is off
the beaten tourist track, and isn't overshadowed by manufactured
charm. Standing at the shore, looking across the Chedabucto Bay,
you can see Cape Breton rise in the distance. There's little wonder
why Stan was drawn to this place all his life.

Valerie's father arrived in Canso a few years after World War I.
Sidney Bushell worked as a telegraph operator for the Commercial Cable Company, owners of the transatlantic communication
cable that linked North America with the Old World. Sidney was
originally from Tunbridge Wells, Kent, England and had spent
some time working for the cable company in South America. He
was also something of an amateur writer who'd had several of his
poems published. One was "Yeastcake Jones," which Stan later set
to music and recorded on his 1983 album FOR THE FAMILY.

Sidney married Letitia Mary Narraway Hart soon after arriv-
ing in Canso. She was from a prominent local family of United
Empire Loyalist stock. Her mother was one of the Halifax
Smiths, well-to-do merchants who considered themselves upper
crust. Stan characterized his grandfather as a "poor telegraph
operator," but this is misleading. In an area of the country where
unemployment was always high, Sidney enjoyed steady work,
and, although there were 12 children, the family was comfortable. The Commercial Cable Company had its own clubhouse,

tennis courts (proper "whites" were the only acceptable attire), ballroom, boats on the lake — all accessible to employees only. Even the company houses were better than average. They had running water and plumbing, while the rest of the community made do with wells and outhouses.

Valerie Bushell was in her teens in 1946 when she moved from Hazel Hill to find work. She wound up in the town of Amherst on the New Brunswick border. There, she went to business school, worked in a jewelry store, and in the fall she met a young man named Nathan Allison "Al" Rogers, fresh from his stint in the Royal Canadian Air Force. They were engaged a year later, married in July 1948, and moved to Hamilton shortly thereafter to find work. On November 29, 1949, their first son was born and duly christened Stanley Allison Rogers.

Prodigy

On the ridge above Acadia's town to the valley down below
The evening falls upon the families listening to the radio
And watching the apples grow.

— *Watching The Apples Grow*

This is Stan Rogers' first memory: sitting in his grandmother's kitchen in Hazel Hill, Nova Scotia, in his hand a slice of still-warm bread lathered in peanut butter. The room is hot, filled with the loamy heat of the wood stove and the smells of the kitchen — birch wood burning, bread baking, a giant and perpetual pot of stew. Around him sit his mother and father and grandparents and various aunts and guitar-playing uncles, everyone singing and laughing. In years to come, Stan would recognize the individual songs — by Hank Williams, Jimmie Rodgers, and Nova Scotia boys Hank Snow and Wilf Carter — but for now the sounds blend together and that is enough. Other children had fairy tales: Stan had country and western.

Young Stan was by all accounts cheerful and precocious, and from the start he had an affinity to music. According to his family, he could sing almost as soon as he could talk. On visits to Hazel

Hill, Stan impressed his grandfather with his perfect pitch and uncanny ability to improvise. Stan's parents recognized and encouraged his musical talent. Valerie, in particular, had refined tastes and made sure that both her boys were exposed to the classics of music and literature. But it was those family gatherings on the East Coast that stuck out most in Stan's mind. In the liner notes for FOGARTY'S COVE, he recalls those special times. "Mom's brothers, most of them, anyway, played or sang, or both, and I guess it naturally followed that one of my earliest memories would be of my uncles sitting around my grandparent's kitchen, 'half shot', playing guitars (some of them home-built) and singing old tear-jerkers by Wilf Carter, Hank Snow, and Hank Williams, with Aunt June and Mum and all the rest joining in, in more-or-less harmony, while dad looked on, smiled, and played referee."

Stan got his first guitar when he was five. It was hand-built by Stan's Uncle Lee Bushell, one of those kitchen uncles. The boy had hounded his uncle for months until finally the guitar appeared. As an adult, Stan remembered the "depression-model" Bushell guitar fondly in the winter 1983 issue of the folk magazine *Come for to Sing*. "The frets are cut from brass welding rods," he explained, "the nut and saddle were carved from an old toothbrush, the bridge pins are brass beads, and the top, back, sides, neck, fret-board and strap pin were all hand-cut from hardwood birch. It weighs nearly twenty pounds, has a tone vaguely resembling that of a small-body Martin . . . I still play it often, keep it near me in my living room, and will never, ever part with it."

Not long after getting the guitar, Stan made another important discovery. He found that if he took his toy ukulele around to the neighbors and sang a little song, something magical happened. People gave him money — a couple of pennies, maybe, the odd nickel, and every once in a while a shiny, silver dime. This first crack at a musical career didn't last long. Stan's mom was not happy to hear that Stanley was going to the neighbors for money and his public performances came to a sudden end.

Stan did practice at home, and Garnet remembers how the two of them would sing themselves to sleep each night — Stan instructing his brother, who was six years younger, on the fine points of two-part harmony — listening to country music on a giant RCA Victor tube radio.

———————

"Pumpkinhead . . ."

The voice trailed off in the singsong refrain of a school-yard taunt. The fat kid in the duffle coat stood silent, this time determined not to let his anger show. But his eyes welled with tears. These kids were relentless. Day in, day out, they would pick on Stan. It didn't take much, just a couple words, and Stan would lose it. It's not hard to understand why the kids baited him. He was a smart kid, the kind, his mother says, who liked to use big words nobody else understood. But smart was not always a smart thing to be in a rural Ontario schoolyard in 1960. At 11, Stan was big for his age. He'd never been well-coordinated. He shied away from sports, except for mud football, and despite his size, he was strangely passive when things got rough. He wouldn't fight back. Stan did have some friends, though. Neighbor Dave Murray was one of his closest. Murray recalls that Stan was mouthy, argumentative and a first-class bullshitter even then. But he also saw another side of Stan.

"We built tunnels in the hay in the old barn behind my house," Murray recalls. "Me and Stan and a couple of other kids from the neighborhood, we'd play for days." The old barn was, of course, forbidden territory to the boys. Many of the boards were loose or rotten, and there was always the danger that the floor could collapse. It was the perfect place for an 11-year-old: it had an element of cozy peril and offered a sense of complete seclusion. "We'd smoke cigarettes in the hay bale tunnels. Can you imagine that? Here we were under 12 feet of hay, in a little compartment we'd made, maybe four feet by six feet, smoking cigarettes, lighting little fires in the hay. And we'd talk to each other, about our hopes, our dreams, our fantasies. And Stan was right there with us. He wasn't trying to show off or be the center of attention. He was just being himself and letting his true thoughts come out."

Around such friends as Dave Murray, Stan did not seem unusually musical. He would sing on Friday nights with the rest of the gang as they walked the gravel roads near Stan's home in Tapley Town. Out with the guys, Stan was best known for his volume, rather than his pitch or harmonies. They'd sing the popular songs of the day: *Lollypop*, *Wake Up Little Susie*, *Leader Of The Pack*. Those were faceless days for pop music. Rock 'n' roll, the white man's rhythm 'n' blues, had flowered in the mid-fifties, and by 1962 it was dead. Elvis was six years past his prime, and flat pop with a tempered backbeat — the music of the Johnnies and Frankies and Bobbies — ruled the radio charts. But popular music was about to change, and when it did, Stan's life changed as well.

BUSHELL BROWN BREAD

To understand the stuff that came out of Stan Rogers' mouth, it helps to know what went into it. Bushell Brown Bread, from his grandmother's recipe, was a lifelong favorite of Stan. You don't need to allow this bread time to rise. If you pan the dough right after the first kneading, it makes a delicious dense bread. It's perfect for busy households — which makes sense when you think of Mrs Nita Bushell and her 12 children.

> *Ingredients*
> 8 cups white flour
> 8 cups whole-wheat flour
> 3-4 tablespoons shortening
> 1 cup white sugar
> 4-5 tablespoons salt
> 1 cup molasses
> 2-3 cups lukewarm water
> 2 envelopes dry yeast

Directions
1. Proof yeast in 1 cup lukewarm water. Cut shortening into dry ingredients.
2. Make a well in the flour mixture. Add yeast and molasses.
3. Add water a little at a time, until dough feels pliable.
4. Pan immediately for dense bread. For lighter bread, raise until dough doubles in size. Then pan.
5. Bake slowly at 315° F for 1 hour.

Folk **B**oom

We live in fear of no one to love us
Of feeling like an empty hole
No kind heart or strengthening hand
To light the dark and secret soul.

— *Matter Of Heart*

There are probably as many definitions of folk music as there are folk fans. Historically, and to purists and academics, it means something quite specific — traditional music, played on traditional instruments, passed on from generation to generation with little variation. But today, most people use "folk" in a much more general sense to refer to popular acoustic-based music, often with an emphasis on introspective or political lyrics.

The term can be used in a positive sense to distance a favorite artist from mainstream commercial pop ("After all these years, Dylan remains essentially a folk artist . . . ") or in a negative sense ("Bob Dylan? He's just a tired old folkie . . ."). In Canada, a large body of "pure folk" music has been preserved, thanks to scholars like Kenneth Peacock, Roy MacKenzie, and Helen Creighton, who alone collected more than 4,000 folk songs in the Maritimes.

Since the 1950s, the aptly named Edith Fowke, a scholar and broadcaster, and her frequent collaborator, the singer Alan Mills, have brought traditional Canadian folk songs to millions through their books, radio work, and records.

Those who maintain the strict definition of folk music are often maligned by others within the folk community. Stan himself called them "folk nazis." But the purists have a good point. Without clear boundaries, the term becomes almost meaningless. When you get right down to it, there's little difference between what most people consider folk music and pop music in general; folk music has always been a popular and populist medium, while most of the popular music of this century was based on two folk forms, country and the blues.

This more general meaning of "folk" arose in the 1960s as a result of a revival movement known as the "folk boom." The roots of this revival go back to 1950 when the Weavers' reworking of a traditional song *Good Night Irene* hit Number One on the pop charts, stayed there for 13 weeks and sold over two million records. Led by Pete Seeger — one of folk music's most influential figures — the Weavers continued to enjoy success, charting 10 hits in two years. But in the mid–fifties, the notorious House Committee on UnAmerican Activities branded members of the band "communists," a blow to both the band — radio wouldn't touch them for years — and to folk music in general.

As the 1960s approached, most of the music on commercial radio was pretty bland, and audiences were ready for something new. Along came the Kingston Trio, who sang traditional folk songs. With their conservative haircuts and freshmen good looks, they appeared the antithesis of communist agitators. From 1960 to 1962, the Trio recorded six platinum albums and a host of Top Ten singles. The success of the Kingston Trio kicked off the so-called "folk boom." Peter, Paul and Mary had a huge hit with *If I Had A Hammer* — co-written by Pete Seeger and fellow Weaver Lee Hays — which gave voice to a growing mood of political and social discontent.

Today, people often use "folk boom" as a generic term, but it really refers to a specific period, starting from the Kingston Trio's first hit, *Tom Dooley*, in 1958 and lasting to the British Invasion in 1964. During that period, like-minded performers who sang contemporary versions of folk songs or wrote their own songs in a traditional style were a dominant commercial force in American music.

At the forefront of the folk boom was the Canadian duo of Ian and Sylvia Tyson. Sylvia — who would later play a role in Stan Rogers' career — was born in Chatham, Ontario, in 1940. In the late 1950s, she teamed up with Ian Tyson, a one-time logger and rodeo rider, but originally from Victoria, B.C.'s staid capitol. The two sang in folk clubs around Southern Ontario and eventually made their way to New York, where Albert Grossman, who managed the likes of Bob Dylan and Peter, Paul and Mary, saw the duo and signed them up. Soon, Ian and Sylvia had a contract with Vanguard Records. They recorded half a dozen albums for this company, all of them reaching Billboard's pop charts, and had a number of hit singles, including Ian's classic *Four Strong Winds* and Sylvia's *You Were On My Mind*, a Top Five single in 1965 for The We Five.

———

In 1964, Stan Rogers wasn't worried about issues of definition. For an intelligent, romantic outsider like Stan Rogers, folk music was the perfect form of expression. It offered a sense of community, folk singers encouraged their audience to "sing along" — and appealed to his sense of history. It also proved that intelligence and compassion had a place in popular music. And best of all, it was portable: all you needed was a guitar, a good strong voice, and a love of the spotlight, three things Stan could count among his assets.

More and more, music became Stan's saving grace. In his brother Garnet's words, music "took the place of a normal adolescence." It gave Stan a new role: the troubadour. When he showed up at a party with his guitar, people were happy to see him. The odd girl — Stan would probably say very odd — might even park herself beside him for the evening. In his early teens, Stan experimented with rock. He sang and played bass in several bands with names like "Predator" and "Stanley and the Living Stones." But despite his technical proficiency, Stan was not at ease with rock. He had the temperament — he liked to show off and take center stage — but he wasn't comfortable with the music. And he certainly never looked like a rock star. He tried, but with his heavy black glasses and fluffy pompadour, he wound up looking like a Cro-Magnon Buddy Holly.

By now, Stan was developing a network of musical friends. Though he remained something of an outcast at high school — Stan would later refer to his teenaged self as a "geek" — he fell in with people who shared his love of song. Stan's closest friend at that time was Bill Jurgenson, a schoolmate at Saltfleet High. Jurgenson recalls that while Stan may have flirted with rock, his real love was folk. He had an innate feel for the music. "I'd bought an album, one of those how-to-play-guitar things," Jurgenson says. "I managed to pick up a couple finger-picking styles and passed them on to Stan. He just took them and went with them. He was so damn good, and so quick to pick up this stuff."

In 1963, at the ripe old age of 14, Stan started playing at coffee houses in Hamilton. His first solo show was at a place called the Ebony Knight, run by painter Bill Powell. Stan played for two hours and his pay wasn't exactly scale: five bucks and a bottle of cheap wine, according to legend. His set included familiar folk songs of the day: a couple by Dylan, some traditional tunes, like *Black Girl*, *Tom Dooley*, and *Kum Ba Ya*, and an occasional Hank Williams country stomp. Soon, Stan was including an original song or two, although few of these early songs survive.

As Stan began to play more solo concerts, Bill Jurgenson took on the job of manager. Bill, who was a few years older than Stan, would drive Stan to gigs and keep him out of trouble. Stan had always taken his own opinion very seriously, but now there was a new dimension to contend with. At 15, Stan sprouted up by a foot: he was his full adult height and quickly learned to use his size to intimidate. His first priority was to settle a few old scores in the old neighborhood. Stan's finest moment might just have been the night he and Bill Jurgenson stopped at a bar called the Plantation House. "The waiter asked us for our I.D.," Bill recalls. "I pulled mine out, and Stan patted his pockets, then told the waiter that he forgot his wallet. The waiter was persistent. The next thing I knew, Stan stood up, pounded his fists on the table and looked down on the waiter. 'Jesus, man, what do I got to do? Bring my 15-year-old son in here?'" The ploy worked. The waiter apologized profusely and promptly brought them some beer. The two had a good laugh. Stan had meant it as a joke, but was also coming to realize that his size and forceful personality had certain advantages.

By 1967, Stan had a reputation as one of the brightest young performers on the Hamilton coffee house circuit. His chief competition came from another teenager, Nigel Russell, who specialized in bluegrass guitar. The two were aware of each other, but did not meet until they shared billing at the Wrong Side cafe in 1967. Also on the bill was a 15-year-old singer making her professional debut, Terri Olenick. A photographer from the local paper thought it would make a cute picture if the three performers pretended to play something together. Stan feigned reluctance at first, pretending to be shy. But then he joined the other two, unable to pass up an opportunity to get his picture in the paper. While the camera clicked, they improvised a song. It didn't sound half bad. As a matter of fact, it sounded damn good. And so, the Hobbits were born.

The name came from the Tolkien book, a favorite of Stan's. He had read the entire *Lord of The Rings* trilogy in a matter of days when he was 17. The name was supposed to reflect the personality of the bandmates — in Terri Olenick's words, "rolly polly, playful, funny hobbits." At the time, Stan himself looked like an overgrown hobbit. He had a thin beard that he trimmed often. And although he was already balding on top, the hair on the sides was fairly long, with an unkempt look. Because of his size, his mother made a lot of his clothes, and he designed them in a somewhat medieval fashion with lots of tunics and buckles and fringes. The Hobbits marked the first time Stan worked in a trio, the format he came to favor during his career. Stan and Nigel played guitars; Stan and Terri shared vocals. They played a typical folk repertoire, with an emphasis on songs by such Canadian songwriters as Gordon Lightfoot, Joni Mitchell, and Leonard Cohen.

When the Hobbits started playing together, Nigel was a student at Trent University in Peterborough, about 100 miles northeast of Toronto. Stan had tried McMaster University in Hamilton a year earlier, but his studies were sidetracked by more serious pursuits: girls and beer. By 1969, he moved in with Russell in a house dubbed "Little Red" in honor of The Band's Woodstock home "Big Pink." This was the most tumultuous period of Stan's life. He was unclear about his life's direction, a situation that wasn't helped by a couple of heartbreaking love affairs. Meanwhile, Nigel Russell recalls, Stan's flirtation with the music business was creating some tension in his family. His parents had supported Stan's musical interest from the start. But being practical Maritimers, they hoped that he would choose a more secure vocation than folk music.

The pressures of growing up were taking their toll. As Russell saw it, Stan was a walking contradiction: from the outside he appeared strong and confident, but, like any artist, he had his vulnerable side. "To look at him you'd think: 'Here's a tough-assed son-of-a-gun who's been down the road.' Nothing could be further from the truth. Stan was rather naive; this is at the root of his songwriting. His lack of experience freed him to go into his mind and romanticize. He made legends out of stuff that was actually mundane."

Stan seemed constantly at odds with himself. He shielded himself from the kind of rejection that he had known in the playground, but more than anything, he wanted to share himself. He wanted others to recognize his gifts and take them seriously. He would try so hard to express himself that he became nearly inarticulate. This made his music more important than ever to him. It was his saving grace, arrived at only after hours of painstaking rehearsal with attention to the very smallest detail. Performance was not a spontaneous celebration, but a well, earned victory. Nowhere was Stan's difficulty more evident than in his on-stage patter. In those unrehearsed moments between songs, when Stan had to share himself with the audience, he rarely knew where to begin and, rarer still, when to stop.

A review in a London student newspaper tells the story. After praising Stan's rich and resonant voice, the reviewer took exception: "Rogers came close to torpedoing the whole affair with his inane babbling. His between-songs chatter might well have built up the rapport he so obviously wanted if he hadn't been so blatantly self conscious." There were uncomfortable moments, true, but there was also a payoff for Stan. He lived for those moments when his singing and playing would enrapture the audience and carry them away. Near the end of his life, in a backstage monologue recorded for CBC radio, just before he took the stage for his final appearance at the Calgary folk festival, Stan explained how even after a decade in the business, he still got nervous before every show.

"I start thinking about how I'm going to look. How I'm going to get on stage, how I'm going to get off: make sure I don't trip over anything. I don't want anything to disturb that focus, the fine edge that I want when I get out in front of all those people. Too, I feel a responsibility. When folks pay a good piece of change to come to a folk festival or come to a concert, they're expecting something pretty special: they have a right for something pretty special and it's up to me to make it as special as possible."

Stan worked harder and harder at perfecting his performance skills. By the end of 1969, the Hobbits had broken up, but Stan and Nigel continued to play together. Over the next year, Stan took another stab at university, this time joining Nigel at Trent. But his loyalty to the halls of higher learning was not strong. The songs were coming easier now, and sooner or later he'd have to make up his mind. Would he follow his heart and become a professional musician or would he find a more conventional career? The problem would soon take care of itself.

RCA

Way down in the ocean, under the shining sea
The fishes' world is in commotion,
And it's because of me
They think the price of breathing
Is more than I can afford
But I'm living high and doing fine
Without visible means of support

    — *Fishes* (unreleased)

The year was 1970 and suddenly home-grown Canadian music was breaking onto the American pop charts. The "Canadian Invasion" was led by The Guess Who, a quartet from Winnipeg who had five U.S. hits that year, including the Number One two-sided single *American Woman / No Sugar Tonight*. Anne Murray also made the Top Ten with *Snowbird*, and there was a handful of one-off singles like Mashmakhan's hypnotic *As Years Go By* and the Original Caste's enduring pop parable *One Tin Soldier*. The year also saw a change in the rules that governed Canadian radio. The new rules, designed to encourage radio stations to play more Canadian songs, were simple: 33% of the songs played by a station had to fit the special guidelines defined by the MAPLe system. A record got one point for each part of the MAPLe — Music, Artist, Production and Lyrics — that was Canadian. In the early days, one out of four was all that was needed to qualify, so that any song written, performed, or produced by a Canadian was eligible. These Canadian content rules are still in effect, although these days a record needs two points to qualify.

In 1970, these Cancon rules were affecting the kinds of acts record companies signed. Virtually all Canadian record companies were American subsidiaries, which in practice meant two things: the companies weren't very committed to Canadian music, and they didn't expect to make a lot of money from it. The parent companies were reluctant to release Canadian records in the United States, and if a Canadian act met with success, they were quickly signed to the American parent company.

Barry Keane worked for RCA Records in the early 1970s. Best-known as Gordon Lightfoot's drummer, and also featured on some of Stan's early recordings, Keane says things weren't all bad. "In those days, it was easier for a Canadian artist to get a recording contract. One single was easy and cheap to produce, and the risks were lower. We'd slap a song on a record, put a name on it, and see what would happen." The catch was that in order to get a contract, artists often had to hand their publishing rights over to the record company. In other words, the artists gave away ownership of their songs. This is an important concession because every time a song gets played on the radio or performed in concert, its owner gets a residual. "From a publishing standpoint, it made more sense to sign a singer-songwriter," Keane says. "It's because of the MAPLe system. If you sang and wrote the song, that qualified you right away. Radio stations had to play your record, because it met their Cancon requirements, so even if you didn't sell any of those records, just having them played on the radio provided income."

Enter Stan Rogers. By 1970, Stan had dropped out of university for a second time (rumor has it he was kicked out for hitting a professor) and was trying his luck at teachers' college in Hamilton. As a profession, teaching was a reasonable compromise; it was acceptable to Stan's family and it satisfied Stan's own pedantic tendencies. And then there was the added benefit of summers off. Still, Stan was restless.

Faced with the prospect of a serious career, he decided to take one more kick at the musical can. Stan and Nigel Russell sent a demo tape to RCA's Toronto office. Within weeks, Stan got a phone call from the head man at RCA: he had himself a deal.

Stan recorded his first single for RCA in the fall of 1970. It was a rush job; RCA wanted to have the record out in time for the Christmas market. The B side was the traditional *Coventry Carol*, and the lead single was an original called *Here's To You, Santa Claus*. The premise was that Santa, with his share-the-wealth attitude, must be a communist. The story is told from the point-of-view of an all-American kid who decides to take the Santa problem into his own hands.

> Here's to you Santa Claus flying up so high
> And if you come 'round here tonight
> I'll blast you from the sky
> If you get by my toy radar dome
> I'll grant you I can tell.
> The land mine in the fireplace will
> Blow you straight to hell.

While Stan was happy to have a recording contract, he was uncomfortable with what the record company had in mind for him. Stan saw himself as a serious folk musician, but RCA saw him as novelty — as Stan told *Folk Life Quarterly* for its summer 1978 issue, they "wanted to make me into a kind of Ray Stevens, 'Ahab the Arab' kind of thing." This was a problem that plagued Stan his entire career; his talent was unique and defied established market labels. While Stan wasn't happy with RCA's direction, he buckled down and went to work.

———

Stan Roger's first single was recorded at RCA's famous Mutual Street Studio in Toronto during a marathon 48-hour session. The recording went smoothly, Stan taking to the studio like a seasoned pro. As a matter of fact, things went better than Stan could have imagined. As he was improvising some lyrics for the lead single, the door opened and a familiar looking man walked in. It took a moment to sink in, but all at once Stan realized who it was: his idol, Gordon Lightfoot.

Of all the recording artists who influenced Stan Rogers' musical development, none had a more profound effect than Gordon Lightfoot. Born in Orillia, Ontario, on 17 November 1938, Lightfoot was, like Rogers, a musical prodigy. When he was 20, Lightfoot went to music college in Los Angeles, acquiring the theoretical background that most of his songwriting contemporaries lacked. By the early 1960s, Lightfoot was living in Toronto and proving his versatility. He sang in the coffee houses, arranged the music for commercials, and even contributed his square dance talents to the CBC TV show Country Hoedown. He also turned his attention to songwriting. It was the height of the folk boom, and Lightfoot's songs were quickly picked up by Canadian folk artists. Ian and Sylvia were impressed with Lightfoot's work and introduced the young singer-songwriter to their manager Albert Grossman.

The year 1965 was a watershed for Lightfoot. Peter, Paul and Mary's recording of his song *For Lovin' Me* was a Top Thirty hit in the U.S., while Marty Robbins' version of *Ribbon Of Darkness* reached Number One on the country charts. Lightfoot signed a record contract with the RCA's American label and released his self-titled debut album.

For a young Canadian folk singer like Stan Rogers, it was a tremendous lift to see one of his countrymen make the big time. Stan listened to all of Lightfoot's albums over and over, and was particularly impressed with the song *Canadian Railroad Trilogy*, from the 1967 album THE WAY I FEEL. A historical ballad, it uses many elements that would later be found in Stan's best work, including a complicated musical structure and a focus on that

Canadian obsession, the link between transportation and communication.

Lightfoot nodded to Stan and took a seat in the control room. He'd been in the studio next door, doing the final mix on his album SIT DOWN YOUNG STRANGER. He was a friend of Bill Misener, Stan's producer, and had come to check out the new talent. As Nigel Russell recalls, Lightfoot cracked up listening to the words of *Here's To You, Santa Claus* and made a couple of joking suggestions of his own. After Stan's session was finished, Lightfoot invited the two young musicians to join him in his studio. It was just the four of them: Stan, Nigel, Gordon, and the engineer. For Stan, who was then only 22 years old, the day was a dream come true.

But the next day, Stan came stumbling back to reality. He showed up at his class Friday morning, still tired from two days in the studio. The instructor confronted him immediately. "I was making a record for RCA." Stan hoped the professor would be duly impressed and let the matter drop.

"Will this be a regular occurrence?" Stan shrugged his shoulders, "I hope so."

The teacher took off his glasses and offered Stan a long, penetrating look. Stan would have to make a decision, he said: "Music or teaching; you can't do both."

Stan smiled, slightly embarrassed by his own discomfort, but more than a little relieved. If only every decision in life could be this easy.

Home **B**rew

Hello London,
I just had to let you hear,
That my new friends are the best I've ever known
And I just might make this London town my home.

— *Hello London* (unreleased)

The audience sat in rapt attention. Smale's Pace Folk Club was the most popular stop on London's burgeoning folk circuit. It was a classic coffee house of the early 1970s, a hippy's idea of a home away from home. Cheap food, soup and sandwiches mostly, perhaps the occasional low level drug transaction, and cup after cup of strong coffee. That night the crowd was in for a special treat. Stan took his seat, tuned his guitar for a few moments. It was February 1972 and he'd moved to London following a couple of career setbacks. His contract with RCA was terminated after his second single flopped and his partnership with Nigel Russell ended when Russell went solo.

Once his guitar was in tune, Stan spoke to the audience. "After you've lived in Hamilton for a number of years," he commented, "you can appreciate what London is all about. It's nice to have air that you can breathe, and people who smile at you. It's also nice being able to share music with some good people. I just wrote a tune about it."

Hello London,
Had to get back to see you again.
Already I find, I leave behind
The dusty steel mill city that was mine . . .

Stan sat back in his chair, his eyes closed, the room completely silent, except for the two guitars and the sound of his voice.

At the time Stan had joined a group called Cedar Lake, a loose arrangement of musicians — at any given moment, it ranged from eight to 20 members — who got together to showcase their collective talents. They were young men, friends, compatriots — for them, the moment was everything. Cedar Lake was the kind of musical collective that only could have emerged in the early seventies. The name tells it all: it was deliberately generic, evoking an image of a pastoral Anytown, Canada. The goodwill spilled over to the audience, who were as into the music as the performers. That night Stan shared the stage with Doug McArthur, but they hadn't even rehearsed their set. That's what Cedar Lake was all about.

For one brief moment, London was the center of Canada's folk universe. Some of the finest young singer-songwriters gathered in this white-collar city, where education and finance were the main industries. Many of the names are still familiar to folk fans: Gord Lowe, David Essig, Paul Mills, David Bradstreet, Willie P. Bennett, Luke Gibson, Doug McArthur, Frank Wheeler, Jim Ogilvie, Brent Titcomb. Even Garnet Rogers caught the tail end of the London folk comet. As Paul Mills recalls, it was the perfect place for a developing musician. "We had the luxury of an audience that would come to the coffee house and sit through almost anything, and at least appear like they were enjoying themselves. Those were very self-indulgent days. Head down, eyes closed, everybody really got into the music. For all of us, the stage at

Smale's Pace was like a school. We made our mistakes on that very forgiving stage and learned our craft."

Other performers who made regular stops in London included such luminaries as Bruce Cockburn and Murray McLauchlan. Born in Ottawa in 1945, Bruce Cockburn is in many ways the antithesis of Stan Rogers as a performer and an artist. Where Stan was gregarious and outspoken, Cockburn remains aloof, a serious and studied musician. His interest in music was sparked in Grade 10 when he got his first guitar. While he obviously listened to pop and folk music of the time, Cockburn was also strongly influenced by jazz artists like Herb Ellis and Oscar Peterson. In the mid-sixties, Cockburn moved to Boston, where he began formal studies at the prestigious Berkeley School of Music. He has always had a strong commercial sense, and from the beginning of his career has written songs that are both artistic and popular. He was a national sensation in the 1970s and made inroads in the United States in the 1980s, charting several albums and singles. Cockburn is now recognized by music fans around the world. Though he lacks the vocal prowess of some of his contemporaries, he is nevertheless one of the most important figures in contemporary Canadian music. Serious, political, wondrously melodic, he has become as much a voice for the urban experience as Stan was for the rural.

With his working class background and country music sensibility, Murray McLauchlan is much closer to Stan Rogers than Bruce Cockburn. McLauchlan was born in 1948 in Scotland and moved to Canada at the age of five. By 17, he was playing coffee houses, and in the late 1960s signed to Canada's independent True North label, the same record company that had signed Bruce Cockburn. Unlike Rogers, McLauchlan's music has been much more accessible to radio. In 1973, a stellar year for domestic singles, McLauchlan's *The Farmers Song* became the hit that launched his career as a popular artist but pegged him as a country singer. In an effort to reach a broader audience, he released the album BOULEVARD in 1976, featuring songs with a rockier edge and a full-scale back-up band. The album managed to crack the Top 100. In the 1990s, he moved into broadcasting. His popular CBC Radio show, *Swinging on a Star*, brought the best of an eclectic range of acoustic music to Canadian audiences every week, keeping alive the spirit of the coffee houses where he began his career.

In London, Stan settled down after five years of wandering. He had found a circle of friends who accepted him, not just because of his talent, but because they liked him. Stan lived with a couple of transplanted Nova Scotians, brothers Mike and Tom Curry. Apparently, he went to the brothers' place for brunch one Sunday. During the course of the day, five gallons of home brew disappeared and the brothers had found themselves a new roommate.

The house they shared defined Stan's London experience. It was a flophouse-cum-performance center. The music would go on well into the night. And in the morning you'd have to step lightly over all the sleeping bodies to get your bowl of cereal. Rumor has it that Willie P. Bennett lived in a closet for a time, when he had nowhere else to go. It was the kind of place where there was always a pot of stew on the stove, where the homemade beer flowed freely (average consumption: 10 gallons a week), and rent was an afterthought.

Hanging out in London with the Cedar Lake crowd was clearly a special time for Stan; he called it the "most serene of experiences" in his groovy press kit from that era. "These people are all my friends," he wrote. "They are all fine musicians and lovers of good music, and beautiful, warm, unique individuals to boot, and up until the time I met my old lady, the greatest highs I ever had came from sharing a stage with these folks. This is music that is vital, alive and pure Canadian. It speaks to me of the northland lakes, a painfully blue sky, and the warm sweet smell of freshly ploughed ground. It's music to share a fire with, to laugh and cry and clap your hands over, to dance to with your old lady, to find some of the answers to the difficult questions of our living in. Every man needs something in his life to fasten on to and be proud of, and Cedar Lake is lots to be proud of. Come give us a listen, and if you ever bump into me somewhere, give me a smile and let me buy you a beer, because all of this music is for you, you know."

Stan's closest friend in London was Paul Mills (no relation to Alan). The two first met in a university coffee house. Paul was studying to be an engineer at the time, but he was also a damn fine picker. He and Stan got to talking, hit it off, and wound up jamming until six in the morning. Paul was the one who suggested that Stan move to London. By that time, Paul had nearly finished his Master's degree and came to the distressing realization that he had no interest in being an engineer. Early one morning, as the last of the stragglers was clearing out of Stan's house, the two friends were finishing off a bottle of Scotch. Out of the blue, Paul spoke up. "Well, I know what I want to do with my life." Stan put down his class and looked his friend, waiting for the punchline. There wasn't one. Paul really had made up his mind. "I want to be a record producer," he declared.

Stan looked pleased and without missing a beat, suggested that Paul produce the albums Stan one day hoped to record. They shook on it and finished the bottle of Scotch. It was an unassuming start to a working partnership that would last the rest of Stan's life.

———

In the comfort of his new-found Ontario home, Stan was getting back in touch with his Maritime roots. Before London, Stan rarely mentioned the East Coast, and, as a teenager, he seldom visited there. But now, the Maritimes appealed to the young man's sense of history and his romantic nature. Stan included a couple of old-time jigs in his act and would refer to Nova Scotia as "the place where I come from." In Mike Curry's words, "Stan considered himself to be a Nova Scotian and bitterly resented the fact that he wasn't born there."

Stan spent as much free time in Nova Scotia as he could and particularly enjoyed his Uncle Prescott Rogers' little cottage at

Half Way Cove, just a short drive out of Hazel Hill, Nova Scotia. It is here that in late September of 1973 Stan took Diane Ariel McEwen, whom he'd started dating earlier that summer. Ariel was a nurse who was active in the arts scene around Hamilton. They had met when Ariel hired Stan to play at "It's Your Bag Day," a local arts festival, and Stan was immediately taken by her red hair and fiery personality.

Actually, it wasn't the first time they met. She had seen him years before playing in a coffee house and since then they'd seen each other occasionally in church in Hamilton. Their first formal introduction was in the summer of 1970, when Stan was assistant cook at a church camp and Ariel, who'd been camp nurse the summer before, was visiting. One of the girls took Ariel down to the cookhouse to meet Stan, who was asleep. Ariel was introduced to his feet, hanging limply over the end of the bed. So, it wasn't exactly love at first sight, but when they finally did get together, it was love nevertheless.

The weekend at Uncle Prescott's was one of laughter and discovery for the young lovers. And even after Ariel left, Stan felt her presence in that tiny house by the sea. A song was writing itself in his head and slowly made its way onto paper.

> Where the earth shows its bones of wind-broken stone
> And the sea and sky are one
> I'm caught out of time, my blood sings with wine
> And I'm running naked in the sun.

The result was *Forty-Five Years*, a masterful love song. Later Stan would say that this was the only love song he ever wrote, but this was not strictly true. He wrote dozens of them in his early years, having learned the lesson of many young troubadours — that the quickest way into a girl's heart — and bedroom — was to write her a song. Stan's best songs were always love songs of a sort. They didn't speak of mythical or romantic love, the mainstay of pop music; instead, they dealt with the complicated, often ambiguous, and very real relationships we experience in our daily lives.

As *Forty-Five Years* was forming in Stan's mind, he sat down and wrote Ariel a letter that offers a revealing glimpse into his creative process. The images and ideas that would soon make up the song permeate the letter like spirits, waiting to be given form. Stan writes:

> . . . Now that you've been here, and I've seen how you took to the place, I'm sure there will be a next time — many next times. I love you more than I ever thought possible, or mere words could ever say. But I've a song running up today, and this one I'm sure I'll keep. I just want to hold you closer than I've ever held anyone before. Mom says hi, and I hope you get back alright, and I overheard Dad telling my uncle Jim yesterday that "Stan's new girlfriend is really a pleasant type to have around." Whatever that means. I guess that's high praise coming from him.
>
> So far today I've had four cigarettes, and I'm about to light my fifth, which will be my last until after supper. Not bad, I guess. Funny as I sit here writing, the words to the song are coming faster and faster. Pretty soon I'll have to stop for a while and go find that dried up old guitar. Oh, love, I'll never forget the sight of you running naked and laughing in the sun with the water streaming down your breasts. I've never seen anything so beautiful in my life, and I've never seen anyone so happy. I'm sure you deserve that kind of happiness, but I'm not sure I deserve it. I'm still constantly amazed every time I think of the two of us together. I've never thought of myself as good looking, or as being particularly desirable to women, and to find myself loving and being loved by one of the finest women a man could hope to meet is almost miraculous. I can see myself looking into those green eyes of yours fifty years from now and loving it . . .

Enclosed with the letter, Ariel found two sheets of notepaper on which Stan had written the lyrics to his newest song, *Forty-Five Years*.

And I just want to hold you closer than
I've ever held anyone before
You say you've been twice a wife and you're through with life
Ah, but Honey, what the hell's it for?
After twenty-three years you'd think I could find
A way to let you know somehow
That I want to see your smiling face forty-five years from now.

STAN ROGERS MARITIME HOME BREW

This straightforward grog was Stan's favorite. The measurements aren't very precise — it's taken from Stan's handwritten recipe — but Ariel assures me that, with a little experimentation, you'll be able to make a simple and reliable home brew.

1. Start yeast (lukewarm sugared water).
2. Fill dutch oven $3/4$ full with water.
3. Place on high heat.
4. Add:
   1 bag dextrose
   1 can malt
   1 teaspoon salt
   1 teaspoon citric acid
   1 teaspoon finings
5. Stir until finings dissolve. Then pour in vat.
6. Add $4\,1/2$ dutch ovens of cool water.
7. Stir in yeast.
8. Cover.
9. Let beer sit for at least 2 weeks. Then skim off foam and bottle.
10. Add 1 teaspoon sugaring solution (see below) per bottle.

Sugaring Solution:
   $3/4$ cup boiling water
   7 tablespoons sugar. Stir until dissolved.

The Guysborough Line

Now there's no train to Guysborough
Or so the man said
So it might be a good place to be.

— *Guysborough Train*

By the end of 1973, all the pieces were in place. Stan had friends, musical cohorts, and a family of sorts, having moved in with Ariel and her three children — David, the oldest at four, Beth, and Kate. The predator was being domesticated and didn't seem to mind it one bit. "He was drawn to the kids like a moth to a flame," Ariel says. "He would lie on the couch for hours with his little stepdaughter Kate, just reading to her or talking or playing. It answered something inside him. People would ask him how he could take on this woman and her three kids. But he found something in it that was vital; it was absolutely like breathing to him."

As Stan was settling in with home life, his recording career was also starting to take shape. His friend Paul Mills had been hired as producer with CBC Radio and managed to wangle some studio time for Stan. In those days, it wasn't unusual for the "Corp" to record promising artists like Stan. The CBC had a mandate as a public broadcaster to promote and develop Canadian talent. In Stan's case, an EP record was produced for the in-house Transcription Series label.

Stan's three-song EP for CBC turned out to be his most successful recording venture to date. The songs were a kind of pastoral pop rather than pure folk music, as the opening lines of the lead song *Three Pennies* indicates.

> When day comes
> On this mountain
> To your well I will go
> Drink of you deep
> Watch you in sleep
> And down meadows green will softly go . . .

Stan was trying to be a seventies mellow singer-songwriter, in the mold of James Taylor. But Stan did not have a confessional personality. The best he could achieve was a vague spiritual awareness that he tried to explain in the second song, *Past Fifty*.

> I'm going through life like a pilgrim
> Lost in the storm
> With winds that blow to make me cold,
> But the holy body keeps me warm.

In terms of melody, these two songs aren't bad for a young songwriter, but the lyrics don't stack up to Stan's later work. However, the third song was a stand out. *Guysborough Train* became a favorite of CBC programmers and was soon a hot commodity on the folk music black market. Everybody and their uncle-in-law begged, borrowed, or bootlegged a copy.

The idea for the song was based in fact. In the 1960s, the Nova Scotia government promised to build a rail line to Guysborough, a town at the foot of Chedabucto Bay, and, like many government promises, this one was broken.

Now there's no train to Guysborough
Or so the man said
So it might be a good place to be.
I sit in this station
And I count up my change
And I wait for the Guysborough train.

The song has a political basis, but Stan was more interested in the futile imagery of a train going nowhere than he was in the politics. The lyrics to *Guysborough Train* are particularly interesting because of Stan's use of the personal, narrative voice, the I-witness. While other folk singers of the era used this kind of voice to explore their own inner feelings — songwriting as therapy — Stan used it to describe a historic event. In a sense, he was combining the seventies singer-songwriter style with a traditional form, the historical ballad.

And I ride for all time
On the Guysborough line
And I grow by the North County rain
And the North Shore's begun
The man I've become
In rags, on the Guysborough train.

Guysborough Train doesn't have the scope or impact of a true historical ballad, but it was the starting point from which Stan developed his literate and literary style of song-writing: song as story. The narrative voice is always slightly detached, like Stan himself often felt, an observer on the edge of circumstance.

For the next two years, Stan worked hard to establish himself on the Canadian music scene. He had been touring extensively with a trio that included an old Cedar Lake crony Jim Ogilvie on bass and younger brother Garnet on fiddle, flute, and electric guitar.

They played every bar and folk club that would have them. Success seemed within their reach.

Stan took a second stab at a recording career, signing briefly with New York's prestigious folk music label, Vanguard Records, but he didn't stay with Vanguard for long. As Stan told *Folk Life Quarterly* in the summer of 1978, the label wanted him "to cross over into the pop market for them." Pop music just wasn't Stan's interest. The result, as Paul Mills recalls, was that the Vanguard "recording sessions did not go well. I think the problem was that we were all trying too hard. It ended up sounding forced. Vanguard insisted on hearing the rough mixes of the basic tracks and it was on the basis of these unfinished tracks that Vanguard decided to let Stan go."

By the summer of 1975, Stan Roger's hard work began to pay-off in another way as he moved on to the folk festival circuit. At the time, these festivals were the proving ground for folk artists. One great show at the Mariposa or Winnipeg festivals could establish an artist's international reputation.

In the early 1970s, the dream of developing folk musicians was to play the Mariposa Folk Festival. In folk music history, Mariposa ranks second only to the Newport Folk Festival in Rhode Island in terms of impact and longevity. Like all great Canadian cultural events, it began as a tourism initiative when Ruth Jones conceived of a folk festival as a way to attract visitors to Orillia, Ontario. The festival was named after renowned humorist Stephen Leacock's fictitious name for the city. Gordon Lightfoot came from Orillia.

The first Mariposa Festival took place in 1961 and included such performers as Ian and Sylvia, who helped organize it, and Ed McCurdy, a singer of traditional Canadian songs. It was a mild success. Two thousand folk fans turned out, and, although the organizers lost money, the festival continued to grow. By 1964, the festival was so big that Orillia's city council banned it. It changed locations for several years before finding a new home in 1968 on the Toronto Islands. Estelle Klein was Mariposa's artistic director from the mid-sixties through to the end of the seventies.

The festival was originally all-Canadian, out of financial necessity more than any philosophical disposition. Later Klein felt a broad base was important and, though she was criticized by some, transformed the festival into an international showcase.

The Mariposa Festival was a product of the folk boom and throughout its history this was reflected in a tendency toward 'pure' traditional music and a focus on performances as opposed to performers. Acts were generally given half-hour timeslots, and multi-performer workshops were the order of the day. To discourage any sort of star system from developing, there were no evening shows. The 1972 calendar of events makes this point abundantly clear:

All Programs
end at 8:30 pm
Festival Site must be
cleared at this time

Stan Rogers believed that the Mariposa organizers put undue emphasis on traditional folk music and he agreed only reluctantly to participate in the 1975 festival. Stan played three other major festivals that year: the Blue Skies festival in Clarendon Station near Kingston, Ontario; Home County in London, Ontario; and the Winnipeg festival. Although Mariposa was still the most important festival in the country in the mid-seventies, by the end of the decade Mitch Podolak's Winnipeg folk festival surpassed it in importance, leading the way for a host of regional festivals in Vancouver, Sudbury, Owen Sound, London, and more. Stan followed this circuit with annual repeat performances, gathering die-hard fans along the way.

During the mid-seventies, folk music began to change again. Singer-songwriters like James Taylor and Carole King took the lead in creating music with simple arrangements (acoustic guitars preferred) performed by a self-accompanied artist whose original songs featured rich, introspective lyrics. In Canada, Bruce Cockburn and Murray McLauchlan became part of this movement, both recording for True North, one of the few successful independent record companies in Canada at the time. Their contemporary, Valdy, is another interesting example of a successful singer-songwriter. He was one of the first national folk artists to break the Top Forty radio format, achieving this success despite, or perhaps because of, his decision to live outside of Southern Ontario's major entertainment markets.

Valdy came to epitomize the hippy ideal: sort of a one-man version of Cedar Lake. Originally from Ottawa, Valdy was born Valdemar Horsdal and became a resident of Saltspring, an island halfway between Vancouver and Victoria. He sang songs with titles like *Country Man, Simple Life*, and *Hometown Band*. Valdy's easy manner and smooth singing style allowed him to straddle the gulf between folk and popular music. Although he had been involved in the folk music scene since the mid-sixties, it wasn't until 1971 that he made an impact on radio with the single *Rock And Roll Song*. What followed was a succession of Top Forty singles and top-selling albums.

Like Rogers, Valdy knew himself to be a folk artist but found the label "folk" to be a detriment in the popular music world. "I have found this designation to be one hundred-and-ten percent limiting. My manager said, 'DO NOT USE THE WORD FOLK.' But I never listened. And here we are twenty years later and my manager is still saying, 'We are not using the word folk.'"

Valdy and folk singers like him impressed Stan. He realized that if he ever wanted to make it, he had to crack the radio markets. Once again, the CBC entered the picture. The *Guysborough Train* EP had been so popular that Paul Mills got the go ahead to make another record with Stan. But what at first seemed a golden opportunity soon developed into one of the most traumatic episodes in both their recording careers.

The studio was booked for ten o'clock on a snowy morning not long after New Year's Day, 1976. By 10:30, Stan hadn't arrived. At eleven o'clock, still nothing. The radio reported numerous road-closures and a rash of serious accidents. As it neared 11:30, Mills contemplated calling off the session. "I had a room full of musicians who were getting paid and I was responsible for the budget. When Stan and the boys finally arrived, they were all flustered. They unpacked their instruments and started to play. It was just awful. Stan was so agitated that he couldn't play his guitar. Jim Ogilvie's bass had something wrong with it; there was a buzz in one of the strings. Nothing was going right."

With time and money rapidly disappearing, a stressed-out Paul Mills was forced to make an executive decision. He told Stan to put down his guitar; he wanted Stan just to sing. He asked Jim Ogilvie to take a coffee break, effectively kicking the bass player out of the studio. Paul then assigned studio musicians to play in place of Jim and Stan.

After recording the track, Stan was livid. "How dare you defile my music this way?" he demanded. Paul explained that he was trying to do his job, but that didn't cut much slack with Stan. He didn't speak to Paul for three months and the friendship seemed all but over. Two months after the incident, Paul got an angry letter from Stan. At that time, Paul was producing the show *Touch the Earth* for CBC. "Stan wrote this four page letter, tearing me to shreds for what I had done. The letter was about honesty and all the things that mattered to him in terms of the music. The one line I remember was: 'Touch the earth? You wouldn't know it if it crawled into bed with you.' It was the biggest falling out that Stan and I ever had."

Not only did this session result in a lost friendship, Stan Rogers lost a bass player. Jim Ogilvie had felt uncomfortable throughout the recording session. They had been playing together for three years, but suddenly Ogilvie felt like an outsider. "We had evolved the songs in our own fashion and, when we went in to record, that's how we were going to play them. I tried to do it the way they wanted, but I didn't really want to and I think that showed. Stan and I had a little squabble and it blew up. I left and that was it."

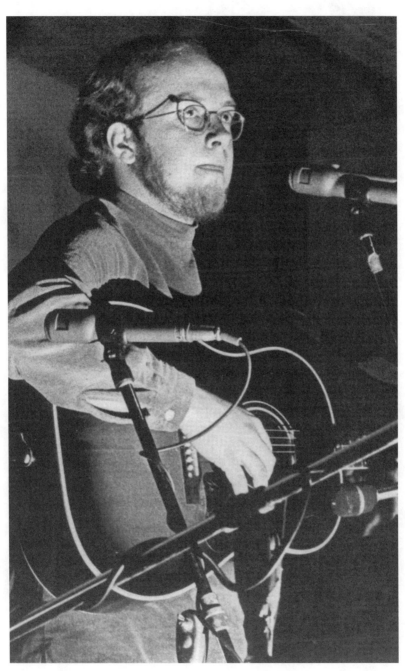

Performing at Smale's Pace, circa 1972.

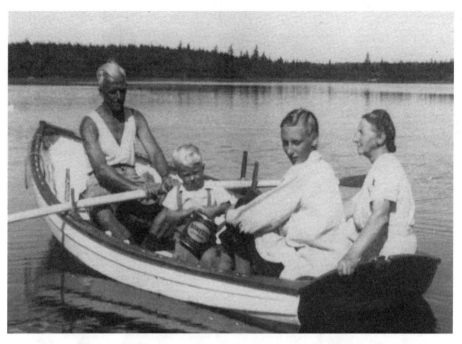

At age three, out for a paddle with his Aunt June and his grandparents (from the Bushell side) near Hazel Hill, Nova Scotia.

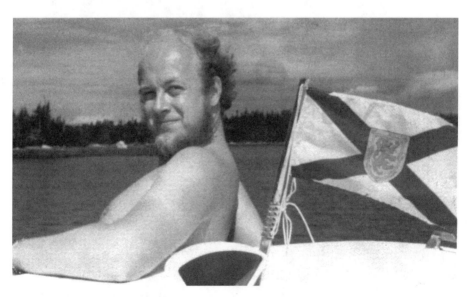

Aboard a friend's boat in Black Duck Cove, near Hazel Hill, Nova Scotia.

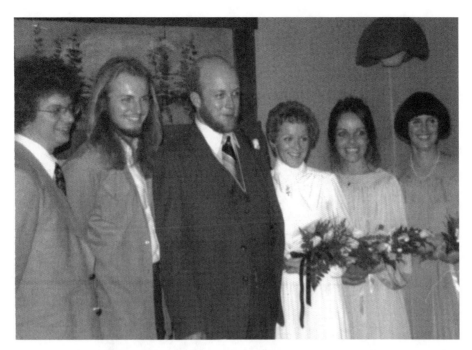

Stan and Ariel were married in a civil ceremony on 30 September 1977. Left to right: Paul Mills, Garnet, Stan, Ariel, Beth McQueen, and Bev Mills.

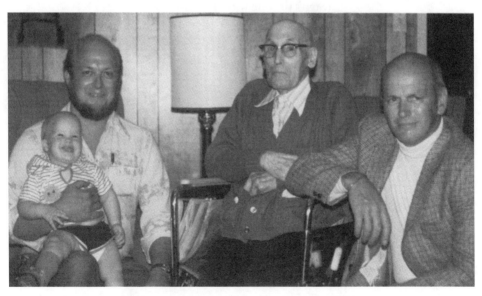

Four generations of Rogers men, in 1981.
Left to right: Nathan, Stan, Al, Stanley.

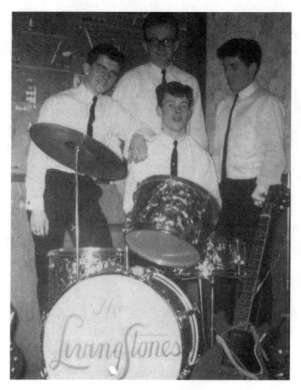

At 16 with his rock band, "Stanley and the Living Stones."
(Stan's the one with the glasses.)

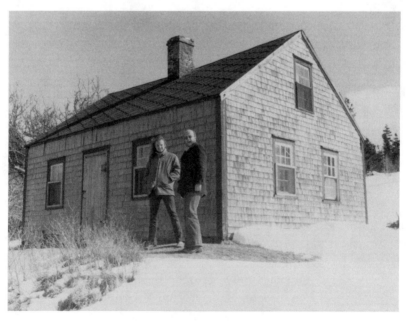

Stan and Garnet outside Uncle Prescott's cabin at
Half Way Cove, near Canso, Nova Scotia.

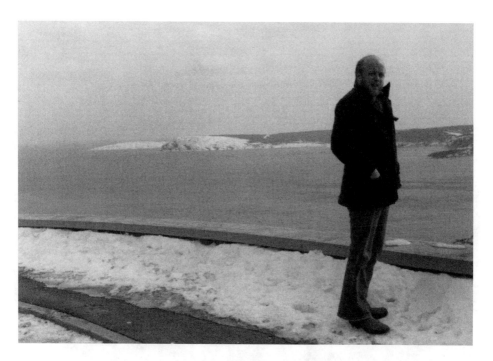

On the road in Nova Scotia.

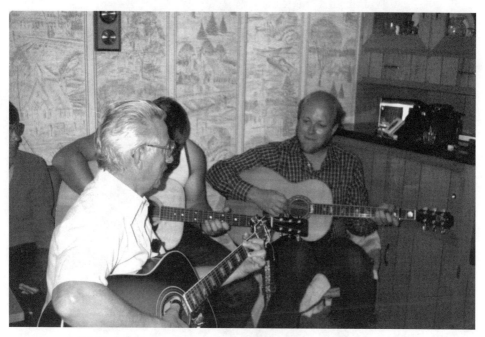

Picking in Aunt June and Uncle Sam's kitchen, 1980, with
Uncle Lee Bushell (left) and Eldon Monroe (rear).

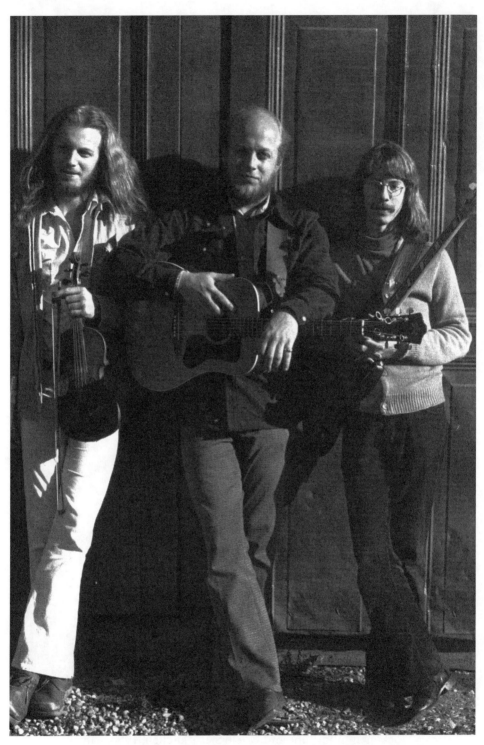

The band in 1975: (left to right) Garnet, Stan, David Woodhead.

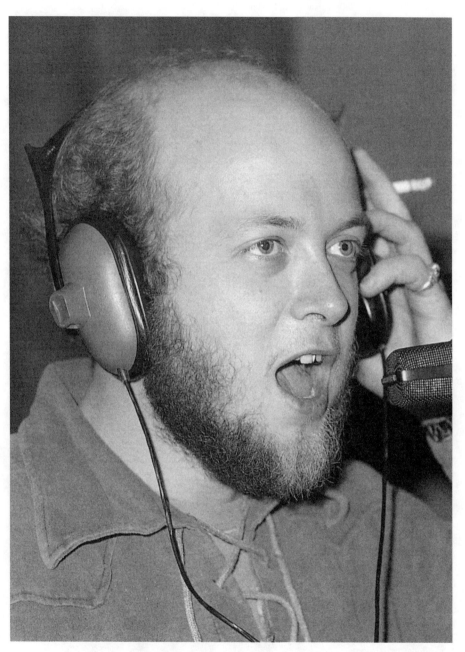

Recording *Turnaround* at Springfield Sound in London in 1977.

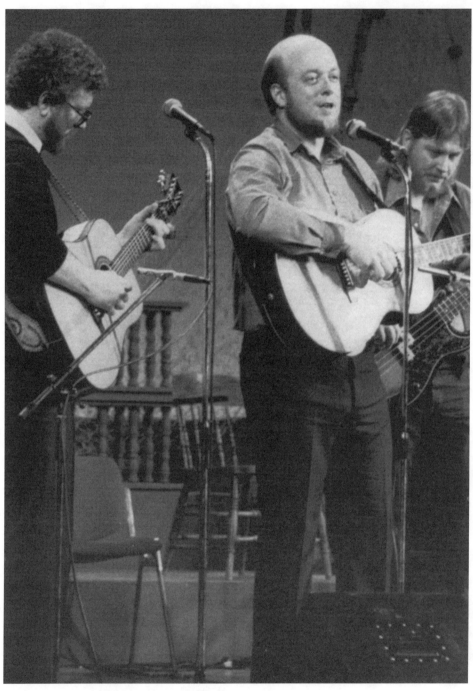

Onstage at the Rebecca Cohn Theatre recording the live
album HOME IN HALIFAX. Stan is joined by Curly Boy Stubbs,
a.k.a. Paul Mills, with Jim Morison in the background.

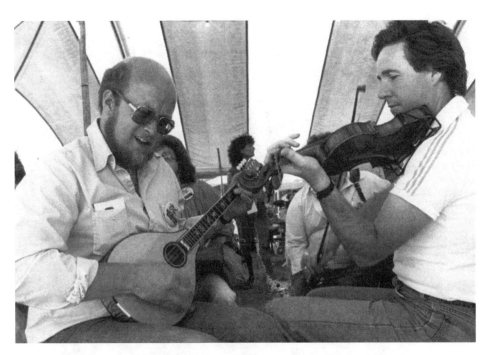

At the Winnipeg Folk Festival in 1980, jamming with John Allen Cameron.

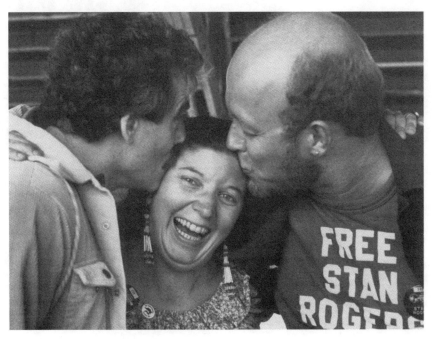

"Free Stan Rogers" t-shirts were in vogue in US folk circles at a time when Stan had trouble getting a visa to perform there. Here he's seen with Emily Friedman, editor of *Come For To Sing*, and Brit Trad folk singer Lou Killen.

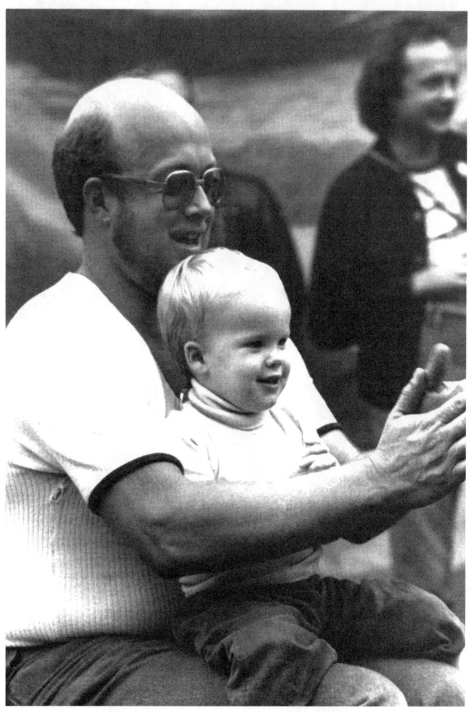

With Nathan in 1981 at Owen Sound Folk Festival.

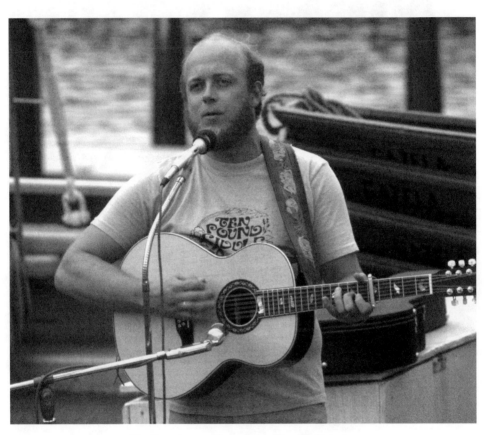
Performing on board the *Gazella Primiero*.

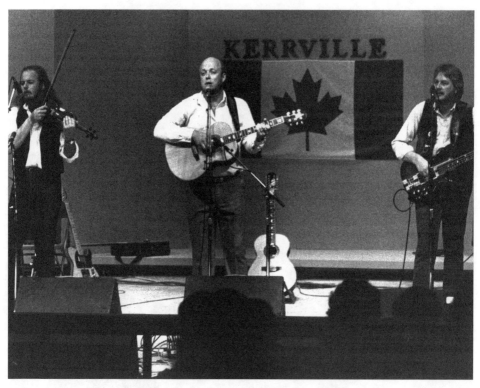

Stan's last concert, in Kerrville, Texas.
Left to right: Garnet, Stan, Jim Morison.

Revival

God damn them all!
I was told we'd cruise the seas for American gold
We'd fire no guns!' Shed no tears!
But I'm a broken man on a Halifax pier
The last of Barrett's Privateers.

— *Barrett's Privateers*

Fans know Stan Rogers as a songwriter and singer, but few appreciate the impact he's had on folk music in general. Other artists, such as Leonard Cohen, used traditional motifs in their music, but Stan went much further. He was a trailblazer, who almost single-handedly established a Canadian folk idiom and helped spark the interest in traditional British and Celtic music that has swept across North America. Because of Stan, we've all come to recognize that there are other American forms of music besides country and the blues. There are jigs, reels, shanties, broadside ballads, hornpipes — all of which deserve a place, not just in music history, but in contemporary songwriting as well.

Although Stan was a child of the American folk boom of the early 1960s, his model was the so-called Brit Trad Revival in

Britain during the early 1970s. The folk boom of the early 1960s was by-and-large an American phenomenon that had a limited effect on British popular music. There was "skiffle" in the late fifties, which combined elements of American traditional music — simple instruments like acoustic guitars and washboards and songs by the likes of Leadbelly and Woody Guthrie — with British dance band sensibilities. The skiffle craze swept through England, and many of Britain's pop music heavyweights, such as Lennon and McCartney, cut their teeth in skiffle bands.

British traditionalists resented the American origins of skiffle and sought to revive their own musical heritage. This "Brit Trad Revival" was spearheaded by Bert Lloyd, a musicologist and singer, and Ewan MacColl, a singer and songwriter of distinction, whose elegant ballad *The First Time Ever I Saw Your Face* was a hit for Roberta Flack in 1971. The idea was to incorporate the traditional music of the British Isles in contemporary rock and folk forms. Brit Trad gained momentum in the early 1970s, with the rise of bands such as Fairport Convention, Incredible String Band, and Steeleye Span. Its influence could be heard in the generations of artists that followed, such as the Clash, U2, the Pogues, and Billy Bragg.

In Canada, the unofficial home base for the British revival music was a coffee house in Toronto called Fiddler's Green. The club was formed in 1970 by a group of transplanted Brits, including Tam Kearney and Jim Strickland. Fiddler's Green quickly became one of the most popular folk music venues in the city. Grit Laskin, a guitar maker and a member of the Friends of Fiddler's Green, the club's house band, remembers the club in all its glory. "Technically the building was condemned," he recalls, "but we used it anyway. The upper floors shouldn't have been stepped on, but we had a secret way to get in and set up our equipment. When it was at its peak, it was running two nights a week, and each night was so jammed that there were line-ups in the parking lot. It was crazy; we would pack in over 120 people, way beyond any type of fire code limit."

Stan Rogers was a frequent visitor to Fiddler's Green. Even

when he wasn't featured on the bill, he would show up and just join in. He loved the atmosphere of the club: the performances were free flowing and the club's format was as loose as its floorboards. It was a sharp contrast to Stan's polished and well-practiced stage show.

Another Fiddler's Green regular was a mysterious guitarist and singer who went by the name Leon Redbone. Redbone is interesting both as a folk artist and as an example of the difficulties the general public has in understanding folk idioms. Unlike the other Fiddler's Green regulars, Redbone wasn't into Brit Trad. Rather, he sang folk interpretations of popular songs from the American songbook of the thirties and forties and even earlier. His repertoire included *Ain't Misbehavin'*, *When You Wish Upon A Star*, and *Your Cheating Heart*.

Leon Redbone became a pop music sensation in 1976, thanks in part to Bob Dylan's outspoken support and to a timely appearance on TV's *Saturday Night Live*. Part of Redbone's appeal was his air of mystery: he looked like a Lebanese Groucho Marx, had a taciturn disposition, rarely gave interviews, and always wore dark glasses. His enigmatic ways weren't just for show; he always surrounded himself in secrecy. Paul Mills recalls occasionally giving Redbone a ride home after a session at the coffee house. "He'd never actually let you drop him off at his house. It was always on a corner or side street. He really like to keep up that air of mystery." Redbone's playful profile from the 1972 Mariposa Festival program is a good example: "I was born in Shreveport, LA in 1910, and my real name is James Hokum. I wear darkglasses to remind me of the time I spent leading Blind Blake throughout the south, and I now live in Canada as a result of the incident in Philadelphia." In response to a request for a photograph for the program, Redbone sent a crumpled snapshot of Bob Dylan. In 1976, Redbone recorded the album ON THE TRACK for Warner Brothers. Over the next 10 years, he released half-a-dozen albums.

Leon Redbone started out as the darling of music critics and record buyers, but with each album their disenchantment grew. Fewer and fewer albums sold, although most made the Top Forty chart. Meanwhile, some critics concluded that he was nothing more than a novelty act whose novelty had worn off. The problem for Redbone was that pop music demands change. Enduring pop artists, such as David Bowie and Neil Young, understand this dynamic and go to great pains to re-invent themselves. Folk artists who enter the mainstream always have a hard time staying there because folk, by its very nature, doesn't change, and theyalways run the risk of being relegated to the status of a novelty act.

———

Once Stan Rogers got the notion to become a one-man traditional music revival movement, he explored different traditional forms. His first success came as much by accident as design. In the summer of 1976, he was playing the Northern Lights Festival in Sudbury, Ontario, and between shows he would join the other performers, including the Friends of Fiddler's Green, for a beer and a song. Chorus songs were a favorite at this type of gathering: a leader sings the verse, then the group joins in for the chorus. Stan had one problem with chorus songs. Since he didn't know any, he was never able to sing lead — and there's only so long that Stan Rogers could stay in the background. Later, in an interview with *Folk Life Quarterly*, Stan recalled how he took matters into his own hands. "I was hanging out with all those guys — they'd rather sing than eat — almost rather sing than drink — and they were hanging out in their own rooms, all into singing sea-shanties," he explained. "I loved the parts, it was great fun, but I wanted to sing lead and have them sing the harmonies for a change. But I didn't know any of these songs, because I was a total neophyte in traditional music — still am, for that matter — so I went back to my room and I thought over a story a poet friend had told me, about Nova Scotian privateering in the time of the American Revolutionary War. I got this little bit of a tune running through my head, and twenty minutes later I had *Barrett's Privateers* written down. I went back to the room where the Friends all were, and said, 'Hey-hey! I've got a new song!' And Tom Kearney said, 'Aw — look out folks — Rogers is gonna make us all cry again!' And I said, 'No! No! You don't understand! This is a different kind of song!' So I started singing it, and by the time I got to the second chorus, they were all crowded around, reading the page over my shoulder, and singing perfect bloody harmonies. So I knew that the song had satisfied my desires. I never expected it to go beyond that point — I just wanted a song that I could sing lead on that one night."

The genesis of *Barrett's Privateers* went back at least four months before the festival, though. Stan had come across the general outline of the story the previous spring when he was working with Bill Howell in Halifax. During one break in the action, when the two friends had settled into a bottle of Scotch and a long conversation, Howell played a radio piece he had written called *MacMechan's Ocean*, a profile of a turn-of-the-20th-century popular historian and Dalhousie literature professor named Archibald MacMechan. Today MacMechan is lost to the dustbin of history, but in his time he was a well-know academic and author of numerous authentic seafaring tales. One of his most famous works was *Godfrey of the Rover*, the story about a privateer, or licensed pirate, plying his trade for England during the Napoleonic Wars. The story was based on an earlier poem, which might also have been written by MacMechan (although some accounts put it as anonymous) called *The Ballad of the Rover*.

> Come all you jolly sailor lads, that love the cannon's roar,
> Your good ship on the briny wave, your lass and glass ashore,
> How Nova Scotia's sons can fight you presently shall hear,
> And of gallant captain Godfrey of the *Rover* privateer

The poem tells the tale of the *Rover*, an actual Nova Scotian privateering ship, captained by one Alex Godfrey. Godfrey and his crew were legendary figures in early Canada, having single-handedly defeated a convoy of seven French ships in one battle, and three Spanish ships in another. The *Rover* did indeed have a Letter of Marque, giving it permission to attack any ships enemy to Britain (and there were lots of those back then) and operate out of British ports.

The whole concept of privateering intrigued and amused Stan. This all came rushing back to him that night in Sudbury as he sat down to write his own *a capella* chorus song. As Stan told an interviewer a year later at the Winnipeg Folk Festival, "I remembered the story of the privateers and I invented this fellow Elcid Barrett who took a sloop of war out on a privateering venture. I decided to tell it in the first person; the story of this 17-year-old boy who shipped out as a privateer and made it back to Halifax 6 years later missing both legs . . ."

Perhaps it was this firm grounding in reality that gave the story such narrative power. In any case, the song was an instant classic, in every sense of the term. Ian Robb, a Friend of Fiddler's Green and one of Stan's favorite performers, was at the Northern Lights Festival. He remembers well what happened that afternoon when Stan turned up with his new song. "We were doing our usual singing around, and Stan was there. Finally Stan said with a smile, 'I've had enough of playing second fiddle to you guys!' and he went away." No more than 20 minutes later, Stan returned to the group with a new song in his hands, and from the moment Stan sang the first line, it was obvious that he had just created a modem classic.

> Oh, the year was 1778,
> How I wish I was in Sherbrooke now!
> A Letter of Marque came from the king
> To the scummiest vessel I'd ever seen.

Quickly the other singers joined in the chorus, many thinking it was a song right off the top of Stan's great head, while others frantically searching their memories to remember the source of what they presumed to be an ancient sea shanty. None of them realized that the song — "Barrett's Private Parts" as he came to call it with mock disdain, once it had been established as a fan favorite — had been the result of detailed research in the Halifax public archives.

Regardless of what anyone thought, it was a turning point in Stan's career. Musical artists are only as good as the songs they sung: now, Stan had created a signature song, which in one rousing chorus managed to grab the audience's attention and present to them the simple, powerful image of Stan Rogers, Maritime Man.

Fogarty's Cove

She will walk the sandy shore so plain
Watch the combers roll in
Til I come to Wild Rose Chance again
Down in Fogarty's Cove.

— *Fogarty's Cove*

"You know, Stan . . ." June Jarvis placed a bowl full of homemade Blueberry Grunt in front of her ever-hungry nephew. "I was just thinking . . ."

Stan scooped a spoonful of blueberry and biscuit into his mouth. "Well, don't hurt yourself."

Aunt June continued. "You spend so much time down around Canso, it's like a second home."

Stan grunted. Apparently the dessert was having its desired effect.

"I mean, you're always looking for something to write about. Why don't you write some songs about right here?"

At his Aunt June's suggestion Stan Rogers did try his hand at writing a song about the Eastern Shore in 1974. A simple idea, it proved to be an important step in Stan's career, the beginning of a process that culminated in his 1976 debut album FOGARTY'S COVE. Stan had written songs about Nova Scotia before — *Guysborough Train* and *Pocketful Of Gold* come to mind — but *Fogarty's Cove* was different. It wasn't just about the Maritimes; the song itself had the feel of traditional Maritime music.

Stan made a demo of *Fogarty's Cove* that summer, recording it in the basement studio of an aspiring young producer, Danny Lanois. In the 1980s, Lanois emerged as one of the world's top producers while working with artists like U2, Bob Dylan, the Neville Brothers, and Robbie Robertson.

At that time, Paul Mills had just started producing CBC Radio's *Touch the Earth*, hosted by Sylvia Tyson. The show quickly became a popular and influential program that helped advance Stan's career. Directly, he got national exposure from his numerous appearances. Indirectly, *Touch the Earth* brought Stan together with Mitch Podolak, the driving force behind his first album. Podolak, a freelance journalist from Winnipeg, approached Mills with an idea. He told Paul that he wanted to start a folk festival in Winnipeg, and asked the producer to chip in some of his budget to get the ball rolling. To Mitch's surprise, Paul said yes. Thus the CBC, through Paul Mills, was the first to offer financial support to the Winnipeg Folk Festival.

From the start, Winnipeg was a different kind of festival than Mariposa. The focus was more on the performers than on the music itself, which suited Stan fine. While Mariposa was a product of the folk boom in the sixties, which had strong ties to the academic world, Winnipeg came out of the seventies, when tepid pop songs and disco's mechanical rhythms ruled radio. Festivals such as the Winnipeg Folk Festival provided a musical alternative, a place where music fans could rediscover the excitement of live music. Winnipeg proved to be the best of them all, and by the late seventies, it had surpassed Mariposa in prestige and influence.

In September 1974, a month after the first Winnipeg Festival,

Mitch Podolak was in Toronto. He decided he owed Paul Mills a phone call. The two met for dinner, and Paul brought along a tape of *Fogarty's Cove*. "I was sitting there listening to this tape and getting my mind blown," Podolak recalls. "So Paul called up Fiddler's Green where Stan was playing that night and said to Stan: 'Listen, when you're finished, get your ass over here right away. There's someone I want you to meet.'" Mitch was so impressed that he invited Stan to play at the Winnipeg Folk Festival the following summer.

Despite a serious case of the jitters, Stan was in top form. The audience was bowled over by the sheer energy of the man. Until Winnipeg, Stan had been a regional phenomenon with pockets of support in Southern Ontario and on the East Coast. Thanks to Winnipeg, the folk world sat up and took notice. At some point during the festival, Mitch Podolak asked about Stan's recording career.

"Stan, how come you haven't made a record?"

"Well, that's a long story," Stan replied, giving a capsule history of his hard luck relationship with record companies. The simple truth was that nobody was knocking on Stan's door. His music was so far out of the mainstream that even folk labels weren't interested in taking a chance on him.

"Well, you've got all these songs about the Maritimes — why don't you do an album of them?"

"That's all well and good, Mitch, but I don't have the kind of money it takes to make an album."

There was a long pause, as both men considered their fate. On the spur of the moment, Podolak had a great idea. "Look," Mitch finally said. "I'll get the money, and I'll start a label, and I'll record you."

Podalak was as good as his word. With five grand already saved up, he went to the bank and borrowed another $5000. With this money he started Barn Swallow Records and paid for Stan's first album. "All of a sudden," Podalak told me, "I was a record company. And the best part was that I knew nothing about making records."

FOGARTY'S COVE was recorded in September 1976 at the Spring-field Sound studio in London, Ontario. The budget was tight, so the band had to work around the clock.

David Woodhead was Stan's bass player at the time. He recalls that the record was finished in, well, record time. "It took us two days to do FOGARTY'S COVE, which was unheard of back then. This really relates to Stan's professionalism. He liked to get the job done. But also, he did have a certain show-off quality. I think it was important to him to be able to do a record faster than any-body else."

Stan assembled his band and a crew of his old friends to help put FOGARTY'S COVE together. Paul Mills produced and per-formed under the alias "Curly Boy Stubbs." John Allen Cameron appeared on one track. Grit Laskin turned up on several tracks using the alias "The Masked Luthier Of Dupont Street." The reason for the false name was that Laskin didn't belong to the musician's union and, technically, couldn't play with other union musicians.

The songs on this album were influenced by Stan's numerous trips to Nova Scotia, and in particular by the work he did with his friend, the poet and CBC producer Bill Howell. Howell was living in Nova Scotia at the time, and the two collaborated in an ongoing artistic experiment called "Anecdote," which aired periodically on the CBC Radio show *Music Maritimes*. "Anecdote" had an inter-esting premise: the poet and songwriter carried on a dialog through their artistic mediums. This on-demand writing helped Stan hone his skill as a songwriter, while his close association with Howell gave Stan a greater understanding of the techniques of poetry. Several of the songs from "Anecdote" wound up on FOGA-RTY'S COVE.

Stan wanted to use the album to start his own Can Trad Revival, and to use his personal, mythical relationship with the Maritimes as a starting point to create a unique vision of what it meant to be Canadian. "There is no such place," Rogers wrote of Fogarty's Cove in the liner notes to the album. "At least on any map. But if you trace with your finger along the shore of Chedabucto Bay, Nova Scotia, from the town of Guysborough northeast toward Canso Town (as differentiated from the Canso Strait), you will encounter names like Half Way Cove, Queensport, Half Island Cove, Fox Island, Hazel Hill, and Canso herself, where my mother was born, and where she grew up."

Of the 12 songs on FOGARTY's COVE, 11 relate to the East Coast. As Stan told interviewer John McLaughlin, for the summer 1978 edition of *Folk Life Quarterly*, he had a clear idea in mind of the kind of songs he wanted to create for the album. "I wanted to write the kinds of songs that more closely reflected the Maritimes themselves than stuff I'd heard before," he explained. "There are fine Maritime writers, but they tend to write in a very uptown style — they write pop songs about the Maritimes. I wanted to write 'old' songs about them. I wanted to write some songs that would sound like anything from thirty to two hundred years old. *Fogarty's Cove* was the first tune, and I did that mostly just to satisfy my aunt. Out of that tune, and out of the realization that I could write stuff like that, came the whole album. I think there were three songs on the album that were written within about three days of its being recorded. In fact, *The Wreck of the Athens Queen* I wrote as we were going to record it — reading the lyrics off the music stand — and it took us eleven takes to record that. *Giant* was written during rehearsals. *Fisherman's Wharf* was written during the little 'Band-aid' session, on a separate day apart from the main session."

Side One was a powerful introduction to an important new folk artist, featuring *Forty-Five Years*, *Fogarty's Cove*, and *Barrett's Privateers*, all standout tracks. The second side is a mini-suite that summarizes the range of Stan's Can Trad vision. The songs include the historical ballad *The Rawdon Hills*, *Plenty Of Hornpipe*, the first of many ship salvage songs, *The Wreck Of The Athens Queen*, *Make And Break Harbour*, and a recitation, *Finch's Complaint*. The side opens and closes with the haunting, Celtic-inspired song *Giant*.

Considering that FOGARTY'S COVE was a young artist's first album, it is surprisingly dark and gloomy — folk gothic, as it were. In fact, the album is one long meditation on the relationship between vitality and decay. Stan was particularly fascinated with working people: time and time again the people of his songs struggle to be productive, to make a buck, only to encounter forces of destruction. In *Maid On The Shore*, sailors search for love and find death instead. In *Barrett's Privateers*, one young man searches for wealth and winds up literally without a leg to stand on. In *The Rawdon Hills*, all that's left from a Maritime gold rush are "the worn down shacks of labour past on a hill of broken stone." In *The Wreck Of The Athens Queen*, the image of decay is reversed; a shipwrecked boat yields her treasures. In *Make And Break Harbour*, the fish boats return with "a dry empty hold" and "too many are pulled up and rotten." And in *Finch's Complaint*, the last piece on the album, Stan's mood is summed up; as the song's hero says, "We're working men with no work left to do."

In terms of Stan's career, the timing of FOGARTY'S COVE was perfect. The album, dedicated to Stan's grandfathers and to "the people of Canada's Atlantic Provinces," was an ideal introduction for the record-buying public because it presented a clear image of the man and his music, something the audience could readily identify. The album almost worked too well. For the rest of his career, the public recognized Stan not as a singer of songs about the Maritimes, but as a Maritime singer. His public persona was so firmly entrenched in his audience's mind that it became harder and harder for him to move outside of the box he'd created.

BLUEBERRY GRUNT

This dessert, one of Stan's favorites, comes courtesy of his aunt June Jarvis. She explains the significance of the name: "The idea is that you eat so much of it that all you can do is push your bowl away and grunt."

1. Mix 3 parts blueberries (fresh preferred) to 1 part white sugar.
2. Cook on low until sugar is dissolved and berries are boiling.
3. Drop spoon sized blobs of sweet biscuit dough into the mixture, just like adding dumplings to a stew. Add two blobs per serving.
4. Cover. Cook on low heat for 12 minutes.
5. Serve, when just cool enough to eat, with cream or vanilla ice cream.
6. Eat until full. Then grunt.

Turnaround

Bits and pieces you offered of your life
I didn't think they meant a lot or said much for you
And all the chances to follow didn't make a lot of sense
When stacked against the choices you made.

— *Turnaround*

FOGARTY'S COVE was an immediate success. Stan sold 8,000 copies within nine months of its release, with a timely appearance on CBC's *Morningside* boosting sales. Critics also picked up on the album, and quickly recognized its importance. *The Montreal Gazette* called it "a superbly executed collection of songs about the Maritimes. . . . One of the finest folk music albums to yet come out of Canada." The L.A-based *Folk Scene* singled out FOGARTY'S COVE as top contender for Best Folk Record of the Year and concluded it was "a great achievement in every respect." At a moment when folk music threatened to implode under the pressure of self-indulgence, Stan Rogers was a breath of fresh sea air.

Although FOGARTY'S COVE opened a lot of doors, Stan wasn't completely happy with the results. His knack for writing authentic-sounding songs and his attempt to establish a Canadian folk identity made him the darling of folk purists, a group Stan had long avoided. He decided that what he needed was another album to showcase his versatility as a songwriter and prevent himself from being pigeonholed.

Stan started recording his second album, TURNAROUND, in late September 1977, and finished just in time for his marriage to Ariel on the thirtieth of that month. The record was something of salvage job, an apt image since it is one that Stan returned to again and again in his songwriting. Stan searched through the songs he had written over the last 10 years to find ones that would best represent his diverse songwriting repertoire. As he explained in the album liner notes, TURNAROUND was a cathartic experience for Stan. True, he was cleaning out his closet. But the hard work was anticipation of the new direction his life was taking.

"To all the friends and relatives that hounded me so ruthlessly and sweetly over the years," he wrote, "I'd like to say 'Here are some of them. I always agreed they were good songs, and I'm proud of them. But I had to wait until I could do them justice.' The songs on this album span, although they don't entirely represent, some nine years of writing. Some were written in the damndest places, too, and under very odd circumstances. I'll leave you to guess which ones are more or less autobiographical . . . . In any event, this thing has really become a labour of love, and was something more difficult to do than FOGARTY'S COVE. The strain on all concerned was at times well-nigh ludicrous, and I can only applaud and thank those that are close to me for putting up with so much. My long-suffering father, for example, has had to put up with the birth of a fledgling record company in his living room, and the transformation of his wife from a quiet, funny and witty country lady to an energetic, talented and harassed corporate executive. As for my wife . . . well, check the recording dates on the cover, and maybe you'll understand that she put up with a lot when I tell you we were married on Sept. 30, 1977."

In the end, out of 10 songs, only *The Jeannie C.* was written specifically for the album. The project began under the auspices of Mitch Podolak's Barn Swallow Records, but, after the recording began, Podolak pulled out. He simply had no more money. Without the cash, TURNAROUND seemed dead in the water. Enter Stan's parents. Valerie had recently started up a mail-order business in her kitchen to help meet the demand for FOGARTY'S COVE. In reality, Valerie's decision wasn't completely voluntary. She started off mailing some albums for her son, just to help, and the next thing she knew, Stan presented her with a business license and a vision of a corporate empire which would one day, he hoped, span recording, wholesale and retail sales, management, and artist promotion. The mail order side was going quite well. Buoyed by its success, Al and Valerie decided to take a bigger chance on their son. They invested part of their life savings to complete TURNAROUND and in the process started a new recording and publishing company called Fogarty's Cove Music. Having already made his money back on the first album, Mitch sold Barn Swallow Records to the new Rogers family label for $2,500, retaining half the publishing rights. Garnet, a talented graphic artist, sat down and designed the company logo: a boat on posts, out of the water, waiting for refitting and its ultimate return to the sea.

Throughout his career, Stan struggled with the fact that, on the one hand, he wanted commercial success, while on the other, he didn't want to be seen as a sell-out to the folk community. In other words, he wanted stardom without compromise. With TURNAROUND, Stan's struggle is clearly laid out: one side features the traditional music his fans wanted to hear, while the other offered the singer-songwriter material that Stan hoped would get him radio play. As Stan explained to *Folk Life Quarterly* in 1978, he was attempting to show that there was more to his music than the mythic Maritime Man. "I'm very much interested in traditional music, and I hear more and more of it all the time . . . . But I'm also a contemporary writer, and popularity such as FOGARTY'S COVE got me also gave some of the people who heard it the wrong impression. They kind of got the idea I was strictly a singer of the traditional-sounding songs, and I don't want to get myself locked into that. I want to do popular music, pop-folk, too."

Side One of the new album contained work of the revivalist Stan: *Dark-Eyed Molly* by Scottish folksinger Archie Fisher and a version of the traditional *Oh No, Not I*, which Stan described as "folk punk" and earned the singer the nickname "Steeleye Stan," a reference to the British revival band Steeleye Span. *Second Effort* was a countrified tune culled from a CBC Radio special *So Hard To Be So Strong*. *Bluenose*, originally written for a Government of Nova Scotia promotional film, was actually one of Stan's least favorite among his Maritime tunes. But the final cut on Side One was a standout: *The Jeannie C.* It's the story of an old fisherman who loses his beloved boat to the sea, and along with *Barrett's Privateers* and *Northwest Passage*, one of Stan's most powerful Can Trad songs.

Side Two of TURNAROUND is reserved for the singer-songwriter Stan. *So Blue* is an unabashed tribute to Canada's Joni Mitchell, whose jazz-influenced songwriting style had a tremendous impact on Stan. *Front Runner*, another song rescued from *So Hard To Be So Strong*, and *Try Like The Devil* both betray Stan's country roots. *Song Of The Candle*, a holdover from his pre-London days, showed that Stan could be as introspective and as obscure as any other singer-songwriter. The title track, one of the first songs Stan ever wrote, finishes the album.

Stan was very proud of the song but never talked about the story behind it. Nigel Russell was there in 1969 when Stan wrote *Turnaround* and he interprets it as an attempt by Stan to come to terms with his own limitations. At the time it was written, the Hobbits had just broken up and Stan was visiting Nigel in Peterborough. Nigel was going out for a jog, and had tried unsuccessfully to talk an out-of-shape Stan into joining him. "After I'd gone a few blocks, I heard somebody call me; I turned around and there was Stan. He figured that he could catch me and keep up, even though he was totally out of shape. He figured that all he had to do was put his mind to it. But already he was fading, and when I looked at him, he had given up."

Never one to waste his energy, Stan went to work as soon as he got back to the house. By the time Nigel retuned from his jog, Stan had finished composing *Turnaround*.

> And if I had followed a little ways
> Because we're friends you would have made me welcome out
>   there.
> But we both know it's just as well, 'cause some can go
> But some are meant to stay behind and it's always that way.

Only by a fluke did Stan wind up including *Turnaround* on the album. They were nearing the end of the recording session and the crew was relaxing after dinner. As Stan recalled to an interview in 1978 with *Folk Life Quarterly*, he'd forgotten the song even existed. "One night after we were finished we were downstairs, in the living quarters below the studio, and Mike Curry, our Spiritual Advisor — he advises us on matters of spirits — picked up my brother's guitar and just started playing this old song of mine. He made it sound so good, and it fitted in so well with what we conceived this album to be, that the next night we went into the studio and recorded it."

At Curry's insistence, Stan put the song on his new release. What began as an after-thought summed up the mood of the entire album, as well as pointing to the direction Stan's life was about to take.

Stan had high hopes for TURNAROUND, but the public response was disappointing. The album sold reasonably well, thanks to Stan's touring and his mother's relentless mail-order work, but without the benefit of a showstopper like *Barrett's Privateers* or *Forty-Five Years*, TURNAROUND lacked bite. To this day, it remains one of Stan's least commercially successful albums.

Still, the album served its purpose. TURNAROUND established Stan as a reliable recording artist and as a songwriter of unlimited potential. And because they produced the album on the cheap, the family soon sold enough copies to break even.

The year 1978 started with a setback. David Woodhead, the

bass player, announced that he was quitting the band. Stan should have seen it coming. Woodhead was a brilliant, creative player who liked musical challenges. He wasn't cut out to be Stan Rogers' sideman for life. It was too bad because, musically, the combination worked well. Stan provided a firm foundation which allowed Woodhead room to improvise. Meanwhile Garnet was developing into a superb accompanist, his relaxed manner and off-the-cuff remarks providing the perfect foil to his brother's more practiced and measured performance. In the trio, Stan had found a format which allowed him to present his best assets — his voice and songs — upfront and pushed his liabilities to the background. Once known for marble-mouthed song introductions and abrasive attempts at humor, Stan was now earning a reputation for his crisp, professional show.

Soon after TURNAROUND was released, Stan started to make inroads into the United States. One of his earliest American fans was Emily Friedman, editor of the prestigious Chicago-based folk journal *Come for to Sing*. The two first met at the 1975 Winnipeg Folk Festival, although, as Friedman recalls, it was a rough introduction. "I wound up being in an elevator with Stan. He was a little standoffish at the time. What I didn't know was that Stan disliked America and Americans. So he barely acknowledged me."

Their next meeting went better the following year, again in Winnipeg. This time, when Stan saw Emily, he ran over to her and gave her one of his trademark bear hugs. Presumably he was pleased with the positive press he had gotten in her magazine. In time, Friedman became a devoted and influential friend. Stan would often visit her when he was down in the States and became a regular columnist in her journal. Friedman sang his praises to anyone who would listen and even acted as his one-woman distribution company in the United States, selling albums from her living room.

Stan tried to get U.S. club dates numerous times. At first, no one wanted to book him. But as his reputation grew, Stan ran into a different obstacle: U.S. Immigration. Immigration seemed reluctant to give an unknown performer the proper papers, and Stan, unlike some other Canadian performers, would not work in the U.S. without a visa. Stan was finally allowed to perform at a benefit concert for *Come for to Sing*. In the eyes of the U.S. government, as long as he wasn't making any money, he was welcome.

Among the first major American performers to recognize Stan's talent was Tom Paxton, a central figure in the sixties folk boom who remains a potent musical force to this day. Paxton was born in Chicago in 1937 and moved to Oklahoma as a youngster. In the early sixties, he hooked up with the Greenwich Village crowd that included Bob Dylan, Phil Ochs, Pete Seeger, and Peter, Paul and Mary. And in 1965, he released the landmark folk album, RAMBLIN' BOY.

Paxton's first introduction to Stan was at the 1978 Summerfolk Festival in Owen Sound, located about three hours northeast of Toronto on Georgian Bay. Paxton was walking across a field early on a Sunday morning. "I heard this incredible voice coming over the loud-speaker," Paxton recalls, "singing *Amazing Grace*. This huge voice. And I thought, 'Who the hell is that?' Then I realized it must be Stan Rogers. I'd been hearing so much about him. Folk music is a very small world and we quickly get to hear about the people we haven't met yet. The word was out that he was a definite comer."

Paxton met Rogers a half hour later and they became friends. The American singer had a tremendous respect for Stan and considered him the Canadian equivalent of the American folk giant, Woody Guthrie. Paxton even wrote a song for Stan, now forgotten, although in Paxton's opinion there's no great loss since the song "turned out not to be very good."

Stan's immigration problems had a positive side. American folk fans were itching to get a look at him. His first major show was at the Philadelphia Folk Festival, the premier American festival since the decline of Newport in the late sixties. As Garnet Rogers recalls, the band had a chip on its shoulder and set out to prove to the Americans just what they could do. "The festival organizers didn't want to give us an evening concert — they gave us a cheesy afternoon slot. We felt ill-used. We just had a bad attitude, brought about by three guys being in the same van year after year, grinding it out. We just decided that we were going to go out there and tear their faces off."

They parked their van in a secluded spot and just sat there with the windows shut, psyching themselves up for the show. "We just huddled," Garnet continues. "Finally we opened the door of the van, fixed bayonets on our guitars, and went over the top."

These were the days when jeans and t-shirts were the standard folk uniform, but Stan's band dressed up for all their shows. In the end, they put on the kind of show that wouldn't be out of place at a rock concert. "We'd leap around stage: three guys thrashing around, running from one end of the stage to the other. We finished the last chord of *Witch of the Westmorland*. Everyone went nuts because we weren't just a bunch of folk singers up there farting around. Needless to say, they gave us the evening spot the next night."

Why was Stan an immediate hit with American audiences, while it took him years to catch on in Canada? For starters, his personality probably better suited the American temperament. Like it or not, Canadians tend to be compliant and polite, two adjectives rarely used to describe Stan Rogers. He was brash and demanding, which is exactly how Americans expect talented people to behave. And then there's the prodigal son theory: Canadians don't acknowledge their artists until they become successful somewhere else. At home, Stan was just another wannabe, but in the States they recognized his merits without prejudice. In fact, being Canadian was a selling point in the United States. Stan seemed, well, exotic. Because Canadians and Americans live so close together, sharing a common language and similar cultures, the differences between the two countries aren't always apparent. But Nigel Russell, who grew up in Canada and now makes his home in Texas, says a performer can always tell what country he's in without looking at a map. "Canadian audiences clap on the 'on' beat; American audiences clap on the 'off' beat. That's not a bad thing, except that Canadians feel bad for clapping on the 'on' beat. It doesn't sound right, because it's not what the Americans are doing." This seems a small point, but performer after performer has commented on it. And it does suggest that at the very heart, for rhythm is the heartbeat of song, Canadians and Americans approach music differently.

Given the number of Canadian songwriters who have found success in the States, there must be some common quality or attribute that sets them apart. Stan's friend and fellow folksinger Doug McArthur believes that the difference lies in Canadian songwriters' tendency to be less political and more literary than their American counterparts. "Canadians are perceived by American audiences as having a more balanced point of view. Canadians like to distance themselves from their subjects. In our country, we're physically so far apart from each other that we've become fascinated by distance; we are fascinated by the spaces in between."

Nigel Russell agrees. "Canadian songwriters have a view that comes from not having grown up in violent cities. It's the same kind of feel that country music has: heartfelt, optimistic and wholesome."

All these "Canadian" qualities are found in the music of Stan Rogers. At home, they often went unnoticed, but in the United States, they only added to his appeal.

Between the **B**reaks

We grow but grow apart –
We live but more alone –
The more to be, the more to see,
To cry aloud that we are free
To hide our ancient fears of being alone.

— *Delivery Delayed*

The world got a little bigger for Stan Rogers in 1979. He put out another album, his third in three years. He played major club dates and festivals throughout North America. And best of all, he and Ariel had a child together.

The new album was called BETWEEN THE BREAKS, dedicated to Emily Friedman, who talked Stan into making a live record. "I was hoping Stan would achieve that high-energy spontaneity on record that he had in his live performances," she explains the genesis of the album, "but which had been missing in his previous two albums. The production on his studio albums tended to drift further and further away from how he sounded live, as his career progressed. I thought a live album would be a great way to show off the songs."

The album was recorded in a restaurant-cum-folk club in Toronto, The Groaning Board. To fill out the sound, Stan expanded his usual complement of three musicians to five. Garnet was there, along with David Allen Eadie, the new bass player in the trio. Grit Laskin joined in on an eclectic selection of instruments that included the long-necked mandolin, Northumbrian smallpipes, and the concertina. Curly Boy Stubbs, a.k.a. Paul Mills, kicked in on guitar. Mills also retained his job as producer, while his co-producer on *Touch the Earth*, Bill Garrett, lent a hand in the mobile recording truck. The recordings took place over the span of four nights, during what was one of the most hectic weeks in Stan's life.

As Stan described this wild ride in the album's liner notes, "The rest was a simple matter of finding the right gig to record, finding a mobile sixteen-track recording facility that didn't cost the moon, frantically rehearsing Grit and Curly Boy in not only the tunes intended for the album but enough to do the rest of the show as well, arranging for a cover photograph, trucking sound equipment all over the place, helping publicize the week at The Groaning Board (a live album requires a live audience, preferably a large live audience), sending out nearly a hundred invitations, making endless phone calls, driving close to two hundred miles a day for two weeks, and most importantly, trying to do a good show every night for the folks who, to our immense relief, turned out in large numbers to see the whole thing go down. . . . The end result of all this you hold in your hands, and we're quite pleased with it. Valerie's fingernails are healing nicely, thank you, and she no longer trembles and sweats when the word 'album' is mentioned."

Grit Laskin has a similar recollection of the experience. He put in a full day at his workshop, where he repaired and handcrafted custom guitars. In the evenings, to save time, the band would meet in Grit's workshop to practice. "We performed the same two fifty-minute sets each night," Grit explains. "Out of those, we chose the best version of each particular song. We wound up with more material than we needed, but that suited

Stan fine. He was always in the habit of recording more than he needed, just to play it safe."

The public response to BETWEEN THE BREAKS was over-whelming. The hard-core folkies, who liked Stan's traditional side, loved the album, but Stan also won over a truckload of con-temporary music fans, especially in the United States. The album did what it set out to do: capture the energy of Stan Rogers live in concert. As Emily Friedman notes, this was as much due to Stan's growing awareness of his audience as it was to the live recording format. "The energy level on TURNAROUND was down; that's what turned a lot of listeners off. The energy level on BETWEEN THE BREAKS was up, partly because it was recorded live, and partly because Stan was beginning to understand that high-energy material was selling."

In terms of song styles, BETWEEN THE BREAKS had a little bit of everything. It contained traditional songs like *Rolling Down To Old Maui* and Archie Fisher's *The Witch Of The Westmorland* — even a new version of *Barrett's Privateers* because, as Ariel reports, Stan didn't feel the original sounded "manly" enough. There were also a couple of tunes — stunning, heart-wrenching ballads — from Stan's old singer-songwriter repertoire, *First Christmas* and *Delivery Delayed*. The material Stan wrote specifi-cally for this album was outstanding, an indication of how his songwriting skills were still developing. Of the nine tunes on the album, three were new: *Flowers Of Bermuda*, *Harris And The Mare*, and one that was to become his signature song, *The Mary Ellen Carter*. It is from that genre peculiar to Stan Rogers, the salvage song.

> She went down last October in a pouring driving rain
> The skipper, he'd been drinking and the Mate, he felt no pain.
> Too close to Three Mile Rock and she was dealt her mortal blow
> And the *Mary Ellen Carter* settled low.

An instant classic, the song secured Stan's reputation as a song-writer and was the kind of sales-boosting "hit" TURNAROUND lacked. It is also his most inspirational song and, given the circumstances of his death, his most poignant.

> Rise again, rise again — though your heart it be broken
> And life about to end
> No matter what you've lost be it a home, a love, a friend
> Like the *Mary Ellen Carter*, rise again.

As much as anything, *The Mary Ellen Carter* is a patented Stan Rogers political statement. He never attacked politicians or parties directly. But he often took a swipe at the unspoken relationship that underlies all politics: the relationship between the powerful and the powerless. This level of politics is evident in a previously unpublished piece giving background to the song from one of several radio plays Stan wrote but were never produced. This play was called, aptly, *The Mary Ellen Carter*. "Maritime insurance fraud has become big business," the narrator comments, "so big in fact that whole shipping conglomerates have been formed in recent years whose sole purpose is not, as one would expect, the movement of goods in ship, but rather the sinking of ships in as profitable a manner as possible. A company buys a smallish freighter, as old and rickety as possible, registers it under any of four or five 'flags of convenience' like Panama, Sierra Leone, or Hong Kong, secures a cargo for a voyage, and insures the whole lot for as much as possible; usually several times the value of the ship. As soon as the ship is in deep water, it will mysteriously spring a leak and sink. The crew takes to the boats, reports the loss, and after an investigation, the insurance company pays off."

While the live album played an important role in the development of Stan's career, it seems to lack a unifying theme. Stan used to say that the live album was "about heroes," but then, what Stan Rogers song wasn't? If there is a theme, it is probably one of loss. In *Barrett's Privateers*, the narrator has lost his legs and his youth. In *First Christmas*, families are separated and lost. In *The Mary Ellen Carter*, a ship is lost, as is the workers' faith in their employers, while in *White Collar Holler*, the employees lose their identity. And in *The Flowers Of Bermuda* and *Harris And The Mare*, what's lost is life itself. The song *Delivery Delayed* deals with what for Stan seems the most potent loss of all: the separation between the mother and her child. In this song, he describes birth from the baby's point of view.

> By giant hand we're taken from the shelter of the womb
> That dreaded first horizon, the endless empty room
> Where communion is lost forever, when a heart first beats alone.
> Still, it remembers, no matter how it is grown.

Stan wrote the song in 1975 to commemorate the birth of Paul Mills's son. Ariel says that in writing the song Stan became fascinated with the birth process, and, in particular, with the woman's experience of childbirth. He read books on it, asked questions, watched films in an effort to bring himself as close as possible to this experience, one he would obviously never have.

In many ways, *Delivery Delayed* sums up Stan's interests as a songwriter. He was deeply curious, and like any good Canadian songwriter, compelled by the distances between people. Perhaps this is why he returns over and over again to the theme of separation and loss: he was less interested in how far apart people were than he was in how they became separated in the first place.

To many fans, *Delivery Delayed* seems out of place on BETWEEN THE BREAKS. The song is low-key, reflective, more suited to Side Two of TURNAROUND than to the energy of a live album. But there were two good reasons for its inclusion, one sacred, the other, profane. The latter has to do with sound quality on the vinyl records. In this day of digital CDs and cassettes, physical placement of a song has no bearing on the quality of the sound produced. But on vinyl, the grooves get closer together as the record "progresses." Near the end of a side, the grooves are so tight that there isn't room for a lot of sound. That is why many albums end a side with a slow song, and that may be why BETWEEN THE BREAKS ends with *Delivery Delayed*. The sacred reason is simple. In the second-to-last week in April 1979, when the album was recorded, Ariel was six months pregnant. On July 16 of that year, their first and only child was born: Nathan Prescott Warren Rogers (Ariel did have three children, David, Kate and Beth from a previous marriage, all of whom considered Stan as their father.)

Those were the early days of natural childbirth, and Stan, a Lamaze graduate, was right there in the delivery room coaching Ariel — "Breathe, honey, dammit!" — and holding her hand. In the morning, he stood on his porch and whooped and shouted and ran down to his old van, affectionately named "Clank," and honked and honked and honked. One by one, the neighbors opened their eyes and awoke to the realization that Stan and Ariel Rogers had a son.

By the time of Nathan's birth, Stan had achieved such stature that he was becoming a source of humur for a lot of people. Not the laugh-behind-your-back humor of the disenfranchised or envious, but the gentle, chiding humor of peers sharing in Stan's success and at the same time warning him not to let that success inflate his already enormous ego. Because his music was so powerful and his lyrics so appealing, Stan's songs were favorite targets of parody. The finest example is *Garnet's Home Made Beer*, a take-off on *Barrett's Privateers*. Fittingly, it was written by Ian Robb, from the Friends of Fiddler's Green, who had been with Stan in Sudbury when he wrote the original. According to Robb, the parody was based on a wild party at the Rogers home, circa 1978.

"Everyone was in a funny mood, and people started throwing various liquids around," he recalls. "Originally it was water, but it quickly devolved into beer. My wife happened to be on the receiving end of a large jug of home-made beer, which Garnet poured over her. She was not terribly pleased." Suitably inspired, Robb went off to write of the adventure, in a song that has reached semi-legendary status among Stan Rogers' fans.

Garnet's Home-Made Beer
(to the tune of *Barrett's Privateers*)

Oh, the year was 1978
(How I wish I'd never tried it now!)
When a score of men were turned quite green
By the scummiest ale you've ever seen.

CHORUS

God damn them all! I was told
This beer was worth its weight in gold;
We'd feel no pain, shed no tears.
But it's a foolish man who shows no fear
At a glass of Garnet's home-made beer

Oh, Garnet Rogers cried the town
(How I wish I'd never tried it now!)
For twenty brave men, all masochists, who
Would taste for him his home-made brew

CHORUS

This motley crew was a sickening sight
(How I wish I'd never tried it now!)
There was caveman Dave with his eyes in bags;
He's a hard-boiled liver in the staggers and jags.

CHORUS

Well, we hadn't been there but an hour or two,
(How I wish I'd never tried it now!)
When a voice said: "GIMME SOME HOME, MADE BREW"
And Steeleye Stan hove into view.

CHORUS

Now Steeleye Stan was a frightening man
(How I wish I'd never tried it now!)
He was eight feet tall and four feet wide
Said, "Pass that jug or I'll tan your hide!"

CHORUS

Stan took one sip and pitched on his side
(How I wish I'd never tried it now!)
Garnet was smashed with a gut full of dregs,
And his breath set fire to both me legs.

CHORUS

So here I lay with me twenty-third beer,
(How I wish I'd never tried it now!)
It's been ten years since I felt this way –
On the night before my wedding day.

God damn them all! I was told
This beer was worth its weight in gold;
We'd feel no pain, shed no tears.
But it's a foolish man who shows no fear
At a glass of Garnet's home-made beer

What was Stan's reaction to the song? Ian Robb and his Fiddler's Green cronies had gone to great pains to keep the song a secret — no easy task in the insular folk music community. When he finally did sing it for Stan, Robb says he was completely tickled and, whenever he played in Robb's hometown of Ottawa, Stan would drag his friend on stage to sing the parody. "I know what it's like to have your songs parodied," Robb says. "No one is really offended by it: a parody indicates that the song is well-loved."

The biggest joke of all was played on Stan in the summer of 1980. He spent an entire month on, of all things, a school bus. He was part of a traveling folk show put together by Stan's first backer, Mitch Podolak, for Alberta's 75th anniversary celebration. The Alberta government gave Podolak $200,000 and an old bus, then let him loose. Podolak assembled a collection of his finest musical friends: Stan Rogers, Sylvia Tyson, Connie Kaldor, the American folk singer Jim Post, John Allen Cameron, Stringband, Duck Donald's Bluegrass Band, Paul Hann, and Joan MacIsaac. In all, there were 45 people on the bus tour, including roadies, technicians, and back-up musicians. Like the other musicians on the bus trip, Joan Besen had an experience she'll never forget.

Today Besen is best known for her songwriting and keyboard work with Prairie Oyster, Canada's premier country music band, but in 1980, she was part of Sylvia Tyson's Great Speckled Bird. Joan recalls that the trip was an absurdity on wheels, a kind of demented high-school outing for a cast of characters, the youngest of whom hadn't seen the tail end of high school in years. "It was not a luxurious tour," she recalls. "You did a high-intensity show, then climbed back onto a school bus? My god! No one was 20 years old. But, while there was something amateurish about the conditions under which we were working, there was nothing amateurish about the quality of the shows."

For Stan, the money was good: he made close to $8,000 for 33 days of work. He was able to build on the strong support he already had in Alberta; he often referred to Calgary as his "second home," which put the city in contention with his other 'second homes' on the East Coast and in the United States. Stan had a prestigious spot in the line-up. Although Sylvia Tyson was the undisputed star, Stan was second on the list and closed the show many nights. "Stan definitely had one of the most powerful and moving shows you would ever see," Joan Besen recalls. "And you could count on him, night after night."

Besen knew Stan before the tour. They'd always got along, mostly because Besen had an instinctive understanding of how Stan ticked. "Stan was the classic gruff-exterior-with-the-heart-of-gold guy. He really enjoyed presenting this rough exterior. It was kind of a test, I think, but there was also a perverse sense of humor at work. There are certain elements in the folk world that are very serious, very politically correct. Stan was a big guy with a certain amount of renown and power. And it gave him great delight to take a shot at these people whenever he could."

Mitch Podolak's biggest concern at the start of the tour had nothing to do with logistics. He was terrified that Stan and Jim Post would wind up killing each other. Podolak was witness to their first meeting at the 1978 Winnipeg Folk Festival when he introduced the two folk singers.

"Why, he's just a little guy," Stan said, without offering his hand. "I could lift him right up and break his neck, couldn't I?"

"You put your hand on me and I'll poke your eyes out," Post replied.

"Feisty too, isn't he?"

The problem was that Post intimidated Stan. The Texas-born folk singer had a great reputation as a performer and songwriter. Even though he was on the verge of stardom, Stan was still insecure at heart, but then, such insecurity is often what makes a great performer tick.

As it turned out, Podolak's worst fears never materialized. Once they got used to each other, once Stan felt he could trust Post, the two got along famously. But that's the way it often was with Stan. It took a while for Stan to feel he could trust a stranger.

While there were lots of memorable moments on the bus tour — like Post dancing naked in a field at Drummheller just as a bus full of elderly American tourists pulled up — the highlight of the trip was the High River show. This was Joe Clark's hometown, and, in 1980, its native son was prime minister. Stan was the fourth act that night. He climbed up on stage, then strummed a chord to get the crowd's attention. "Good evening!" he called into the mike. He stepped back and strummed another chord.

"Well, High River . . . ," he said, a twinkle in his eye. The other performers held their collective breath; they could tell Stan had something on his mind. "You've given us a prime minister. . ." Stan paused and smiled. "Better luck next time."

Although meant as a joke . . . let's just say the fans didn't appreciate the humor. Stan played the rest of his show to a cold and stony silence, watching with embarrassment as audience members left in droves. The performers who followed Stan tried to win back the half-empty auditorium, but their efforts were largely in vain.

In a way, this was the story of Stan's life. Because of his size and his talent — or maybe just because he was a folk singer — people took him seriously all the time. This reaction confused and hurt Stan as much as his ill-fated attempts at humor confused his audience, sometimes leaving him feeling confused as well.

Delineation

Ah, for just one time, I would take the Northwest Passage
To find the hand of Franklin reaching for the Beaufort Sea
Tracing one warm line through a land so wide and savage
And make a Northwest Passage to the sea.

— *Northwest Passage*

With BETWEEN THE BREAKS, Stan Rogers accomplished what he
set out to do and then some. The album captured the feel of his
live concerts and made him a hit in the American folk market.
"The live album was really quite a success," Stan wrote in his song
book *Songs from Fogarty's Cove.* "And it opened a lot of doors. We
started touring even farther afield, particularly in Western
Canada, and these new scenes had a profound effect on my writing and indeed my whole attitude about what I did for a living."

Stan's next step was clear. Above all else, he wanted commercial success and mainstream acceptance, but on his own terms.
When he first started in the music business with RCA, there was
only one route to success: singles. In that kind of market, with
artists vying for airtime on commercial radio, Stan could never
make it. But times had changed. Albums had surpassed the 45 single

in importance, and album-oriented FM radio stations opened new markets. It was also possible for an artist to reach this album-buying market without even making a dent on radio, as Stompin' Tom Connors was consistently proving.

Stompin' Tom Connors is perhaps the only other artist who can match Stan Rogers' power in creating a contemporary identity for traditional Canadian music. The two men approached music very differently. While Stan was studied, literate and serious, Stompin' Tom remains experienced, lyrical, and lighthearted. While Stan consciously tried to invent a Canadian folk idiom based in part on his childhood fascination with the East Coast, Connors plays and sings in the tradition of the music that surrounded him as he grew up. Tom Connors lived the life of Stan Rogers' imagination. Born on Prince Edward Island in 1937, he was orphaned quite young and ran away from his foster home in Skinner's Pond at the age of 14. Eventually, he made his way to a boarding house in St. John, New Brunswick, where he first learned to play guitar. Then he was off to work the boats. He traveled the country coast to coast with his guitar, playing every backwoods bar and makeshift club that would have him. In 1964, Connors found himself at the Maple Leaf Hotel in Timmins, a mining town 150 miles north of Sudbury. Soon, the crowds were streaming to the beer hall to watch a kid in black cowboy clothes sing his tunes, all the while stomping time with his boot on a piece of plywood. Over the next year, Connors played sold-out shows at the Maple Leaf. The owners had to expand the place three times to keep up the demand.

Connors made his first record in 1964, with his own money. Since that time he's made almost 40 more. Along the way, he started his own company, Boot Records, which in its heyday distributed 60 Canadian artists, Stan Rogers among them. Connors formed Boot Records out of sheer frustration with the Canadian music industry, having had more record company doors shut in his face than he cares to remember. "No recording company would have anything to do with me," he recalls. "So I saved up my pennies by working in hotels and started making 45 singles on my own and selling them in bars. I'd go to the jukebox owners and give them 45s. Sometimes they'd put them in the jukebox; other times they'd throw them in the garbage. That's the chance you take."

Connors's tenacity paid off. Before he got fed up with the music business and retired in 1978, he had 12 gold albums — 50,000 units of each sold — and half a dozen Juno Awards. His albums had titles like BUD THE SPUD, STOMPIN' TOM AT THE GUM-BOOT CLOGGEROO, STOMPIN' TOM MEETS 'MUK TUK' ANNIE, and THE UNPOPULAR STOMPIN' TOM, reflecting his love of homegrown stories and his less than mainstream appeal. While he might have made more money with a bigger label, Connors says he made a choice to protect the integrity of his music. "I think that anybody who writes his own material and feels strongly about the content and subject matter is probably better off, in the beginning, with a smaller company. Stan felt strongly about his desire to represent his country through his music, and that's something a big record company just wouldn't let him get away with."

In 1990, after a 12-year hiatus during which Connors worked on his farm and managed his other businesses, the singer returned to the public eye. The president of Capitol Records Canada, Dean Cameron, sought out the singer and persuaded him to end his self-imposed retirement. Although he personally thought Capitol was making a big mistake, Connors relented and his first release, FIDDLE AND SONG, went gold. Of the 14 albums re-released from Connors's back catalog, 12 went gold, an extraordinary success story.

Still, Connors doesn't get any airplay outside of the CBC and the occasional spin on a country or Maritime station. "I learned very quickly that radio had no use for people who wrote songs about their own country," Tom remarks. "And I also knew that in Canada there is such a great need for people to write about this country. Everybody needs to know about their own country. This is why the music industry in the U.S. has thrived so well; they're always singing about themselves."

While BETWEEN THE BREAKS was a success, Stan was frustrated with the limited scope that a single album afforded him. He wanted to incorporate the whole country in his music, something he couldn't do in 10 songs. To achieve this grand plan, he planned a series of linked albums, starting, retrospectively, with FOGARTY'S COVE.

NORTHWEST PASSAGE was number two in a planned five-part series, built around FOGARTY'S COVE, which would take him from one coast to the other. On this album, Stan looked at Western Canada. Others in the series would look at the Great Lakes, Quebec and Acadia (songs in French and English), and the Far North. Regrettably, Stan was unable to complete the last two albums in the series before he died.

NORTHWEST PASSAGE was recorded at London's Springfield Sound late in 1980. The album turned out to be Stan's most complete artistic achievement to date, fulfilling the promise of FOGARTY'S COVE. It's no surprise then to read in the NORTHWEST PASSAGE liner notes that the "album came about in much the same way" FOGARTY'S COVE had five years earlier. "As the result of much traveling in the West and North of Canada," Stan wrote, "I had amassed a number of songs that dealt specifically with that area and some bright soul suggested that this album become yet another 'theme' album, and incorporate the Western tunes." By the time he hit the studio, Stan was more or less ready with what he termed "a fairly eclectic brew" of songs. But one key ingredient was missing. He knew that he wanted to call the album "Northwest Passage." Only problem was, he didn't yet have a song of that title.

Stan knew that he wanted it to be another *a capella* chorus song. Every album except TURNAROUND had one, and, besides, they were fun to do. But it was down to the wire, the night before the recording session was to end, and Stan still didn't have anything on paper. As Stan later recalled in a 1982 radio interview with Howard Larmen,

"I was helpless with fatigue at that point and I remember at one point I was lying on the floor of the studio looking up.

Everyone else had gone to bed and I was completely alone in the place and I was lying there and I could hear the sort of machinery cooling, that had been heated up during the day, some sort of electronics. I could hear the cabinets sort of cooling or clicking or something and just dead silence, and I started thinking about the silence of the north and what John Franklin must have felt on that last fatal voyage of his, where he got so close to breaking into the Beaufort Sea. He had gotten within 40 miles of breaking through and he would have been the first man through the Northwest Passage, but instead he and all of his men and both ships were lost and it was kind of a terrible saga. And I got thinking again about the first people who went across Canada. There was an explorer called Kelso or Kelsey, depending upon where you thought he was from, who first saw the Canadian prairies and described it as a 'sea of flowers' and that always stuck in my head. David Thompson was the first person to accurately survey and map the Canadian Rockies. Alexander Mackenzie was one of the first people to reach the Pacific through the Canadian Rockies. Simon Fraser another, the Fraser River that runs into Vancouver was named after him. All of these great explorers who were equally as intrepid as people like Lewis and Clark or Kit Carson or any of them you know. Canadians don't know much about these people. I mean we study them in grade 5 or 6 history and that's the last we hear of them. Canadians don't know how Canada was developed. I mean they have a smattering of history from the time of Confederation, the founding of our country in 1867. They know who Sir John A. MacDonald was. He was the first Prime Minster in many ways the father of our country. But they don't know who the other Fathers of Confederation were. I'm descended from one of them so I take an interest in them. At any rate through my songs, for the past couple of years, I've been trying to satisfy my own lust for dramatizing these things or perhaps injecting them into popular culture, but I've also had the motive of trying to make my countrymen a bit more aware of just how fascinating their own history is, and to sort of help them become a bit more small "n" nationalist. I wrote *Northwest Passage* with all of that in mind lying on my back, on the floor of the studio at 3 in the morning."

The next morning at breakfast, producer Paul Mills asked Stan if he had a title song yet.

"We got to finish today or else," Paul said.

Stan, still groggy from a lack of sleep, shrugged. Yeah, it was finished, he said, then, at Paul's prompting, sang it right there at the kitchen table, reading the words off a piece of paper.

> Westward from the Davis Strait 'tis there 'twas said to lie
> The sea route to the Orient for which so many died;
> Seeking gold and glory, leaving weathered, broken bones
> And a long-forgotten lonely cairn of stones . . .

Stan raised his head at the end of the song to see Paul crying. "That's a very stirring and solid piece," the producer said, pulling himself together. They went straight into the studio and recorded it. The album had it's title song — and Canada had what may well be the greatest song ever written about this country.

> How then am I so different from the first men through this way?
> Like them, I left a settled life, I threw it all away.
> To seek a Northwest Passage at the call of many men
> To find there but the road back home again.

> Ah, for just one time I would take the Northwest Passage
> To find the hand of Franklin reaching for the Beaufort Sea;
> Tracing one warm line through a land so wild and savage
> And make a Northwest Passage to the sea.

NORTHWEST PASSAGE has a unifying theme that goes beyond geography, with Stan once again exploring the idea of separation. Lines, especially lines of communication, are the central image of the album. In some songs, the lines are clearly drawn. In *Northwest Passage*, Stan speaks of "one warm line" of people across the snow.

In *Field Behind The Plow*, he talks of "straight dark rows." The hero of *Night Guard* put his "life on the line."

In other songs — *Canol Road, You Can't Stay Here*, and *The Idiot* — the lines are implied. *Lies* offers Stan's fullest contemplation of the theme. The story is of a woman, a farmer's wife, looking at her aging face in a mirror.

> She'd pass for twenty-nine, but for her eyes,
> But winter lines are telling wicked lies.
> Lies! All those lines are telling wicked lies.

The linear quality of communications is a very Canadian concept. We see it in routes of transportation: rivers, railway, roads and even airways, all of which are orientated along an east-west line. The irony is obvious to anyone who lives in this country: lines distance even as lines connect.

> Then she shakes off the bitter web she wove,
> And turns to set the mirror, gently, face down by the stove.
> She gathers up her apron in her hand.
> Pours a cup of coffee, drips Carnation from the can
> And thinks ahead to Friday, 'cause Friday will be fine!
> She'll look up in that weathered face that loves hers, line for line,
> To see that maiden shining in his eyes
> And laugh at how the mirror tells her lies.

Stan was interested in connections because at that point in his life he was becoming more connected to the world around him. Parenthood, in particular, was helping Stan open up. Having understood distance, Stan was now drawn more towards connections. He was a father, after all, and Ariel says that he found being a parent both frustrating and rewarding. "He was away from home almost 200 days of the year. His children seemed like strangers at times, and Stan had a difficult time keeping up with the subtle changes in rules that go on in a home."

The demands of fatherhood had also changed since Stan's own

childhood, when children were seen and not heard, and fathers were the detached patriarchs of the family kingdom. By the early 1980s, the pressure was on dads to be involved, sensitive and — yikes — nurturing. Like many men, Stan was ill-prepared for the job. On the other hand, Stan truly connected with his children. Perhaps it was because he, himself, was such a child at heart. That youthful combination of insecurity and limitless faith in one's own ability was a quality Stan could appreciate.

Whatever the reasons — fatherhood, greater career and financial security, simple maturity — Stan seemed more comfortable with himself and even more focused on his career. He needed some new challenges. He had toured Canada and criss-crossed the United States several times. Now it was time to visit the source of his musical roots and begin building his fan support around the world.

Letter from **S**cotland

'Twas the same ancient fever in the Isles of the Blest
That our fathers brought with them when they "went West"
It's the blood of the Druids that never will rest
The giant will rise with the moon.

— *Giant*

Carlton Hotel
Edinburgh, Scotland
25 May 1981

Ariel, Sweetheart:

I remember a time when writing letters was one of my favourite recreations, chiefly because, I suppose, it was a way of easing what I conceived of to be blasted boredom, or perhaps more likely, loneliness. I also couldn't afford the phone calls I would otherwise have had to make. Whatever the reason, I know I spent a lot of time at letter writing, and was told that I wrote a good one. More than once in the past few years, I wondered how I fell out of the practice, when I used to enjoy it so much. It occurred to me this morning, that perhaps I'm not lonely anymore. Of course I miss you like crazy, but that's not the same thing at all, because I only have to look at the ring I wear to remember where I left the other half of my heart. I know that no matter where I am, I'm not really lonely anymore. So I guess letters are not as essential to my well being as they used to be . . .

The folk world had come to expect the unexpected from Stan Rogers, but no one anticipated the scope and beauty of NORTH-WEST PASSAGE. Emily Friedman, in *Come for to Sing*, called the album "another brilliant and innovative record from the emerging genius of Canadian songwriting." Although the album fell short of breaking Stan into mainstream radio markets, it certainly brought him a wider audience.

Not long after NORTHWEST PASSAGE was released, Stan made his first trip to Great Britain. He was part of a ceilidh, a Gaelic word which means roughly "musical party," sponsored in part by the International Gathering of the Clans. The feature act was Stan's old friend, guitarist and fiddler John Allen Cameron. The two had already shared the stage many times at folk festivals and clubs. Cameron even put in an appearance on the FOGARTY'S COVE album. The idea of this ceilidh was to present the Scottish culture of Nova Scotia to the people of Scotland. A working title for the show could have been the Coals To Newcastle Tour. Predictably, it was a disaster.

The trouble started, Cameron recalls, as soon as the plane landed. "We went to find our hotel, but the group in Scotland forgot we were coming. There was nothing booked, so we had to make hotel arrangements at the last minute. The next thing we found out was that there had been no promotion. We ended up filling out little hand-drawn posters ourselves, and walking all over Edinburgh, posting them."

The Canadians had two hours of singing and dancing and

piping and fiddling, a great show, which lacked nothing except an audience. Over 10 days, the biggest crowd they played to was 22. They finished up in a small theater right below a punk music club.

"Stan would be doing a nice soft song, and right above us in the hall all we would hear was pounding of feet and loud drums."

John Allen Cameron is a story in himself. He was born near Mabou, in Inverness County on Cape Breton Island, a part of the world steeped in Celtic traditions, where 50 years ago, Gaelic was the mother tongue for many. John Allen grew up admiring the two most important people in the community: the parish priest and the local fiddler. As a teenager, John Allen entered the seminary, but dropped out before completing his vows. He eventually took a teaching degree and wound up with a job in London, Ontario. But his first love was music, and he soon quit teaching to hang out in the folk clubs with other like-minded musicians, including an exceptional picker by the name of Paul Mills. Thanks to his work with another Nova Scotian, Anne Murray, John Allen became an internationally known entertainer.

Although he started out on fiddle, John Allen is best known for guitar arrangements of traditional Cape Breton pipe tunes. In his heyday, John Allen thought nothing of taking his act to Las Vegas or the American talk-show circuit. For the dyed- in-the-wool folkie, these are usually acts of treason. "I preach that music has no boundaries," Cameron says. "If it's performed well, there is no reason why traditional music can't be palatable to the unconverted. We tend to be slaves to definition, without ever really thinking things through."

Canadian music owes a debt to John Allen Cameron because he was the first performer to popularize the country's indigenous Celtic music, in particular, the music of Cape Breton Island. He blazed a path that has been followed by some of Canada's best contemporary artists: Rita MacNeil, the Rankin Family, Spirit of the West, Loreena McKennitt, the Crash Test Dummies, and, of course, Stan Rogers himself.

Stan and John Allen decided that they owed themselves a treat. With the tour mercifully finished, they rented a car and set off to see Scotland. They headed north to Argyll, where a folk festival was under way. When they arrived at the festival, they were coaxed into performing. "We got on the stage that night, and they wouldn't let us off," John Allen recalls. "Our encore was over an hour and a half. Between the songs and the fiddling and Stan's marvelous voice — he blew them away — we took the place by storm."

The two Canadians never got to sleep that night. They stayed in a pub until seven o'clock in the morning, playing, singing, and swapping songs with the local musicians. Inspired by their success, the duo went out in search of more authentic Scottish music.

. . . I managed to get a good reception in a crowded pub last night. It was straight out of a British Airways ad, decorated like the deck of a wooden sailing ship, and jammed full of people singing and laughing at the top of their lungs. I got to do a half-hour set, and they hollered for more. I had the place dead quiet at one point, too. I guess I haven't lost my touch . . .

Stan and John Allen's search for traditional Scottish music did not go well. The best they could find was a cheesy music hall revue. Later, acting on a hot tip, they wound up in a smoky folk club where a kid with ripped jeans and an acoustic guitar sang Rolling Stones and Beatles songs. Stan was displeased, to say the least. The two Canadians eventually talked their way into *Studio Two*, a radio show on the BBC's Glasgow station. It was 40 minutes of near chaos, songs, and tremendous musicianship that left the listeners reeling, in more ways than one. Among other things, the audience was treated to Stan singing in Gaelic and John Allen's guitar arrangements of traditional pipe tunes. They were also treated to a healthy dose of Canadian candor, courtesy Stan Rogers.

It started innocently enough.

"What's your impression of our music?" the host asked.

Stan took a breath, then started up. "The indigenous, traditional music of Scotland I love, and always have. But we've spent three nights listening to local musicians. The first night was wonderful, and the other two nights were simply . . . " At this point, Stan offered the BBC's Highland Service listeners to a loud "raspberry" noise. "They were terrible. We wanted to hear what highland music played by highlanders sounded like. What came out was this plastic doll dressed in a kilt that was way too short, and a jacket that was much too tight, and great knobby knees, and an English accent — or at least an anglicized Scot's accent — with a big plastic smile set on his face, doing these music hall tunes."

Not satisfied with telling the Scots how to run their own house, Stan took a swipe at the powers that be. He admonished the main sponsor of his trip — "The International Gathering of the Clowns," Stan called them — for charging Scots the equivalent of over $10 to see the ceilidh. He realized that he was biting the hand that fed him, but what the hell. He was on a roll, and he was never one to hide from authority.

. . . A whole lot of things have changed in me. In a very real sense, I guess I've taken living, and making a living, very much more seriously than I ever did before. Like most of the other things I do, I overdid it. My present lousy physical condition is the end result.

I've been worried that I might not have the self-discipline I need to pull myself back into shape. But I also find that I love my life too much these days to risk screwing things up totally. In a very real sense, loving you is loving life itself, and while I suppose I should have saner reasons for wanting to lose weight and harden up my body, I really feel I want us both to live a long time together. If I make it to 83, for example, I will have loved you for sixty years. That's a pleasant thought, if ever I've had one.

love always,
Stan

On The **H**eights

And I know what it is to scale the heights
    and fall just short of fame
And have not one in ten thousand know my name.

    — *MacDonnell On The Heights* (original lyrics)

Stan Rogers turned the corner so quickly that no one saw the moment coming or realized when it was past. One instant he was just another folk singer, grunting it out on the club and festival circuit, the next he was a star. Sure, they still had to run their asses off. There were lots of nights working crummy clubs, humping gear, going home with a small percentage of the door. Even back in 1982, 10% of nothing was nothing. But the good gigs were getting better: auditoriums like the Rebecca Cohn Auditorium in Halifax and the choicest spots at all the major festivals. The biggest difference was attitude. The folk world now acknowledged what Stan had been saying for years: he was worth listening to. The Mariposa program said it all: "He is considered by many the finest singer and writer Canada has produced in decades."

Jim Morison now joined the band on bass. David Allen Eadie had left after NORTHWEST PASSAGE and Stan and Garnet were content to work without a bassist until Morison showed up at Stan's door. Jim had met Stan the previous year during the bus tour of Alberta when Morison and his friend Bill Bourne were added to Stan's bill on the tour's last stop in Red Deer. The following spring, Stan was back in town. Someone heard that Stan was out one bass player and urged Morison to approach him. As Morison recalls, Stan was busy that summer, but offered to give the bass player an audition in the fall if he made his own way to Hamilton.

In September, Morison arrived at Stan's door. The singer looked a little puzzled; maybe he'd forgotten his offer or maybe he figured the kid would never show. But Stan always stood by his word. "We sat and rehearsed and drank a lot for three days. Then we went over to Garnet's place to rehearse. It didn't go over well at all. Mind you, I was extremely hung over; so was Stan. Then we drove to Ottawa to do the gig. I thought, well this is it. We'll suffer through it for two nights then I'll be sent packing."

That night on stage, however, everything clicked. The Rogers boys had a new bass player. Morison had the skill, the temperament, and the size to take anything Stan and Garnet threw at him. At Garnet's age, he was bigger than Stan. That just added to the impression that the band was larger than life.

Around the same time, Stan got himself a real agent to book his engagements, a young American by the name of Jim Fleming he'd met at the Winnipeg Folk Festival. Until then, Stan had been doing all the business himself. His normal system was to start off with a patchwork schedule of appearances across the continent, then add gigs along the way. Although Fleming was fairly new to the folk music scene, he was rapidly building a reputation for his honesty, sensitivity, and intelligence, a rare combination in the management side of music.

Jim Fleming did more than just book Stan into clubs. He helped Stan form a viable business plan. "There was something happening with Stan," Jim recalls. "His career was just growing in leaps and bounds, primarily through word of mouth. Some of it had to do with the attention he was getting on the radio, but, even then, radio wasn't that strong. Folk music wasn't getting the attention it is getting today. Stan was making it on word of mouth alone."

Folk festivals had made a comeback, and Stan was their featured performer. Paul McGrath, writing in the July 1982 *Maclean's*, talked of the "summer celebration of folk music" and singled out Rogers in particular. "Stan Rogers could be forgiven for any confusion he might have about what year or even what decade it was," McGrath commented. "Looking out over the crowd at the newly reborn Mariposa Folk Festival in Toronto two weeks ago, the stocky, balding singer could easily have been stuck in the middle of 1972 with no hope of escape. Long skirts flowed to the ground, male hair flowed to the shoulders and babies flowed out of control at the edges of the crowd, chased by young parents who looked as if they believed that Woodstock II was really just around the corner."

As McGrath noted, Mariposa was part of a folk music revival. "The scene into which Rogers, easily Canada's most under-recorded balladeer, will slowly immerse himself over the summer as he and a large number of other Canadian folk performers make the rounds of eight major folk festivals that have sprouted up over the past decade . . . .What once provided sparse employment in the summer months for a few committed singers, pickers and dancers has grown, especially over the past five years, into a reliable coast-to-coast circuit, the only major outlet of a still-growing list of performers. Few will call it a folk boom, but most of those involved will agree that there has been a steady consolidation of an audience that is likely to stick with the idea for years to come."

On a visit to Halifax months before his death, Stan told his Uncle Prescott that things were finally falling into place. For the first time, Prescott says, Stan could see a light at the end of the tunnel.

With Stan's rising "star" status came a new pressure: he had to live up to the billing. As a songwriter, he was a perfectionist who believed that his audience deserved no less than "the finest kind." It was already becoming tough to maintain his own high standards.

As Stan Rogers' status grew, so did his need to prove himself through his songwriting. When an artist puts this kind of pressure on himself, the result is often a creative block. And Stan was no exception. He started writing songs for his next album, tentatively called "The Great Lakes Project," in the summer of 1981, but didn't finish until the late winter of 1983. As Stan worked on his new album, he was also expanding his record company.

In 1980, Fogarty's Cove Music added Grit Laskin's debut UNMASKED to its list. The company was also working out the details to record THIS SIDE OF THE OCEAN by the Friends of Fiddler's Green and LA RONDE DES VOYAGEURS by the Quebec group Eritage. There were also plans for a record of traditional fiddle tunes by Garnet. Things were going so well, in fact, that Stan was talking about expanding the business and had offered to sell shares to several of his friends.

Eighteen months after he started work on the Great Lakes album, Stan had enough material to record what he now called FROM FRESH WATER. Paul Mills was again producer, and this time he helped to arrange a co-production deal with the CBC. The national broadcaster would chip in with some free studio time. The deal meant that, for the first time in his recording career, Stan's songs would get the kind of care and attention that they deserved.

FROM FRESH WATER was a homecoming for Stan Rogers. It marked the first time he had turned his artistic attention to his true home, the province of Ontario. It was an indication of how Stan had changed, how he could now, comfortably, explore his own world. It was also a deliberate attempt to win over his home province. He was well-known in the Maritimes and the eastern United States, with pockets of support in Alberta and along the West Coast, but at home, to paraphrase the song lyrics, "not one in ten thousand know his name."

Ironically, just as he was paying attention to one part of his history, the opportunity came for him to explore another. An organization out of the United States called Folk Tradition, dedicated to an "acoustic approach" to folk music, commissioned Stan to do an album. The result was FOR THE FAMILY, a selection of songs inspired by Stan's Nova Scotia roots. For once Stan didn't write any of the lyrics. They were all tunes he remembered from his childhood, including three songs by his Uncle Lee Bushell and a poem by his grandfather Sidney Bushell, which Stan set to music.

FOR THE FAMILY was recorded on a weekend in the midst of the From Fresh Water sessions. This is how "in demand" Stan had become. And things didn't ease up when he finished his new albums. In April 1983, as soon as FROM FRESH WATER was in the can, the band was on the road for one of its most exhaustive tours to date. According to Jim Fleming, Stan was looking forward to a day in the not-too-distant future when he would be a big enough star to get by on just 60 live shows a year. But for now, he spent most of his days packing and unpacking his suitcase.

Stan and his band started off that April on a working holiday in Bermuda, playing one of Stan's favorite venues, the Bermuda Folk Club. Then it was on to one of their coast-to-coast grinds, playing both near-empty school halls and capacity theaters. In late May, they hit the West Coast with gigs in Vancouver, Victoria, Seattle, and Los Angeles. Soon, they were back at Fiddler's Green in Toronto. Then to the States to clubs like Tiger Hills and Folkway and Town Crier and Godfrey Daniel's. Next was Ottawa and the Home County Folk Festival in London, then Winnipeg for five grand and College of St. Francis a week later for six hundred dollars. Eventually, it would seem one long blur, club after club, city after city: Grand River Holstein's Music Hall Golem Welcome Table RPI Ottawa Ark Bunky's Blue Whale Moorehead Duncan Victoriortalbernigoldriver . . . and so on, well into the New Year.

But first, Kerrville, Texas.

Kerrville

He was the captain of the *Nightingale*
Twenty-one days from Clyde in coal
He could smell the flowers of Bermuda in the gale
When he died on the North Rock Shoal

— *The Flowers of Bermuda*

Quiet Valley Ranch, Kerrville, Texas. 1 June 1983. Garnet Rogers changed his flight to leave early Tuesday morning. Stan understood. There was really no reason to stick around the Kerrville Festival. They had no more shows to play and, after two-and-a-half months on the road, Garnet just wanted to get home to his wife, Gail. In the back of his mind, Stan considered going home too; he needed a break as much as anyone. But there was still lots of glad-handing left to do, and Stan felt he had an obligation to the festival organizers to stay to the bitter end.

There was nothing on the agenda for Tuesday, except a trip to Y-O Ranch, a 40,000-acre game preserve stocked with wild animals from Africa and South America for the benefit of Texas hunters. At one point, the tour bus was attacked by a 10-foot tall ostrich, which tried to peck its way through the windows. Stan laughed until his belly ached and his head turned red, all the time rooting for the heroic bird.

That night, some of the performers went to Kerrville's only French restaurant. Folksinger Connie Kaldor, who along with Stan and Al Simmons made up the Canadian contingent at Kerrville, recalls that Stan seemed unusually reflective at dinner. "He was almost eulogizing himself. He was talking about his life and what he felt strong about and what he felt good about, and he said, how wonderful it was to have tasted success. He was basically saying 'If I die tomorrow I'll be content.'"

When Stan got back to his hotel at one o'clock in the morning, he ran into Jim Morison in the lobby. Morison was a little pissed off, having been stuck at the Holiday Inn all day with no money, while Stan was out having a good time. Stan had thought Morison had already headed home with Garnet. Jim had a new baby boy at the time. He figured that if he was just going to sit around, he might just as well be at home. In a fit of pique, he decided to skip the closing concert and catch the next flight out.

They gathered on stage for the Wednesday night grand finale. The singers linked arms and swayed in time to the music, with most of the audience — "kerrverts," as the regulars proudly called themselves — joining in. By the end of the song, everyone gathered in a big circle, half on the stage, half off, arms around shoulders, singing and swaying together, united in music. Usually Stan loved to join in at times like this, but that night he was off to the side, alone. Perhaps he was trying to catch his breath after the long tour. In any case, he seemed deep in thought. When the song finished, Stan perked up and headed to the hospitality trailer, where he ran into Al Simmons. Without a word, Stan took out his guitar and started to sing.

> I used to love these lazy winter afternoons
> Starting out too late, giving up too soon. . .

Al recognized the song, Stan's *Working Joe* and realized what Stan was up to. He took out his harmonica and played along. Simmons was surprised that Stan remembered: it was a routine they'd worked up several years earlier when Stan was a guest on Al's TV show. Al's cue came when Stan reached the chorus.

But now there's just too much to do in any given day
The car, the phone, the kiddies' shoes, too many bills to pay . . .

Al pulled out a handkerchief and pretended to cry. He cried and cried, and finally blew his nose, at which point, Stan yanked the handkerchief out of his hand. The small audience that had assembled loved the routine, thinking Al and Stan had just made it up on the spur of the moment.

The laughter and applause renewed Stan's energy. He urged Al to join him at the campfires that dotted the adjacent fields. It was a Kerrville tradition. Fans and performers got together around the firelight to share music, talk, and laugh. But Al was tired and homesick, too, and decided to head offto bed. As he watched Stan tromp off into the darkness, his guitar slung over his shoulder like a rifle, Al could see the campfires glowing in the distance and he smelled the mesquite in the air. He called out a final goodbye to Stan, who turned and smiled at his friend for the last time.

The Last **W**atch

It's the last watch on the Midland
The last watch alone,
One last night to love her,
The last night she's whole.

— *The Last Watch*

It was a Friday night. Jim Morison was playing with his newborn when the phone rang.

"Have you heard?" It was Jim Fleming.

Morison was exhausted after Kerrville, and had spent the day sleeping and hanging out with his family. He didn't know what Fleming was talking about.

"Stan's plane went down in Cincinnati."

It took a moment for Fleming's comment to sink in.

"Did it go down soft?" Morison asked.

"It went down hard."

"Is everything cool? Did Stan make it?"

Fleming didn't speak. He was searching for the words.

"Well?"

"No. Stan didn't make it. Turn on your TV. It's on every station."

Stan Rogers went down hard, and the folk fans who were just getting to know and love him took his loss equally hard. They just couldn't believe that at 33 he was already gone. As often happens when a young artist suddenly dies, Stan was quickly elevated to the status of myth. The rumors started soon after the plane touched down. A woman — no one remembered who — recalled being pushed out the plane's emergency exit by a giant, bald-headed man. It could have only been Stan Rogers. The story was embellished with each retelling: two women were pushed out the exit, then three. A near-unconscious woman was carried by a giant man to the emergency exit. As she reached the bottom of the evacuation slide, she looked up to see her rescuer turn back into the fire. Soon, Stan's friends and fans were spreading the story — so widespread that it must have been true — of how he valiantly carried two women, one under each massive arm, out onto the wing of the plane before diving back into the inferno, in search of more survivors. What is true? The survivors I talked to said that the smoke was so thick and the heat so intense that it would have been difficult for anyone to return to the cabin once they got out. Timing, too, was critical. There was only a brief chance to escape the smoldering plane before it exploded in a fireball. But one story is definitely true: Stan's twelve-string guitar — crushed, broken, twisted, and damaged on many routine flights — survived the fire with only minor damage.

At the funeral, it is said, a statue of the Virgin Mary began to vibrate. A lone eagle soared above the gravesite and landed on the casket just as it was about to be lowered. Since in truth there was no burial at all, it's clear that some of these rumors are the product of overactive imaginations.

From the ashes of Flight 797, a new figure emerged: Saint Stan. He was an extension of Rogers' Maritime Stan persona, only rougher and saltier still, with a heart of gold, a golden voice, and not a spot on him. Garnet calls it the "Elvisization" of his brother. In death, we discovered Stan Rogers, bigger than ever.

Meanwhile, his family tried to pick up the pieces. Dealing with the grief and guilt and anger that accompany the sudden death of a loved one is tough enough. The existence of the record company added another dimension of difficulty. Even before Stan's death, there had been tension between Valerie and Ariel. Given the added stress of their tragedy, and without Stan around to mediate, things boiled over. Stan had owned 51% percent of Fogarty's Cove Music Inc., his independent record label, while his brother owned 49%. Since Stan didn't leave a will, it was up to the lawyers to decide who now owned the record company. Within the year, Ariel assumed full control, and in the fallout, the family became divided: Ariel on one side, Garnet and his parents on the other. It is a rift that is only now beginning to close.

In spite of the grief and confusion, the family completed the two recording projects Stan had begun before his death. The albums were released separately, eight months apart, and stand as a testament to the remarkable range of Stan Rogers' talent. The first album, FOR THE FAMILY, was released a few months after Stan's death. He had often referred to it as his favorite album because of the straightforward arrangements and production — guitar, bass, fiddle, and vocals. Here was Stan's voice in its purest form, out in front, the way many said it should always have been recorded. Since the songs are very traditional, they tend to be less appealing to mainstream ears. But even though the album lacked any songs written by Stan himself, it offered a fascinating look at the man's musical roots — a real treat for hardcore Stan fans.

The second album, FROM FRESH WATER, was something else entirely. It is Stan's most ambitious and personal work, a perfect blending of the traditional and singer-songwriter styles, and in terms of theme, offers a prolonged meditation on triumph, achievement, and attainment.

White Squall is a powerful start to the album, a song in which Stan's impassioned, but detached, narrative style is used to its most successful effect.

Now it's just my luck to have the watch with nothing left to do
But watch the deadly waters glide as we roll north to the 'Soo,'
And wonder when they'll turn again and pitch us to the rail
And whirl off one more youngster in the gale.

The rest of Side One offers several glimpses of "success," each more personal than the last. In *The Nancy*, Stan uses a battle scene as a metaphor for the victory of substance over style. In *Man With Blue Dolphin*, Stan tells the true story of a man out to salvage the Bluenose's sister ship, the *Dolphin*. The hero's success lies in his efforts; the results, if any, are secondary. As a matter of fact, Stan might be referring to his own career as he sings:

And even afloat, she's a hole in the water where his money goes.
Every dollar goes
And it's driving him crazy.

The first side ends with *Lock-keeper*, which features some of Stan's most adroit lyrics and, once again, seems a cleverly disguised comment on his own career.

But that anchor chain's a fetter
And with it you are tethered to the foam,
And I wouldn't trade your life for one hour of home.

On Side Two, Stan focuses on the destructive side of success. In *Half Of A Heart*, the narrator is "fascinated by the glitter of the flame, Watching wolves steal half of a heart away." In *The Last Watch*, an ancient lake steamer and her old watchman find themselves callously discarded despite years of devoted service. In *Flying*, a kid unsuccessfully attempts to make it in big league hockey. In *MacDonnell On The Heights*, a soldier finds obscurity in the face of victory:

'Twas MacDonnell raised the banner then
And set the heights aflame,
But not one in ten thousand knows your name.

The last song is *The House Of Orange*. Although Stan once vowed never to write a political song, here it was.

> I took back my hand and showed him the door.
> No dollar of mine would I part with this day
> For fuelling the engine of a bloody cruel war
> In my forefathers' home, far away.

The voice is the exact opposite of the detached narrator who opens the album. Stan is now singing of his own heart, his own anger.

Just before Stan went into the studio, a friend was badly hurt by an IRA bombing in London. While the anger in the song was genuine, Stan doesn't let it carry him away. He reshapes it until he uncovers something unique for his songs: forgiveness.

> All rights and all wrongs have long since blown away,
> For causes are ashes where children lie slain.
> Yet the damned U.D.L. and the cruel I.R.A.
> Will tomorrow go murdering again.
> But no penny of mine will I add to the fray.
> "Remember the Boyne!" they will cry out in vain,
> For I've given my heart to the place I was born
> And forgiven the whole House of Orange,
> King Billy and the whole House of Orange.

Forgetting that in terms of ancestry, Stan Rogers was about as English as you could get, these last two albums stand as an amazing testament to the depth and range of Stan's artistry. The albums are a tribute to a performer and songwriter who had only just approached the peak of his talents and underscored the enormity of the loss. He had achieved so much in his short life, and had so much more to give.

Rise **A**gain

Rise again, rise again, that her name not be lost
To the knowledge of men.

— *The Mary Ellen Carter*

In death came the recognition that had eluded Stan Rogers all his life. He was nominated for a Juno Award as Male Vocalist of the Year in 1984. Although he eventually lost to Bryan Adams, he was presented the Diplome d'Honneur, the highest award for artists in the country. Previous winners included classical pianist Glen Gould, jazz legend Oscar Peterson, and Canada's own opera diva, Maureen Forester. Colin Jackson from the Canadian Council of the Arts had this to say about Rogers when he presented the award.

"It is still too soon to sit down and objectively assess the impact that Stan Rogers will have on Canadian culture. But it is not too early to witness the profound effect that he had on Canadians. Like Woody Guthrie, Stan provided an articulate voice for the voiceless. The East Coast fisherman beset by Russian factory ships; the Prairie farmer, mortgage bound and tied to the land; the Great lakes sailor surviving the storm. . . . Those of us who had the privilege of knowing Stan and those of us who have benefited from his writing and music are better people for it. Had he lived, Stan Rogers would have been a legend in his own time. Now he is a Canadian folk hero. Stan said it for us; Stan could inspire . . . "

―――――――

Years after the fact there are two perspectives on Stan's abridged career: celebration for what he achieved and regret for songs that were never written, albums that were never produced, friends that were never made, conversations that were never finished.

Today, Stan Rogers is remembered around the world as a performer who changed the way folk music is presented, a brilliant songwriter who established a contemporary Canadian folk music idiom and whose talent for the modern historical ballad has yet to be equaled. The question in everybody's mind is: What if? It's a question that still troubles no less that Pete Seeger, North America's greatest living folk artist. In an phone interview from his cabin by the Hudson River, Seeger told me that Stan's death was a tremendous loss, not just to Canada or folk music, but to the world. "He had a combination of talents that was very rare in this world: the outgoing extrovert who loved to perform on stage, but who was an extremely thoughtful man and a great songwriter. I just feel sad when I think of the hundreds of wonderful songs he would have given the world if he had lived. He was on the threshold of an extraordinary contribution."

Stan Rogers' potential was unlimited, but equally remarkable was his achievement. In his brief career, he recorded close to 100 songs, many of which were either unreleased or released in such limited numbers that few people have heard them. Ariel Rogers has worked to remedy that situation. In 1993, she released HOME IN HALIFAX, a live concert recorded by CBC one year before Stan's death. It's a treasure for fans and newcomers alike, containing simple arrangements of Stan's best-known songs, some hilarious banter between Stan and Garnet, and a previously unavailable gem, *Sailor's Rest*. This bittersweet song about an imaginary retirement home for seamen has become another Stan Rogers' classic.

No rail on the mess room table
And you're dead if you spit on the floor
There's no grog allowed, no singing too loud
No locks on the doors
But there's always a fire in the card room
And the tucker is always the best
They'll end it together
Down at the Sailor's Rest.

Two year's later, Ariel released POETIC JUSTICE, which offered two CBC Radio plays prominently featuring Stan's music. First aired on Good Friday, 1980, as an episode of the horror series *Nightfall*, "Harris and the Mare" was based on Stan's song, The dramatization filled a need at the time, providing CBC with a more tasteful, less macabre tale for Easter weekend. The other play was Silver Donald Cameron's wonderful "Three Sisters," an original fable that integrated music and song directly into the narrative. First airing in September 1979 on CBC Playhouse, it showed Stan's versatility as a songwriter and storyteller. In presenting another facet of the man, POETIC JUSTICE was a treat for Rogers' fans.

"I was no less fascinated than many of you at the amazing ability of this man I lived with," Ariel Rogers wrote in the liner notes. "I watched him write and I cleaned up the coffee cups and the wastepaper baskets full of rejects. We had our share of unfinished conversations and our life together was not unlike many other couples, but I loved these two radio plays so much that I could not leave them in the can. They belong together somehow. They speak to me of unique Canadian experiences. Yes, I know they can be translated into any language and would fit in to many parts of the world but they are not from there. They are from here. They belong to all of us. They speak on a very intimate level about us. We need to hear them, to feel these things that speak of how we are or might be in our lives."

In 2000, a whole chest of Rogers' sunken treasures surfaced when Fogarty's Cove Music released FROM COFFEE HOUSE TO

CONCERT HALL, a collection of previously unreleased tracks and other rarities. There are some relatively well-known songs here, like the crowd-pleasing *Acadian Saturday Night*, an out-take from the FOGARTY'S COVE sessions, and *Guysborough Train*, which originally appeared on extended EP — essentially a four-song single record — distributed in-house to CBC stations across the country. But there are also some surprises, including the oddly effective hurtin' tune, *Your Laker's Back in Town*, and the stunning *Puddler's Tale*, which must take it's place among the very best songs Stan Rogers ever wrote.

> They neither know of night or day,
> They night and day pour out their thunder,
> As every ingot rolls away,
> A dozen more are split asunder.
>
> There is a sign beside the gate,
> "Eleven Days" since a man lay dying,
> Now every shift brings fear and hate
> And shaken men in terror crying.

These three albums have added to the Rogers' legend, but Stan's legacy goes beyond the songs he recorded. Throughout his life, he struggled to change the face of Canadian music so that young artists could stay at home without sacrificing their national identity. Steve Macklam, who managed guitar hero Colin James and now represents a who's who of musical artists — including Diana Krall, Joni Mitchell, Norah Jones, and up-and-coming Liam Titcomb, son of proto-folkster Brent — notes that Canada's music industry has become self-supporting. "Today, a musical artist can survive in Canada. They might make a lot more money if they go down to the States, but they no longer have to do that in order to survive. There's a new level of comfort, which allows artists to flourish in a kind of isolation, with less concern for what's happening in other countries."

Resident Canadian artists like kd lang, Colin James, Blue

Rodeo, Jann Arden, Prairie Oyster, Loreena McKennitt, and Rita MacNeil now sell truckloads of records in Canada and get played on every radio station, regardless of whether or not they experience any success in the United States. Although these artists can all be considered "mainstream," they hold on to their traditional roots with a devotion that most American popular artists would never dream of. Known as a blues guitarist, Colin James grew up watching folk acts like Stan Rogers, cutting his teeth playing traditional Celtic tunes on the mandolin on Canada's folk festival circuit. This kind of traditional connection, according to Steve Macklam, is shaping Canadian music today. "I think that Stan started a process that we are only beginning to see come to fruition. Whether people will attribute this to Stan Rogers, or to a deeper tradition of which he is a part, I'm not sure — but I don't think we've heard the last of him."

A deeper tradition.

That's what it was all about for Stan. He didn't just want to report history or recreate ancient musical forms; he wanted to join with that deeper tradition and become part of the musical continuum. "I want to reflect my times," Stan once said. "I want to leave something behind that the world can look at one hundred years from now."

In the years to come, Stan's place in musical history will be a matter of discussion and argument. He couldn't have asked for more. But for now we are left with the stories and the memories and the songs of a true Canadian original.

So, let the conversations end and the music begin.

Ladies and gentlemen, please put your hands together for the one, the only: Stan Rogers . . .

Rise again, rise again — though your heart it be broken
And life about to end
No matter what you've lost, be it a home, a love, a friend
Like the *Mary Ellen Carter*, rise again!

Song Lyrics
(Released and Unreleased)

In his short life, Stan Rogers wrote and recorded almost 100 songs. Always more a craftsman than a technician when it came to songwriting, Stan liked to answer "yes" whenever someone asked him, which came first, the music or lyrics. He had no set pattern when it came to writing. Some songs, like *Barrett's Privateers* and *The Mary Ellen Carter* flowed easily, in single short sessions. Most songs took a lot longer, though.

"I often don't write a song until I need it," Stan told interviewer Jude Johnson, in 1979. "I'll have it in the back of my head somewhere but I won't need it in the repertoire at that particular point and there be no pressure on me to produce something. So I'll just let it percolate, because the longer they sit back there I find the better they turn out. . . . I'm convinced that in order to be a good writer, one has to be at once a little crazy — at least have a very agile mind that darts around a bit — any writer is kind of a synthesis. He's the sum total of everything his heard or listened to or felt or experienced. A good writer can draw from all sorts of influences and experiences and things that are resting subconsciously in the back of his mind: a phrase he's read or a phrase he's heard, a snatch of melody that he might have heard somewhere but has no idea where it came from. You draw on all of these elements when you're writing. And the crazier you are — the more your mind leaps around — probably the better it is for you."

While Stan relied on inspiration, he also believed that discipline was key to success as an artist. When he was working on FROM FRESH WATER, he actually rented an office in Hamilton. He would drive down to work every morning, working on his songs all day, going home at night. "I used to figure that I had to withdraw from the world for a while so I can be creative," he said in the same interview. "Being an artist involves a tremendous amount of self-discipline, you have to discipline yourself to work. With the kind of lifestyle that I'm leading, as a family man with a bunch of small children, they take up so much time and when you are home, they make so much noise, you have to learn to be able to tune the world out at will and just get down and write. . . . You have to be strong to be an artist."

What follows is an alphabetically arranged selection of Stan Rogers' lyrics — old favorites, big hits, unreleased rarities, and some of his earliest efforts — with an account of the genesis of the song. Note that the title is followed by the name of the album where the song can be found and the approximate year the song was written.

True aficionados should check out the official Stan Rogers website at www.stanrogers.net for an up-to-date discography, current news, fan chat rooms, and an online store featuring books, music, and other great gifts for Stan fans.

Discography

FOGARTY'S COVE. 1976. Barnswallow BS-1001/Fogarty's Cove
  Music FCM-1001
TURNAROUND. 1978. Fogarty's Cove Music FCM-001
BETWEEN THE BREAKS . . . LIVE. 1979. Fogarty's Cove Music
  FCM-002
NORTHWEST PASSAGE. 1980. Fogarty's Cove Music FCM-004
FOR THE FAMILY. 1982. Folk Tradition R002
FROM FRESH WATER. 1984. Cole Harbour Music CHM-001/
  Fogarty's Cove Music FCM- 007D
POETIC JUSTICE. 1996. Fogarty's Cove Music FCM-011D.
HOME IN HALIFAX. 1994. Fogarty's Cove Music. FCM-0100.
FROM COFFEE HOUSE TO CONCERT HALL. 2000. Fogarty's Cove
  Music FCM-012.

Stan Rogers' early recordings, from 1970 to 1975, included
two singles for RCA, three songs included on the CBC Transcription Series album LM-416 and four on LM-436. He also had one
song on BEST OF TOUCH THE EARTH, LM-473, issued in 1981.
Stan Rogers albums are available on CD at stanrogers.net

ACADIAN SATURDAY NIGHT
Coffee House to Concert Hall, 1974

This is the most popular Stan Rogers song (almost) never released. Written in 1975, and a last minute cut from FOGARTY'S COVE, the song still managed to become a favorite request at Stan's concerts. It finally made its onto a record with the posthumous FROM COFFEE HOUSE TO CONCERT HALL release. A rollicking story about New Brunswick bootleggers, Stan imbues his story with a sense of detail that brings it to life. I always picture his own grandma at the piano when I read the line about "a fat lady beating her piano like a drum." Trinidad light, by the way, is the illegal rum so precious to the smugglers.

—|—

Uncle Emile, he's gone now nearly ten days
He "tole" his wife's he's gone for the fishing
But in the waters off St. Pierre and Miquellan Isles
The fish come in bottles of gold
If the *Anne-Marie* floats and the Mounties stay blind
He'll be back before the moon is rising
With a very fine catch all safe in the hold
Thirty cases of Trinidad light
For Acadian Saturday night.

Emmeline Comeau works the general store
Papa says she's good for the custom
She's got eyes like fire and hair past her shoulders
As shiny black as ant'racite coal
You can see her Sunday morning on the St Phillipe road
Her mother close behind like a dragon
But her mama doesn't know what she does behind the hall
Away from the music and lights
On Acadian Saturday night.

CHORUS
Oh — don't the fiddles make you roll
'Til your heart she pounds like a hammer
There's a fat lady beating her piano like a drum
And everybody's higher than a kite
On Acadian Saturday night.

Granpa says it was better in his day
The Mounties stayed away from the parties
And he didn't mind a fight when the spirits got high
(You could always throw them out in the snow!)
And the rum was better and it came in bigger bottles
And the revenue cutters were slow -
Still, the old *Anne-Marie* has wings on the water
And there's nothing like Trinidad light
On Acadian Saturday night.

CHORUS

AT LAST I'M READY FOR CHRISTMAS
Coffee House to Concert Hall, 1983

Another song that surfaced on the Rogers' sunken treasures collection, FROM COFFEE HOUSE TO CONCERT HALL, this was one of the last songs Stan wrote, backstage as he waited to go on CBC's 1982 *Joy to the World* Christmas special. Ariel says it's a pretty accurate portrait of Christmas Eve in the Rogers' household, although she contends she was always too damn tired to go out to the Boxing Day sales. To Stan's embarrassment, it took him three tries to nail the song for the cameras — he muffed his lines the first two times.

Last Boxing Day the wife went out
The "White Sales" for to see,
In trunk-load lots bought half-price paper
And tinsel for the tree.

I packed it up for use this year
In a box I marked so plain.
That stuff would sure be handy now,
But it's never been seen again!

CHORUS
At last I'm ready for Christmas,
I've even finished the tree,
At last I'm ready for Christmas,
Like I thought I'd never be.
With my feet propped up by a good hot fire
And a matching inside glow;
At last I'm ready for Christmas,
With nearly two hours to go!

We swore this year we'd start off early,
No need to rush around.
The intention was to start in August
When the prices still were down.

But it was dentist-this and new bike-that
And the money melts away.
So I had to wait for Christmas bonus
And did it all yesterday.

CHORUS

We must be fools, just look at that pile,
You can hardly see the tree.
We said this year we'd keep things simple,
Then did our usual spree.

But it feels so good when the kids go nuts,
It's worth the toil and strain.
These kids are only this young once
And they'll never be so again.

CHORUS

BARRETT'S PRIVATEERS
Fogarty's Cover, *Between the Breaks*,
and *Home in Halifax*, 1976

Many of the most distinguished families in Halifax made their fortunes from privateering — a form of legalized piracy. In the 1700s, Britain was weighed down waging war across the seven seas, and to help their cause the Crown would grant loyal captains a "letter of marque," giving them permission to attack and pillage enemy ships. Today this song is sung around the world and has been recorded dozens of times — often without proper permission, since many people do not realize it was written in the 1970s, not the 1790s.

———+———

Oh, the year was 1778,
(How I wish I was in Sherbrooke now!)
A Letter of Marque came from the king,
To the scummiest vessel I'd ever seen,

CHORUS

God damn them all!
I was told we'd cruise the seas for American gold
We'd fire no guns-shed no tears
Now I'm a broken man on a Halifax pier
The last of Barrett's Privateers.

Oh, Elcid Barrett cried the town,
(How I wish I was in Sherbrooke now!)
For twenty brave men all fishermen who
would make for him the *Antelope's* crew

CHORUS

The *Antelope* sloop was a sickening sight,
(How I wish I was in Sherbrooke now!)
She'd a list to the port and sails in rags
And the cook in scuppers with the staggers and the jags

CHORUS

On the King's birthday we put to sea,
(How I wish I was in Sherbrooke now!)
We were 91 days to Montego Bay
Pumping like madmen all the way

CHORUS

On the 96th day we sailed again,
(How I wish I was in Sherbrooke now!)
When a bloody great Yankee hove in sight
With our cracked four pounders we made to fight

CHORUS

The Yankee lay low down with gold,
(How I wish I was in Sherbrooke now!)
She was broad and fat and loose in the stays
But to catch her took the *Antelope* two whole days

CHORUS

Then at length we stood two cables away,
(How I wish I was in Sherbrooke now!)
Our cracked four pounders made an awful din
But with one fat ball the Yank stove us in

CHORUS

The *Antelope* shook and pitched on her side,
(How I wish I was in Sherbrooke now!)
Barrett was smashed like a bowl of eggs
And the Main-truck carried off both me legs

CHORUS

So here I lay in my 23rd year,
(How I wish I was in Sherbrooke now!)
It's been 6 years since we sailed away
And I just made Halifax yesterday

CHORUS

BILLY GREEN
From Coffee House to Concert Hall, 1975

This is the true story of one of Canada's forgotten heroes, who helped the British army win the battle of Stony Creek by leading them through the dead of night to the American forces. Stan, who used to buy apples as a child from Billy Green's great-grand daughter, called him a "sort of Canadian version of Paul Revere." The song, which was written and recorded in 1975 for CBC Radio's *Touch the Earth*, was also penciled in for FROM FRESH WATER, but didn't make the final cut.

Attend you all good countrymen,
my name is Billy Green,
And I will tell of things I did
When I was just nineteen.

I helped defeat the Yank invader,
There can be no doubt,
Yet lately men forget the name
Of Billy Green, the Scout.

'Twas on a Sunday morn' in June
When first we heard the sound,
Three thousand Yankees on the road
To camp below Greentown.

Two Generals, artillery
And company of horse,
With many rank and file afoot,
They were a mighty force.

Says I to brother Levi,
"Well, we still can have some fun
We'll creep and whoop like Indians
To try to make them run."

Which then we did both loud and long,
Much to the Yanks' dismay.
They fired their 'pop-gun' muskets
Once and then they ran away.

Well, first they plundered Stoney Creek
And then John Gage's farm.
They cut his fences for their fires
Although the day was warm.

They bound my brother Isaac up
And took him from his home.

They pillaged all the countryside,
No mercy there was shown.

Then says I to myself,
"Now Billy, this will never do.
Those scurvy Yanks are not the match
For Loyalists like you."

My brother's horse I quickly caught
And put him to a run,
And reached the British camp
Upon the heights of Burlington.

Says I to Colonel Harvey,
"Now, let there be no delay,
If we're to reach the Yankee camp
Before the break of day.

I'll take you through the woods by night,
Where I know every tree,
And ere the dawn you surely can
Surprise the enemy."

With men and guns we then set forth
The enemy to seek,
Across the beach at Burlington
And then to Red Hill Creek;

We came upon their sentries;
We surprised them every one.
One died upon my sword,
And all the others off they run.

And so it was we were in place
One hour before dawn.
We fired three times upon the camp
And then we marched along.

We fired again and charged
As Colonel Harvey gave the word,
And put the enemy to fight
With bayonet and sword.

With great confusion in the camp,
Two Generals were caught.
The Colonel and his men made
Their artillery as naught.

We killed over two hundred
And we captured all the rest;
Nor did we lose but eighty men;
Of them we had the best.
And so it was I played the man
Though I was but nineteen.
I led our forces through the night
That this land would be free.

I foiled the Yank invaders
And I helped put them to route,
So, let no man forget the name of
Billy Green, the Scout.

—————

THE BLUENOSE
Turnaround, 1976

Originally written for the Nova Scotia tourism documentary
Bluenose N.S. 116, this song ended up on Stan's second album. It's
an ode to the legendary racing schooner, a source of enduring
pride to Nova Scotians (whose collective nickname "bluenosers"
gave the vessel her handle.)

Once again with the tide she slips her lines
Turns her head and comes awake
Where she lay so still there at Privateer's Wharf
Now she quickly gathers way
She will range far south from the harbour mouth
And rejoice with every wave
Who will know the *Bluenose* in the sun?

Feel her bow rise free of Mother Sea
In a sunburst cloud of spray
That stings the cheek while the rigging will speak
Of sea-miles gone away
She is always best under full press
Hard over as she'll lay
And who will know the Bluenose in the sun?

CHORUS

That proud, fast Queen of the Grand Banks Fleet
Portrayed on every dime
Knew hard work in her time
Hard work in every line

The rich men's toys of the Gloucester boys
With their token bit of cod
They snapped their spars and strained to pass her by
But she left them all behind

Now her namesake remains to show what she has been
What every schoolboy remembers and will not come again
To think she's the last of the Grand Banks Schooners
That fed so many men
And who will know the *Bluenose* in the sun?

So does she not take wing like a living thing
Child of the moving tide
See her pass with grace on the water's face
With clean and quiet pride
Our own tall ship of great renown still lifts unto the sky
Who will know the *Bluenose* in the sun?

CANOL ROAD
Northwest Passage, 1981

The greatest cabin fever song ever written. The Kopper King Tavern really exists, as does Canol Road, which heads north from Whitehorse.

———+———

Well you could see it in his eyes as they strained against the night,
And the bone-white mackerel crepe upon the road,
Sixty-five miles into town, and a winter's thirst to drown,
A winter still with two months left to go.
His eyes are too far open, his grin too hard and sore,
His shoulders too far high to bring relief,
But the Kopper King is hot, even if the band is not,
And it sure beats shooting whiskey-jacks and trees.
Then he laughs and says "It didn't get me this time, not tonight,
I wasn't screaming when I hit the door."
But his hands on the tabletop, will their shaking never stop,
Those hands sweep the bottles to the floor.
Now he's a bear in a blood-red mackinaw with hungry dogs at bay,
And springtime thunder in his sudden roar,
With one wrong word he burns, and the table's overturned,
When he's finished there's a dead man on the floor.

CHORUS
Well they watched for him in Carmacks, Haines, and Carcross,
With Teslin blocked there's nowhere else to go,
But he hit the four-wheel-drive in Johnson's Crossing,
Now he's thirty-eight miles up the Canol road.
He's thirty-eight miles up the Canol road
In the Salmon Range at forty-eight below.

Well it's God's own neon green above the mountains here tonight,
Throwing brittle coloured shadows on the snow,
It's four more hours 'til dawn, and the gas is almost gone,
And that bitter Yukon wind begins to blow.
Now you can see it in his eyes as they glitter in the light
And the bone-white rime of frost around his brow.
Too late the dawn has come, that Yukon winter has won,
And he's got his cure for cabin fever now.

CHORUS
Well they watched for him in Carmacks, Haines, and Carcross,
With Teslin blocked there's nowhere else to go,
But they hit the four-wheel-drive in Johnson's Crossing,
Found him thirty-eight miles up the Canol road.
They found him thirty-eight miles up the Canol road,
In the Salmon Range at forty-eight below,
They found him thirty-eight miles up the Canol road . . .

DELIVERY DELAYED
Between the Breaks, 1975

Written on the occasion of the birth of Paul Mill's son, and originally included in the folk opera So Hard To Be So Strong, this song was also recorded by Peter, Paul and Mary and led Peter Yarrow of the group to call Stan "the best young songwriter alive today."

———+———

How early is "Beginning"? From when is there a soul?
Do we discover living, or, somehow, are we told?
In sudden pain, in empty cold, in blinding light of day
We're given breath, and it takes our breath away.

How cruel to be unformed fancy, the way in which we come —
Over-whelmed by feeling and sudden loss of love
And what price dark confining pain, (the hardest to forgive)
When all at once, we're called upon to live.

By a giant hand we're taken from the shelter of the womb
That dreaded first horizon, the endless empty room
Where communion is lost forever, when a heart first beats alone.
Still, it remembers, no matter how it's grown.

CHORUS
We grow, but grow apart —
We live, but more alone —
The more to see, the more to see,
To cry aloud that we are free
To hide our ancient fear of being alone.

And how we live in darkness, embracing spiteful cold
Refusing any answers, for no man can be told
That delivery is delayed until at last we're made aware
And first reach for love, to find 'twas always there.

———

FAT GIRL RAG
RCA single, 1972

Here it is, in all of its politically incorrect glory, Stan's first single
for RCA. Written around 1972, Stan used to introduce this song

by saying how the record company wanted to make him into another Ray Stevens. "I made the record but it bombed. It deserved to. But I'd like to share this tune with you now, because it's a piece of my history, and it deserves to be. So this here's a love song for a fat girl, 'cause nobody ever writes love songs for fat girls, except me."

———+———

Now Saturday night on Highway Eight,
A two-ton blimp derailed freight,
The shock broke windows fifteen miles away.
They declared the train a total wreck,
Stella was treated for scratches on her face and neck,
She's my two-ton sweetie,
My darling Stella Grey.

Sixty-six bust and a forty-eight waist,
Eighty two hips and elephant legs,
And looking at Stella Grey from the behind,
Just makes me go outta my mind,
Woh! How I love Stella Grey!

One-quarter ton of bounce and play.
She's my mammoth mamma,
My darling Stella Grey.
Now she's so fat that if you want,
You can see her backside from the front,
She gives me a thrill when she bellows "Honey!"
Twice as much girl for the money.

(Spoken): Now you gotta remember friends
that this was in the days before Women's lib . . .
(Sung): Now she's my bulgy baby,
My darling Stella Grey.

Now she's not much for looks but she's hell on strong,
Trims her beard when it gets long,
Keeps her hair cut close to her head,
Never lets me into her bed.
(Spoken) and I'm glad!
But still I love Stella Grey . . .

Since I've known her my life has really been so gay,
She's my heavy duty honey,
My darling Stella Grey . . .
I say, my darling Stella Grey.

THE FIELD BEHIND THE PLOW
Northwest Passage, Home in Halifax, 1981

Very early one morning, driving across the Prairies, Stan saw a farmer working his field. That moment inspired this song, which many consider the definitive statement about Canadian wheat farmers. These kinds of every-day heroes were the mainstay of Stan's artistry because, as he told CBC Radio in Calgary in an interview weeks before his death, he liked anybody who puts themselves on the line. "I take my life in my hands on the road a fair bit. We have to drive in some really impossible conditions and we had some near misses in the air too. Twice now we've come very close to being smeared all over the landscape in aircraft. In hanging it out yourself you begin to understand people who do it routinely for a living. So a lot of my songs deal with people who are involved in jobs where they could be killed or seriously injured: fishermen, miners, oil refinery workers, even farmers. I think people who work in hard, extractive industries that require constant vigilance and constant bravery are the real backbone of the country. We don't make enough of them. For some reason we tend to admire bankers and politicians more than we admire people who put their lives on the line to keep the country going."

———+———

Watch the field behind the plow turn to straight, dark rows
Feel the trickle in your clothes, blow the dust cake from your nose
Hear the tractor's steady roar, Oh you can't stop now
There's a quarter section more or less to go

And it figures that the rain keeps its own sweet time
You can watch it come for miles, but you guess you've got a while
So ease the throttle out a hair, every rod's a gain
And there's victory in every quarter mile

BRIDGE
Poor old Kuzyk down the road
The heartache, hail and hoppers brought him down
He gave it up and went to town
And Emmett Pierce the other day
Took a heart attack and died at forty-two
You could see it coming on 'cause he worked as hard as you . . .

In an hour, maybe more, you'll be wet clear through
The air is cooler now, pull you hat brim further down
And watch the field behind the plow turn to straight dark rows
Put another season's promise in the ground

2ⁿᵈ BRIDGE
And if the harvest's any good
The money just might cover all the loans
You've mortgaged all you own
Buy the kids a winter coat
Take the wife back east for Christmas if you can
All summer she hangs on when you're so tied to the land.

For the good times come and go, but at least there's rain
So this won't be barren ground when September rolls around
So watch the field behind the plow turn to straight dark rows
Put another season's promise in the ground.

FINCH'S COMPLAINT (A Recitation)
Fogarty's Cove, 1976

Originally, *Finch's Complaint* was a song, but Stan didn't like the music, so Paul Mills suggested he try it as a recitation. In this form, it fits perfectly into the Can Trad design of FOGARTY'S COVE. As Stan explained in the album liner notes, "A recitation in the old tradition, to be learned by ear and not from the printed (or written) page. The event is very nearly fact, and is included to perhaps illustrate that the Maritimes cannot always be thought of in terms of eating blueberry pie and drinking black rum." The story is based on a true incident. The government had converted an old fish-packing plant near Canso into a fish meal operation, promising everyone in the area steady work. It quickly went under, leaving lots of the locals high and dry. Alpine, by the way, is a kind of beer.

———+———

Tom Finch turned to the waitress and said:
"Bring me another Alpine. I'll have one more before I go to tell Marie the news. Well boys, we're for it this time. The plant is closed for good. Regan broke his promise, and we're through. We're working men with no work left to do.
"I always thought I'd have a boat, just like my dad before me. You don't get rich, but with the boats you always could make do. But the boats gave way to trawlers, and packing turned to meal. Now that's all gone, and we're all for the dole. And the thought of that puts irons in my soul."
Tom Finch stood up and said good-bye with handshakes all around. Faces he'd grown up among, now with their eyes cast down. Slow foot along familiar road to the hills above the harbour. With a passing thought, "Now all this is through and I wonder how Marie will take the news?"
The house had been so much of her, though it had hardly been a year. She's done his father's house so proud, and held it all so dear. But there was hot tea on the table when Tom came through the door. And before he spoke, she smiled and said,

"I know. The plant is gone. Now how soon do we go?"

"We won't take a cent. They can stuff all their money. We've put a little by. And thank God we've got no kids as yet, or I think I'd want to die.

"We Finches have been in this part of the world for near 200 years, but I guess it's seen the last of us. Come on Marie, we're going to Toronto . . ."

———

FIRST CHRISTMAS
Between the Breaks, 1978

Stan believed that Christmas was as much a time for reflection as it was for celebration. "Christmas music tends to be pretty cheerful," Stan told interviewer Jude Johnson shortly after release of BETWEEN THE BREAKS. "I always thought that there should be more songs about the serious side of Christmas, particularly songs that point out that a lot of people get neglected at that time of year." The song was written for, and first performed on, a 1978 CBC Radio Christmas special, recorded live from Sylvia Tyson's living room. While most of the verses were pure invention, the last one was based on the experiences of Stan's elderly grandfather, who'd recently moved into a nursing home and was about to spend his first Christmas there.

———+———

This day, a year ago, he was rolling in the snow
With a younger brother in his father's yard.
Christmas break — a time for touching home
The heart of all he'd known, and leaving was so hard —
Three thousand miles away, now he's working Christmas Day
Making double time for "the minding of the store". . .
Well, he'd always said he'd make it on his own
He's spending Christmas Eve alone.
First Christmas away from home.

She's standing by the train station, panhandling for change
Four more dollars buys a decent meal and a room.
Looks like the Sally Ann place after all,
In a crowded sleeping hall that echoes like a tomb
But it's warm and clean and free and there are worse places to be,
And at least it means no beating from her Dad
And if she cries because it's Christmas Day
She hopes that it won't show . . .
First Christmas away from home.
In the apartment stands a tree, and it looks so small and bare
Not like it was meant to be
The Golden Angel on the top, it's not that same old silver star
You wanted for your own
First Christmas away from home.

In the morning, they get prayers, then it's crafts and tea
    downstairs
Then another meal back in his little room
Hoping maybe that the boys will think to phone before the
    day is gone
Well, it's best they do it soon.
When the old girl passed away, he fell more apart each day
Each had always kept the other pretty well
But the kids all said the nursing home was best
'Cause he couldn't live alone . . .
First Christmas away from home.

In the Common Room they've got the biggest tree
And it's huge and cold and lifeless,
Not like it ought to be
And the lit-up flashing Santa Claus on top
It's not that same old silver star you once made for your own
First Christmas away from home.

———————

FISHERMAN'S WHARF
Fogarty's Cove, 1976

A glimpse of great things to come. Stan takes a kind of simple hippy sentiment — the long for the old ways — and digs inside it a little. What stands out most for me in this song is the voice in parenthesis; this is the first glimpse of the prototype first-person narrator who will come to tell many of Stan's best songs. Fittingly, this was last song written for FOGARTY'S COVE and marks the point where the uncertain singer-songwriter Stan gives way to a historic, narrative voice of tremendous power and authority.

It was in the spring this year of grace with new life pushing
    through
That I looked from the Citadale down to the Narrows and asked
    what it's coming to
I saw Upper Canadian concrete and glass right down to the water
    line
And I heard an old song down on Fisherman's Wharf
Can I sing it, just one time?
Can I sing it, just one time?

CHORUS
Then haul away and heave her home
This song is heard no more
No boars to sing it for
No sails to sing it for
There rises now a single tide of tourists passing through
We traded old ways for the new . . .

With half-closed eyes against the sun, for the warm wind giving
    thanks
I dreamed of the years of the deep-laden schooners
Thrashing home from the Grand Banks
The last lies, one, in the harbour sun, with her picture on every dime

But I heard an old song down on Fisherman's Wharf
Can I sing it, just one time?
Can I sing it, just one time?

CHORUS

Now you ask "What's this Romantic boy who laments what's
    done and gone?
There was no romance on a cold winter ocean
And the gales sang an awful song."
But my father knew of wind and tide and my blood is Maritime
And I heard an old song down on Fisherman's Wharf
Can I sing it, just one time?
Can I sing it, just one time?

CHORUS

THE FLOWERS OF BERMUDA
Between the Breaks, 1978

Stan's favorite vacation spot was Bermuda, and this song was written with the Bermuda Folk Club in mind. The story has a basis in fact, as Stan comments in the album liner notes. "I discovered that the whole area around Bermuda is a kind of ship graveyard. I found a map showing the location of most of the known wrecks, and the dates, and discovered that a coal carrier called the *Nightingale* sank off the North Rock in the early 1880s. The rest of the details are pure invention, except for the fact that Bermuda is lovely." Paul Mills, who played guitar on the live album, says because of this song's intricate structure and difficult time changes, it's one of the hardest of Stan's tunes to pull off. Stan's advice, from *Songs from Fogarty's Cove*, his official song book, is to "get a good breath at the end of each chorus, and a short one after the word coal. In the verses, you are on your own."

He was Captain of the *Nightingale*
Twenty-one days from Clyde in coal
He could smell the flowers of Bermuda in the gale
When he died on the North Rock Shore

Just five short hours from Bermuda, in a fine October gale
There came a cry "Oh, there be breakers ahead!"
From the collier *Nightingale*.
No sooner had the Captain brought her round, came a rending
    crash below
Hard on her beam ends, groaning, went the *Nightingale*
And over side her mainmast goes.

"Oh, Captain, are we all for drowning?" came the cry from all the
    crew.
"The boats be smashed! How then are we all to be saved?
They are stove in through and through!"

"Oh, are ye brave and hardy collier-men or are ye blind and can-
    not see?
The Captain's gig still lies before ye whole and sound,
It shall carry all o' we."
But when the crew was all assembled and the gig prepared for sea,
'Twas seen there were but eighteen places to be manned
Nineteen mortal souls were we.
But cries the Captain "Now do not delay, nor do ye spare a
    thought for me.
My duty is to save ye all now, if I can.
See ye return as quick as can be."

Oh, there be flowers in Bermuda. Beauty lies on every and,
And there be laughter, ease and drink for every man,
But there is no joy for me;
For when we reached the wretched *Nightingale* what an awful
    sight was plain

The Captain, drowned, was tangled in the mizzen-chains
Smiling bravely beneath the sea.

FLYING
From Fresh Water, 1982

A true-life story of a young hockey player who got injured before he had a chance to play in the pros, this is one of Stan's many songs about men defeated on the verge of success. Some fans see the last line of the chorus as a chilling prophecy, adding to the myth of Saint Stan.

—+—

It was just like strapping 'em on and starting again,
Coaching these kids to the top, and calling them men.
I was a third-round pick in the NHL
And that's three years of living in hell,
And going up flying, and going home dying.

My life was over the boards and playing the game,
And every day checking the papers and finding my name.
My dad would go crazy when the scouts would call;
He'd tell me that I'd have it all
Ninety-nine of us trying, only one of us flying.

CHORUS
And every kid over the boards listens for the sound;
The roar of the crowd is their ticket for finally leaving this town
To be just one more hopeful in the Junior A,
Dreaming of that miracle play,
And going up flying, going home dying.

I tell them to think of the play and not of the fame.
If they've got any future at all, it's not in the game.

'Cause they'll be crippled and starting all over again
Selling on commissions and remembering
When they were flying, remembering dying.

CHORUS

———————

FOGARTY'S COVE
Fogarty's Cove, 1974

This is the song that started it all. If the chorus rhythm sounds a little strange, it's because Stan plays around with the time. At one point where he sings "chance again," he switches from common time, four beats to a bar, to waltz time, three beats per bar, then switches back again. The result is a song that sounds rushed for a moment, and gives the song a real "traditional" feel. The name "Fogarty's Cove," by the way, is fictitious. Stan appreciated the artistic license granted by creating an imaginary place. The name was suggested by a line in *Up On Fox Island,* a song written years earlier — and recorded on FOR THE FAMILY — by his uncle, Lee Bushell:
It's in this big city great people do dwell
Ten-story houses, you all know them well
There's Dailys, and Reinholds, McDuffs by the score
The Fogarty boys have there huts by the shore.

———+———

We just lost sight of the Queensport light down the bay before us
And the wind has blown some cold today with just a wee touch of
    snow
Along the shore from Lazy Head hard a-beam Half Island
Tonight we'll let the anchor go down in Fogarty's Cove.

My Sally's like the ravens wing her hair is like her mothers'
With hands that make quick work of a chore and eyes like the top
    of a stove
Come suppertime she'll walk the beach wrapped in my old duffle
With her eyes upon the masthead reach down in Fogarty's Cove.

CHORUS
She will walk the sandy shore so plain
Watch the comber's roll in
'Till I come to Wild Rose Chance again
Down in Fogarty's Cove.

She cries when I'm away to sea nags me when I'm with her
She'd rather I'd a Government job or maybe go on the dole
But I love the waves as I pull about, nose into the channel
My Sally keeps the supper and a bed for me down in
    Fogarty's Cove.

CHORUS

FORTY-FIVE YEARS
Fogarty's Cove, Home in Halifax, 1973

A late night skinny dip formed the basis for what would become one of Stan's best-known and most recorded songs. Ariel still has the handwritten lyrics Stan sent her from Half Way Cove — the real life inspiration for Fogarty's cove — shortly after he wrote the song. This song was a hit of sorts in the United Kingdom for Irish singer Mary O'Hara and remained, until his death, Stan's most requested piece.

Where the earth shows its bones of wind-broken stone
And the sea and the sky are one
I'm caught out of time, my blood sings with wine
And I'm running naked in the sun
There's God in the trees, I'm weak in the knees
And the sky is a painful blue
I'd like to look around, but Honey, all I see is you.

The summer city lights will soften the night
'Til you'd think that the air is clear
And I'm sitting with friends, where forty-five cents
Will buy another glass of beer
He's got something to say, but I'm so far away
That I don't know who I'm talking to
Cause you just walked in the door, and Honey, all I see is you

CHORUS
And I just want to hold you closer than I've ever held anyone before
You say you've been twice a wife and you're through with life
Ah, but Honey, what the hell's it for?
After twenty-three years you'd think I could find
A way to let you know somehow
That I want to see your smiling face forty-five years from now.

So alone in the lights on stage every night
I've been reaching out to find a friend
Who knows all the words, sings so she's heard
And knows how all the stories end
Maybe after the show she'll ask me to go
Home with her for a drink or two
Now her smile lights her eyes, but Honey, all I see is you

CHORUS

———

FREE IN THE HARBOUR
Northwest Passage, 1981

A sequel to *Make And Break Harbour* and, for my tastes, the superior song. While the former was a rather basic protest song, *Free In The Harbour* uses humor, irony, and imagery to produce a much more subtle effect. It's written in three-quarters "waltz" time, a rhythm Stan often used in his songs about the sea because of the rolling, up-and-down effect it produces. Blackfish are better known as northern pilot whales.

———+———

Well, it's blackfish at play in Hermitage Bay
From push through across to Bois Island.
They Broach and they spout and they lift their flukes out
And they wave to a town that is dying.
Now it's many the boats that have plied on the foam,
Hauling away! Hauling away!
But there's many more fellows been leaving their homes,
Where the whales make free in the harbour.
It's at Portage and Main You'll see them again
On their way to the hills of Alberta.
With lop-side grins, they waggle their chins
and they brag of the wage they'll be earning.
Then it's quick, pull the string boys, and get the loot out,
Haul it away! Haul it away!
But just two years ago you could hear the same shout
Where the whales make free in the harbour.

CHORUS
Free in the Harbour,
The Blackfish are sporting again
Free in the Harbour,
Untroubled by comings and goings of men
Who once did pursue them as oil from the sea,

Hauling away! Hauling away!
Now they're Calgary roughnecks from Hermitage Bay,
Where the whales make free in the harbour.

Well, it's living they've found, deep in the ground,
And if there's doubts, it's best they ignore them.
Nor think on the bones, the crosses and stones
Of their fathers that came there before them.
In the taverns of Edmonton, fishermen shout
Haul it away! Haul it away!
They left three hundred years buried up by the bay
Where the whales make free in the harbour.

CHORUS

———

FRONT RUNNER
Turnaround, 1976

Further proof that Stan the songwriter was mortal after all. Maudlin, predictable rhymes and rhythms and hackneyed — but allowing, by comparison, fans to see what made Stan's best songs so great. Another entry for the Olympic folk opera *So Hard to Be Strong*, which made it's away onto the uneven TURNAROUND album. Stan recommended heating cheap sherry on the radiator and chugging it before singing this song: the same advice applies when listening to it.

———+———

Now was it nine years of ten since you last was this friend
Why it seemed like 'twas no time at all
There weren't enough changes to make him a stranger
'Cause we both had old good times to recall

Now he was worn with walkin' so we sat there not talking
But he smiled when out eyes chance to meet
Then I mentioned the past an he spoke up at last
Shook his head and laid his world at my feet.

CHORUS
He said, I've been a front runner
I've been richer than most men you see
I've been mighty, now I'm broken
All seeing, now I'm blind as can be

There are men who don't lose who take what ever they choose
And become what they set out to be
And other men who set the pace but in the end loose the race
And old buddy you know that man is me

CHORUS

You know, I could not feel sorry, tho' it was a such a sad story
That I felt so much I thought I might break
Each man follows his fancies, knows the odds and takes his
    chances
And in the end gets whatever he takes
And neither wisdom nor cunning could sow the pace of change
    the running
Of a race he always knew he would lose.

CHORUS

––––––––––

GIANT
Fogarty's Cove, 1976

This song is based on the legend of Fingal, the Scottish giant
asleep in a cave in the Hebrides, waiting for the day his people

need him. Rogers, a bit of Fingal himself, transported the legend
to the shores or Cape Breton's Bras d'Or. One of Stan's moodiest
pieces, it was always a favorite with the concert crowd. This song
was written during rehearsals for FOGARTY'S COVE.

———+———

Cold wind on the harbour and rain on the road
Wet promise of winter brings recourse to coal
There's fire in the blood and a fog on Bras d'Or
The giant will rise with the moon

'Twas the same ancient fever in the Isles of the Blest
That our fathers brought with them when they "went West"
It's the blood of the Druids that never will rest
The giant will rise with the moon

CHORUS
So crash the glass down, move with the tide
Young friends and old whiskey are burning in-side
Crash the glass down, Fingal will rise
With the moon

In inclement weather the people are fey
Three thousand year stories as the night slips away
Remembering Fingal feels not far away
The giant will rise with the moon

The wind's in the North, there'll be new moon tonight
But we have no circle to dance in its sight
So light a torch, bring the bottle, and build the fire bright
The giant will rise with the moon

CHORUS

———

GUYSBOROUGH TRAIN
From Coffee House to Concert Hall, 1972

From the long out-of-print CBC Transcription Series recording, this song resurfaced in 2000 on FROM COFFEE HOUSE TO CONCERT HALL. An important step in Stan's development as a writer, the song combines elements of '70s singer-songwriters (particularly in its use of vaguely political yet ultimately obscure lyrics) with a complicated musical structure, a strong narrative voice, and Maritime history — all elements that would later become Stan Rogers' trademarks. Still, after dozens of listenings, I have absolutely no idea what this song is about.

———+———

Now there's no train to Guysborough,
Or so the man said,
So it might be a good place to be.
I sit in this station,
And I count up my change,
And I wait for the Guysborough train.

Now I've sat in your kitchens,
And talked about walls,
And I've sung about your withering pain,
Shattered your temples,
And I've brought on your fall,
Now I wait for the Guysborough train.

CHORUS
And I ride for all time, on the Guysborough line,
And I grow by the North Country rain,
And the North Shore's begun, the man I've become,
In rags, on the Guysborough train.

No train to Guysborough
Now ain't that a shame,
Though I know there will be one in time,

And the house that's alone,
It soon will be gone,
Razed for the Guysborough line

CHORUS

People are simple,
Like the rain clouds sweet,
Both grown by that North Country rain,
The Interval is clear,
Will it soon disappear,
Under the Guysborough train?

CHORUS

HARRIS AND THE MARE
Between the Breaks, 1979

This song started when Stan, who considered himself a pacifist, asked: "What would cause me to raise my hand at another man?" The answer: "If they laid a hand on my wife" (although it might have just as easily been, "If they talk out loud at my concerts"). Stan wrote it quickly, in a single evening, to accommodate Grit Laskin's Northumbrian small pipes, which play in the keys of E♭ and F. In 1982, this song was adapted by CBC for a radio play that featured Stan's music: the play forms half of Stan's posthumous release, POETIC JUSTICE.

———+———

Harris, my old friend, good to see your face again.
More welcome, though, yon trap and that old mare
For the wife is in a swoon, and I am all alone
Harris, fetch thy mare and take us home.

The wife and I came out for a quiet glass of stout
And a word or two with neighbours in the room
But young Clary, he came in, as drunk and wild as sin
And swore the wife would leave the place with him

But the wife as quick as thought said, "No, I'll bloody not"
Then struck the brute a blow about the head
He raised his ugly paw, and he lashed her on the jaw
And she fell onto the floor like she were dead.

Now Harris, well you know, I've never struck an angry blow.
Nor would I keep a friend who raised his hand
I was a conscie in the war, cryin' what the hell's this for?
But I had to see his blood to be a man.

I grabbed him by his coat, spun him 'round and took his throat
And beat his head upon the parlour door.
He dragged out an awful knife, and he roared "I'll have your life!"
And he stuck me and I fell onto the floor.

Now blood I was from neck to thigh, bloody murder in his eye
As he shouted out "I'll finish you for sure!"
But as the knife came down, I lashed out from the ground
And the knife was in his breast and he rolled o'er.

Now with the wife as cold as clay I carried her away
No hand was raised to help us through the door
And I've brought her half a mile, but I've had to rest awhile
And none of them I'll call a friend no more.

For when the knife came down, I was helpless on the ground
No neighbour stayed his hand, I was alone
By God, I was a man, but now I cannot stand
Please, Harris, fetch thy mare, take us home.

Oh, Harris, fetch thy mare, and take us out of here
In my nine and fifty years I've never known
That to call myself a man, for my loved one I must stand
Now Harris, fetch thy mare take us home.

HALF A HEART
From Fresh Water, 1983

Stan never did anything half-hearted, although later in his career, the thought of playing a one-night-stand in a dingy bar left him cold. This is his lament over the realities of the music business in Canada.

———+———

That one behind you on the padded velvet throne,
Don't turn around! You've seen that kind before.
Wolves hang around here and they hunt the woods alone,
Waiting for hearts to wander through the door.

This bar has changed now that the hunter's hunted too.
Who is the prey, and who is the hungry mouth?
Go talk with strangers, only nothing said is true.
It's, "Who do you know?" and "When did you last fly south?"

And it's drink bought to catch the eye and make intentions
    known,
The kind they would never buy if they meant to drink alone.
And it's soft words that make the play in warm and winning tones,
The kind words they'd never say if they dared to sleep alone.

But like you, I'm fascinated by the glitter of the flame,
Watching wolves steal half of a heart away.
Watching wolves steal half of a heart away.

HERE'S TO YOU SANTA CLAUSE
RCA single, 1971

Stan's first of many flop singles, at a time when RCA Canada hoped to turn him into Canada's Ray Stevens. What were they thinking?

———+———

CHORUS
Here's to You, Santa Claus,
Come to me tonight,
I've been a thoughtful little boy,
And I'm tucked in bed so tight,
I've always done as I was told,
Always what is right,
Hail to you, Santa Claus,
Come to me tonight!

Yesterday my older brother whispered in my ear,
Words that made me want to cry, I didn't want to hear,
He said there is no Santa Claus, or reindeer for his sleigh,
There are no elves away up north, just lots of ice and Eskimos,
And Northern Lights dance on the snow, and night time lasts all day.

And then I told him Mama said, that Santa'd come tonight,
And the stocking on the mantle piece would soon be full and
    tight,
And the little angel smiling from on top the Christmas tree,
Telling me that I've been good, reminding me I should recall,
The good Lord Jesus who once was, less then five like me.

2ⁿᵈ CHORUS
Here's to You, Santa Claus,
Come to me tonight,
Though your legs are weary
And your eyes are short of sight,
Everybody uses you and
Says that you're to blame,
Although you come round every year,
Your toys are not the same.

Last year for a Christmas gift, I got a tear gas gun,
And on my birthday Auntie sent a toy MIG 21,
It matches all my toy grenades, and the mock-up napalm gun,
And with my helmet on my head, I shoot my little friends all dead,
I blow their families all to bits with a soldier's cruel aplomb,

My kindergarten teacher tells me to hate all that's red,
So if Santa comes round here tonight, I'll hit him on the head,
And with my brand new CIA kit, question him until,
My new toy thumbscrew does its job and he tells me how his
    reindeer fly
Then I move in for the kill and drill him through the head.

(Spoken) "Cause he's a commie and I'm a good American kid!!"

3ʳᵈ CHORUS
Here's to You, Santa Claus,
Flying up so high,
And if you come round here tonight,
I'll blast you from the sky,
If you get by my toy radar dome,
How that be I can't tell,
The land mine in the fireplace will blow you straight to hell.

4th CHORUS
Here's to You, Santa Claus, Better turn and run,
Thanks to democracy,
I've been brought up to know guns,
I'll napalm all your factories,
But don't be so perplexed,
Here's to you Santa Claus,
The Easter Bunny's next!

HOUSE OF ORANGE
From Fresh Water, 1983

Written in 1983, after one of Stan's friends was severely injured by an IRA bomb while on holiday in London. Stan wrote the song in the studio as he neared the end of the FROM FRESH WATER recording session. It was possibly the last song he ever wrote.

I took back my hand and I showed him the door
No dollar of mine would I part with this day
For fuelling the engines of bloody cruel war
In my forefather's land far away.
Who fled the first Famine wearing all that they owned,
Were called "Navigators," all ragged and torn,
And built the Grand Trunk here, and found a new home
Wherever their children were born.

Their sons have no politics. None call recall
Allegiance from long generations before.
O'this or O'that name just can't mean a thing
Or be cause enough for to war.
And meanwhile my babies are safe in their home,
Unlike their pale cousins who shiver and cry

While kneecappers nail their poor Dads to the floor
And teach them to hate and to die.

It's those cruel beggars who spurn the fair coin.
The peace for their kids they could take at their will.
Since the day old King Billy prevailed at the Boyne,
They've bombed and they've slain and they've killed.
Now they cry out for money and wail at the door
But Home Rule or Republic, 'tis all of it shame;
And a curse for us here who want nothing of war.
We're kindred in nothing but name.

All rights and all wrongs have long since blown away,
For causes are ashes where children lie slain.
Yet the damned U.D.I and the cruel I.R.A.
Will tomorrow go murdering again.
But no penny of mine will I add to the fray.
"Remember the Boyne!" they will cry out in vain,
For I've given my heart to the place I was born
And forgiven the whole House of Orange
King Billy and the whole House of Orange.

HOW EASY IT'S BECOME
Unreleased, 1975

An absolute gem for Stan Rogers' fans, this song was never
recorded and nobody recalls Stan ever playing it. All that remains
is a handwritten copy — thankfully with both words and music.
He wrote it, according to his scant notes, for something called
"The Great Canadian Culture Hunt." That may, however, be the
song's subtitle. It's both a prophetic look at Stan's life, and an
accurate picture of the plight of the artist in Canada.

Last night I was taken by the words put in a play
By a young man from Three Rivers I was caught and swept away.
In a theatre half empty, knots of people getting cold
And wanting not to stay.

Oh, the players were a picture that could bring you to your feet
And they spoke of Northern beauty and the lines were so
      complete.
But applause was thin and hollow, and the writer's face was old,
I watched him walk away.

CHORUS
The empty seats all spoke of some old movie on TV
The tired past of Hollywood and Rome,
Which years away and North has brought a writer to his knees,
How easy it's become to stay at home.

In a tiny western gallery was a painter's one-man show
The first time for his children — how he'd loved to watch them
      grow.
He was proud that they were part of him, they needed to be sold
So he could paint again.

All the faces that he painted spoke of laughter, love and sight.
They were real enough to touch, they were strong and full of
      light
And I bought his one self-portrait, and the only one that sold.
He'll never paint again.

2nd CHORUS
The crowded walls all spoke of some old movie on TV
The tired past of Hollywood and Rome,
Which years away and North has brought the painter to his knees,
How easy it's become to stay at home.

Another artist lost in some old movie on TV
The tired past of Hollywood and Rome,
Which years away and North has brought the painter to his
    knees,
What he could be we never would have known,
How easy it's become to stay at home.

THE IDIOT
Northwest Passage, Home in Halifax, 1981

This song about Maritimers who move to Alberta to find work in the oil fields is a companion piece to *Make And Break Harbour*. *The Idiot* uses the same "knuckle-dragging Neanderthal" beat as Stan's Christmas ditty, *At Last I'm Ready for Christmas*. Note too Stan's use of "dole," which shows up in several of his songs. It means unemployment insurance. The term is much more popular in the United Kingdom than in Canada, but it sure was a favorite of Stan's.

———+———

I often take these night shift walks when the foreman's not
    around.
I turn my back on the cooling stacks and make for open ground.
Far out beyond the tank-farm fence where the gas flare makes no
    sound.
I forget the stink and I always think back to that Eastern town.
I remember back six years ago, this western life I chose.
And every day, the news would say some factory's going to close.
Well I could have stayed to take the dole, but I'm not one of
    those.
I take nothing free, and that makes me an idiot, I suppose.

CHORUS

I bid farewell to the eastern town I never more will see
But work I must so I eat this dust and breath refinery,
Oh I miss the green and the woods and streams and I don't like cowboy
*   clothes*
But I like being free and that makes me an idiot I suppose.

So come all you fine young fellows who've been beaten to the
    ground.
This western life's no paradise, but its better than lying down.
Oh, the streets aren't clean, and there's nothing green, and the
    hills are dirty brown.
But the government dole will rot your soul back there in your
    home town.

2nd CHORUS
So bid farewell to the Eastern town you never more will see.
There's self respect and a steady cheque in this refinery.
You will miss the green and the woods and streams and the dust will fill
*   your nose.*
But you'll be free, and just like me, an idiot, I suppose.

IT ALL FADES AWAY
From Coffee House to Concert Hall, 1977

Written during a brief hiatus in his relationship with Ariel. She
really did hate to have those pictures taken, and he liked to bug
her by taking them. This version of the song was an out-take from
TURNAROUND, and never made it to record until the posthumous
FROM COFFEE HOUSE TO CONCERT HALL.

An unfinished conversation
In a picture of the past,
Like the one that I just found of you,
Among many that I had.

I remember I saw you laughing
With my camera close at hand,
We were minutes from a quarrel
And forever from understanding.

You were just a bit excited
and a little more displeased,
How you hated candid pictures
When I took them just to tease.
Then you told me I was crazy,
I said I was born that way,
And we must have said those same two lines
Twenty times a day.

CHORUS
Now, I'd swear you don't remember why we parted,
Just like I cannot remember why we loved.
Ain't it funny how the past
Takes the better memories last
'Cause the pain fades away, it all fades away.

An unfinished conversation
That I'd somehow like to end,
If I just knew where to find you
Or where a letter could be sent.
But I know I'd not be welcome,
I know you'd nearly die;
All conversations fade away
When the love-light leaves the eye.

CHORUS

———

THE JEANNIE C.
Turnaround, 1978

This song was a last minute addition to TURNAROUND. One of Stan's proudest moments as a songwriter came after a concert in Little Dover, not far from the boat shop of the song. After he sang *The Jeannie C.*, an old fisherman came up and told Stan that the song "said things I can only think about." Note that these lyrics, while different from those in the album notes, reflect the actual words Stan sang on the record.

———+———

Come all ye lads, draw near to me, that I be not forsaken
This day was lost the *Jeannie C.* and my living has been taken
I'll go to sea no more.

We set out his day in the bright sunrise, the same as any other
My son and I and old John Price in the boat named for my mother
I'll go to sea no more.

Now it's well you know what the fishing has been, it's been scarce
    and hard and cruel
But this day, by God, we sure caught cod, and we sang and we
    laughed like fools
I'll go to sea no more.

I'll never know what it was we struck, but strike we did like thunder
John Price give a cry and pitched over side. Now it's forever he's
    gone under
I'll go to sea no more.

Now a leak we've sprung, let there be no delay if the *Jeannie C.*
    we're saving
John Price is drown'd and slip'd away. So I'll patch the hole while
    you're bailing
I'll go to sea no more.

But no leak I found from bow to hold. No rock it was that got her
But what I found made me heart stop cold, for every seam poured
    water
I'll go to sea no more.

My God, I cried as she went down. That boat was like no other
My father built her when I was nine, and named her for my
    mother
I'll go to sea no more.

And sure I could have another made in the boat shop down in
    Dover
But I would not love the keel they laid like the one the waves roll
    over
I'll go to sea no more.

So come all ye lads, draw near to me, that I be not forsaken
This day was lost the *Jeannie C.* and my whole life has been taken
I'll go to sea no more.

————————

THE LAST WATCH
From Fresh Water, 1982

Another story of a man — and a ship — who get less than their
just reward, originally titled "The Midland" after a real lake
steamer *The City of Midland*. Paul Mills remembers this being one
of the hardest songs he ever had to mix — not for any technical
reasons, but because he had to work on it just days after Stan's
death.

———+———

They dragged her down, dead, from Tobermory,
Too cheap to spare her one last head of steam,
Deep in diesel fumes embraced,

Rust and soot upon the face of one who was so clean.
They brought me here to watch her in the boneyard,
Just two old wrecks to spend the night alone.
It's the dark inside this evil place.
Clouds on the moon hide her disgrace;
This whiskey hides my own.

CHORUS
It's the last watch on the Midland,
The last watch alone,
One last night to love her,
The last night she's whole.

My guess is that we were young together.
Like her's, my strength was young and hard as steel.
And like her too, I knew my ground;
I scarcely felt the years go round
In answer to the wheel.

But then they quenched the fire beneath the boiler,
Gave me a watch and showed me out the door.
At sixty-four, you're still the best;
One year more, and then you're less
Than dust upon the floor.

CHORUS

So here's to useless superannuation
And us old relics of the days of steam.
In the morning, Lord, I would prefer
When men with torches come for her,
Let angels come for me.

CHORUS

———

LIES
Northwest Passage, 1980

Women were a mystery to Stan Rogers, so it's easy to see why he considered *Lies* one of his finest artistic achievements. He spent six months working on the song. "Belle Heaulmiere" is sculpture, which Stan describes in the liner notes as "a nude of an old woman which forces the viewer to look past the ravages of age to the young person we all are inside." Stan had come quite a long, long, long way from *The Fat Girl Rag*.

———+———

At last the kids are gone now for the day
She reaches for the coffee as the school bus pulls away
Another day to tend the house and plan
For Friday at the Legion when she's dancing with her man
Sure was a bitter winter but Friday will be fine
And maybe last year's Easter dress will serve her one more time
She'd pass for twenty nine but for her eyes
But winter lines are telling wicked lies

CHORUS
Lies!
All those lines are telling wicked lies.
Lies, all lies.
Too many lines there in that face
Too many to erase or to disguise –
They must be telling lies!

Is this the face that won for her the man
Whose amazed and clumsy fingers put that ring upon her hand?
No need to search that mirror for the years
The menace in their message shouts across the blur of tears
So this is beauty's finish! Like Rodin's "Belle Heaulmiere"
The pretty maiden trapped inside the ranch wife's toil and care
Well, after seven kids, that's no surprise
But why cannot her mirror tell her lies?

CHORUS

Then she shakes off the bitter web she wove
And turns to set the mirror, gently, face down by the stove
She gathers up her apron in her hand.
Pours a cup of coffee, drips Carnation from the can
And thinks ahead to Friday, 'cause Friday will be fine!
She'll look up in that weathered face that loves hers, line for line
To see that maiden shining in his eyes
And laugh at how her mirror tells her lies.

CHORUS

LOCK-KEEPER
From Fresh Water, 1982

The locks in this song are the watery kind, although Stan plays with the meaning. Lyrically, this is one of Stan's most mature works and a favorite of both Tom Paxton and Paul Mills. Incidentally, Stan credited the children's book *Wind in the Willows* as being at least partial inspiration for the song, particularly the story of the river rat, who chooses to stay home with family and friends rather than rove the wide world.

———+———

You say, "Well-met again, Lock-keeper!
We're laden even deeper that the time before,
Oriental oils and tea brought down from Singapore."
As we wait for my lock to cycle
I say, "My wife has given me a son."
"A son!" you cry, "Is that all that you've done?"

She wears bougainvillea blossoms.
You pluck 'em from her hair and toss 'em in the tide,

Sweep her in your arms and carry her inside.
Her sighs catch on your shoulder;
Her moonlit eyes grow bold and wiser through her tears
And I say, "How could you stand to leave her for a year?"

CHORUS
"Then come with me" you say, "to where the Southern Cross
Rides high upon your shoulder."
"Come with me!" you cry,
"Each day you tend this lock, you're one day older,
While your blood runs colder."
But that anchor chain's a fetter
And with it you are tethered to the foam,
And I wouldn't trade your life for one hour of home.

Sure I'm stuck here on the Seaway
While you compensate for leeway through the Trades;
And you shoot the stars to see the miles you've made.
And you laugh at hearts you've riven,
But which of these has given us more love of life,
You, your tropic maids, or me, my wife.

CHORUS

LOUISE'S SONG
From Coffee House to Concert Hall, 1976

This song was written and recorded in 1976 for one of the CBC Halifax *Anecdote* series produced by Bill Howell. It's part of that curious sub-set of Stan Rogers' songs: groupie songs. This one finally made the light of day on FROM COFFEE HOUSE TO CONCERT HALL.

I would have been here sooner,
Your note came yesterday,
But, yesterday was crazy;
There was much to square away.
Then I tried to come this morning,
But the old car wouldn't run
And the buses run so slowly,
There was nothing to be done.

But you, you don't need my troubles,
I'm here now, anyway,
And there's nothing left behind me
To say I cannot stay.
When I told you that I love you,
I said' "Call me anytime,
And especially when you need someone
When things get out of line". . .

CHORUS
And oh, there's a burning in your eyes
And the hand you put in mine won't stop trembling.
Oh, tell me what you're going through,
'Cause all I want to do is be protecting.
No! All those shadows on your face,
They look so out of place, they should be sunlight.
I want to take you when the smile returns
And keep you from the night
And wake up to see me in your eyes.

I don't know how we happened,
When we're kept so far apart.
There sure are lots worse prisons
Than the kind with iron bars;
And it almost makes me crazy
To see you hurt inside,

When you're beautiful and really need
To let things open wide.

CHORUS

———————

LOVE LETTER
From Coffee House to Concert Hall, 1976

Another song Stan recorded in CBC Halifax's Studio H in Hali-
fax: this time, for a regional music show called *Music Maritimes*.
This is yet another example of a love song, flying in the face of
Stan's claim that he never wrote any.

———+———

Now here's a picture of me, writing you a love letter,
To make me feel better, 'cause I'm so far from home.
Now, it seems like forever since the last time I saw you,
And I'd sure like to call you 'cause I feel so alone.

Now, it's another cold city but the same old hotel room.
They all look the same to me after a while.
A bed and a window over some dirty alley,
Looking on to the streets meeting nobody's smile.

Now every telephone says, "Hold the line,"
Like the preachers did when I was just a kid;
And it's strange how it still touches me after all this time.
They said, "Keep your light shining brightly."
And I just can't take it lightly; I'm still trying to find it.

Now, every evening brings another show,
To empty faces screaming over too much beer.
And what they find to talk about I guess I'll never, ever know.

But I'm leaving tomorrow and I don't regret it.
Just one more town and then I can forget . . .
It's a picture of me writing you a love letter,
To make me feel better 'cause I've been feeling low.
Hey, it seems like forever since the last time I saw you,
But it won't be much longer, now, look out, honey,
You know I'm coming on home.

MACDONNELL ON THE HEIGHTS
From Fresh Water, 1982

A man named John MacDonnell was an aide-de-camp to General Brock in the War of 1812, and did fight along side the General in the battle for Queenston Heights. The day after Brock fell, Mac-Donnell rallied the troops for another attack on the Yankee inter-lopers — only to die in battle, too. But this song is as much about another forgotten hero, who reached the "heights" but never found fame. Stan's original lyrics tell the tell: "Not one in ten thousand know my name." With MacDonnell, Stan found a part-ner in obscurity.

Too thin the line that charged the heights
And scrambled in the clay.
Too thin the Eastern Township Scot
Who showed them all the way,
And perhaps had you not fallen,
You might be what Brock became
But not one in ten thousand knows your name.

To say the name, MacDonnell,
It would bring no bugle call
But the Redcoats stayed beside you

When they saw the general fall.
'Twas MacDonnell raised the banner then
And set the Heights aflame,
But not one in ten thousand knows your name.

CHORUS
You brought the field all standing with your courage and your luck
But unknown to most, you're lying there beside old General Brock.
So you know what it is to scale the Heights and fall just short of fame
And have not one in ten thousand know your name.

At Queenston now, the General on his tower stands alone
And there's lichen on 'MacDonnell' carved upon that
     weathered stone
In a corner of the monument to glory you could claim,
But not one in ten thousand knows your name.

CHORUS

MAKE AND BREAK HARBOUR
Fogarty's Cove, 1975

Stan completed this song and four others during a wild weekend
of writing alone in Bill Howell's house in Halifax. It was the first
of a series of songs about inshore fishermen. The "long-seeing
eyes" are the drift-nets of foreign trawlers that stretch for miles
beneath the sea.

———+———

How still lies the bay in the bright western airs
Which blow from the crimson horizon
Once more we tack home with a dry empty hold
Saving gas with the breezes so fair

She's a kindly Cape Islander, old, but still sound
But so lost in the longliner's shadow
Make and break, and make do, but the fish are so few
That she won't be replaced should she founder

It's so hard not to think of before the big war
When the cod were so cheap and so plenty
Foreign trawlers go by now with long-seeing eyes
Taking all, where we seldom take any
And so the young folk don't stay with the fisherman's way
Long ago, they all moved to the cities
And the ones left behind, old, tired, and blind
Can't work for "a pound or a penny."

CHORUS
In Make and Break Harbour, the boats are so few.
Too many are pulled up and rotten.
Most houses stand empty, old nets hung to dry
Are blown away, lost and forgotten.

I can see the big draggers have stirred up the bay
Leaving lobster traps smashed on the bottom
Can they think it don't pay to respect the old ways
That Make and Break men have not forgotten?
For we still keep our time to the turn of the tide
And this boat that I built with my father
Still lifts to the sky! The one-lunger and I
Still talk like old friends on the water.

CHORUS

MAN WITH BLUE DOLPHIN
From Fresh Water, 1982

A Stan Rogers' frustration song dressed up as a Stan Rogers' salvage song. Again, it's a true story of a man who spent his life savings trying to raise the *Bluenose's* sister ship, the *Blue Dolphin*. I've tried to track the story down to find out how it ended, but all trails turned out to be dead ends. In any case, Stan called the salvager "crazy" — high praise indeed coming from Stan Rogers.

———+———

It was just like him, he had to pick
A boat gone from dowdy to derelict
In half a dozen years
Of searching for an owner
She may have lost her heart in the harbour mud,
But she really caught his at the flood;
And he wonders how she knew
That she was waiting for a loner.

Blue Dolphin, built by the Rhuland men,
She's lying on the bottom again
With only him to care
That *Bluenose* had a sister.
He lost the house and he sold the car.
His wife walked out; so he hit the bars
And hit up every friend
To raise the *Blue Dolphin*.

CHORUS
And even afloat she's a hole in the water where his money goes.
Every dollar goes
And it's driving him crazy.
He pounds his fists white on the dock in the night
And cries, "I'm gonna win!"

And licks the blood away.
And he's gonna raise the Dolphin.

Blue Dolphin's lying like a wounded whale.
She's hungry for a scrap of a sail
To get her underway
Back to salt water.
Now there's a man lying spent in the winter sun.
He wonders what the hell he has done
And who would ever pay
To save his schooner daughter.

CHORUS

THE MARY ELLEN CARTER
Between the Breaks, Home in Halifax, 1979

On February 12, 1983, Robert M. Cusiak was on board the collier *Marine Electric* when it went down off the coast of Boston. As he lay up to his neck in the frigid water of a swamped lifeboat, fighting off hypothermia, he sang a song to keep his spirits up. The song was *The Mary Ellen Carter*, and to this day Cusiak credits it with saving his life. Stan's signature song, it's still sung to close out folk festivals across the country. Recently, fans have begun to pick up on the not-too-subtle sexual innuendo in the song, leading some to wonder exactly which *Mary Ellen Carter* Stan was talking about. By the way, Stan said that this song and *Barrett's Privateers* virtually wrote themselves, with the lyrics and melody pouring out in brief, 20-minute sessions.

She went down last October in a pouring driving rain.
The skipper, he'd been drinking and the mate, he felt no pain.
Too close to Three Mile Rock, and she was dealt her mortal blow,
And the *Mary Ellen Carter* settled low.

There were five of us aboard her when she finally was awash.
We'd worked like hell to save her, all heedless of the cost.
And the groan she gave as she went down, it caused us to proclaim
That the *Mary Ellen Carter* would rise again.

Well, the owners wrote her off; not a nickel would they spend.
She gave twenty years of service, boys, then met her sorry end.
But insurance paid the loss to them, they let her rest below.
Then they laughed at us and said we had to go.

But we talked of her all winter, some days around the clock,
For she's worth a quarter million, afloat and at the dock.
And with every jar that hit the bar, we swore we would remain
And make the *Mary Ellen Carter* rise again.

CHORUS
Rise again, rise again, that her name not be lost
To the knowledge of men.
Those who loved her best and were with her till the end
Will make the Mary Ellen Carter *rise again.*

All spring, now, we've been with her on a barge lent by a friend.
Three dives a day in hard hat suit and twice I've had the bends.
Thank God it's only sixty-feet and the currents here are slow
Or I'd never have the strength to go below.

But we've patched her rents, stopped her vents, dogged hatch
    and porthole down.
Put cables to her, 'fore and aft and birded her around.
Tomorrow, noon, we hit the air and then take up the strain.
And watch the *Mary Ellen Carter* rise again.

For we couldn't leave her there, you see, to crumble into scale.
She'd saved our lives so many times, living through the gale
And the laughing, drunken rats who left her to a sorry grave
They won't be laughing in another day.

And you, to whom adversity has dealt the final blow
With smiling bastards lying to you everywhere you go
Turn to, and put out all your strength of arm and heart and brain
And like the *Mary Ellen Carter*, rise again.

2nd CHORUS
Rise again, rise again — though your heart it be broken
And life about to end
No matter what you've lost, be it a home, a love, a friend.
Like the Mary Ellen Carter, *rise again.*

MATTER OF HEART
Coffee House to Concert Hall, 1974

Originally written and recorded for Stan's CBC folk opera project
So Hard To Be So Strong about the 1976 Olympics, this is one of
Stan's most personal expressions. He was ostensibly writing about
the break-up of a friend's marriage, but he could have easily been
writing about himself. The song features one of Stan's goofiest —
and most charming — arrangements.

We live in fear of no one to love us
Of feeling like an empty hole
With no kind heart or strengthening hand
To light the dark and secret soul.

Behind the walls of lonely protection
Afraid to give for what we may lose,

And to hide our sin, or let someone within,
Everyone will have to choose!

CHORUS
Put your life on the line
Give your hand and pledge your time
To the love whose lips inflame you
Like some ancient and golden wine;
And to all it's a start
In fulfilling greatest needs in part
For in whatever we dream of what we some day want to be
It's a matter of heart.

We like to think we know what we're doing
We always like to be in control
The rational mind rules the passionate heart
Is what the ancient sages told.

But that can sound a little bit hollow
When you're sitting by the fire alone
And the rarest old wine tastes of ashes and brine
When you've no one there to keep you warm.

CHORUS

The way in which our pride will stall us,
When we know we should be losing control,
Puts us in the fear of falling and we let it go.
Our careful words are self-deceiving,
Though we like to call them "pretence" and "art",
But every old line is held in the mind,
When it's really just a matter of heart.

CHORUS

─────────

THE NANCY
From Fresh Water, 1982

Based on a true story of a British ship that defeated an American cavalry unit during the War of 1812. Written and recorded in that faux traditional style that earned Stan the nickname Steeleye Stan after the Brit Trad Revival band Steeleye Span.

———+———

The clothes men wear do give them airs, the fellows do compare.
A colonel's regimentals shine, and women call them fair.
I am Alexander MacIntosh, a nephew to the Laird
And I do distain men who are vain, the men with powdered hair.

I command the *Nancy* schooner from the Moy on Lake St. Claire.
On the third day of October, boys, I did set sail from there.
To the garrison at Amherstburg I quickly would repair
With Captain Maxwell and his wife and kids and powdered hair.

CHORUS
Aboard the Nancy!
In regimentals bright.
Aboard the Nancy!
With all his pomp and bluster there, aboard the Nancy-o.

Below the St. Clair rapids I sent scouts unto the shore
To ask a friendly Wyandotte to say what lay before.
"Amherstburg has fallen, with the same for you in store!
And militia sent to take you there, fifty horse or more."

Up spoke Captain Maxwell then, "Surrender, now, I say!
Give them your *Nancy* schooner and make off without delay!
Set me ashore, I do implore. I will not die this way!"
Says I, "You go, or get below, for I'll be on my way!"

2nd CHORUS
Aboard the Nancy!
"Surrender, Hell!" I say.
Aboard the Nancy!
"It's back to Mackinac I'll fight, aboard the Nancy-o.*"*

Well up comes Colonel Beaubien, then, who shouts as he comes
    near.
"Surrender up your schooner and I swear you've naught to fear.
We've got your Captain Maxwell, sir, so spare yourself his tears."
Says I, "I'll not but send you shot to buzz about your ears."

Well, they fired as we hove anchor, boys, and we got under way,
But scarce a dozen broadsides, boys, the *Nancy* they did pay
Before the business sickened them. They bravely ran away.
All sail we made, and reached the Lake before the close of day.

3rd CHORUS
Aboard the Nancy!
We sent them shot and cheers.
Aboard the Nancy!
We watched them running through the trees, aboard the Nancy-o.

Oh, military gentlemen, they bluster, roar and pray.
Nine sailors and the *Nancy*, boys, made fifty run away.
The powder in their hair that day was powder sent their way
By poor and ragged sailor men, who swore that they would stay.

4th CHORUS
Aboard the Nancy!
Six pence and found a day
Aboard the Nancy!
No uniforms for men to scorn, aboard the Nancy-o.

———

NIGHT GUARD
Northwest Passage, Home in Halifax, 1980

A modern-day cattle rustling song and a good example of Stan's populist politics. Stan considered this song his first serious foray into rock music. Hoping it would help him reach a wider audience, it was released as the first single from the NORTHWEST PASSAGE album.

———+———

Forty-four's no age to start again,
But the bulls were getting tough and he was never free of pain
Where others blew their winnings getting tanked,
Most of his got banked saving for the farm.

He never thought she'd wait for him at all.
She wanted more than broken bones and trophies on the wall;
But when he quit and finally got the farm,
She ran into his arms and now they've got a kid.

CHORUS
He was star of all the rodeos but now they rob him blind.
It took eighteen years of Brahma bulls and life on the line
To get his spread and a decent herd,
But now he spends his time pulling night guard.

He told her that he'd got it for the game,
A "Winnie" 303 with his initials on the frame
Riding in the scabbard at his knee, tonight he's gonna see
Who's getting all the stock.

Seventh one this summer yesterday;
Half a year of profits gone, and now there's hell to pay.
The cops say they know who, but there's no proof.
The banker hit the roof, and damn near took the car.

CHORUS

He hears the wire popping by the road;
Sees the blacked out REO coming for another load.
This time, it's not one they take but two;
Two minutes and they're through, and laughing in the cab.

And here'll be the end of this tonight,
'Cause all the proof he needs is lying steady in his sights.
It may be just the worst thing he could do
But he squeezes off a few, then make his call to town.

CHORUS

NORTHWEST PASSAGE
Northwest Passage, Home in Halifax, 1982

Along with *The Mary Ellen Carter*, Stan's most inspirational song
and a neat summary of his songwriting strategy of turning the ordi-
nary into the heroic. After the album was released, this song was
featured in stunning 12-part harmony in the CBC radio play,
Famous Inside. Often called "Canada's unofficial national anthem,"
the song was quoted by Governor General Adrienne Clarkson during her installation speech to the Senate, on October 7, 1999. Note:
I've included here Stan's little-known fifth verse, which, sadly, has
never been available on record and never before published.

———+——

CHORUS
Ah, for just one time I would take the Northwest Passage
To find the hand of Franklin reaching for the Beaufort Sea;
Tracing one warm line through a land so wide and savage
And make a Northwest Passage to the sea.

Westward rom the Davis Strait 'tis there 'twas said to lie
The sea route to the Orient for which so many died;
Seeking gold and glory, leaving weathered, broken bones
And a long-forgotten lonely cairn of stones.

Three centuries thereafter, I take passage overland
In the footsteps of brave Kelso, where his "sea of flowers" began
Watching cities rise before me, then behind me sink again
This tardiest explorer, driving hard across the plain.

CHORUS

And through the night, behind the wheel, the mileage clicking
    west
I think upon Mackenzie, David Thompson and the rest
Who cracked the mountain ramparts and did show a path for me
To race the roaring Fraser to the sea.

How then am I so different from the first men through this way?
Like them, I left a settled life, I threw it all away.
To seek a Northwest Passage at the call of many men
To find there but the road back home again.

CHORUS

And if should be I come again to loved ones left at home,
Put the journals on the mantle, shake the frost out of my bones,
Making memories of the passage, only memories after all,
And hardships there the hardest to recall.

————

ONCE IN A WHILE
Unreleased, 1972

Stan Roger loved Sundays. He loved everything about the day: sleeping in, having a giant breakfast, meeting with friends and just relaxing. In fact, "Sunday" rivals "salvage" in the list of Stan's favorite subjects. His catalog includes *Bye, Bye, Sweet Sunday, In Your Sunday Town, Sunday Morning* and others, many which have never been released. This particular song owes a debt to James Taylor, especially the opening line that is very similar to the opening line of Taylor's *Fire And Rain*.

———+———

I woke up this morning and I found that you were gone
I had to smile in knowing that it wouldn't be for long
And so I thought I'd write this song to try and make you smile
Oh, Sunday morning comes once in a while!

As if the days had speedy ways they fly on lightning wings
I dream away the noon light, and at night I only sing
And as I stand before the crowds, I have my special style
Cause Sunday morning comes once in a while!

Now if dreams were made of special days, one would fill my head
I'd carry with me all the things that Sunday morning said
Now I don't care how far away, I never count the miles
As long as Sunday morning comes once in a while!

CHORUS
Now I have played a hundred shows
And walked a thousand miles
And all the freaks and side men
They couldn't make me smile
And sure enough it's lonely,
Heaven only knows.
Oh, Sunday morning.

I woke up this morning and I found that you were gone
I had to smile in knowing that it wouldn't be for long
And so I thought I'd write this song to try and make you smile
Oh, Sunday morning comes once in a while!

PAST FIFTY
From Coffee House to Concert Hall, 1974

More hippy era Stan, but with stronger melodic hooks and a beat you can dance to. All round pretty good singer-songwriter pop, and one of Stan's favorite performance pieces during the Cedar Lake days. First recorded for CBC's in house *Transcription* series, the song caught the attention of folk stalwart Vanguard Records, which signed Stan on the song's hit potential. When the company discovered Stan was not cut out for pop stardom, they cut him loose and the single was never released.

—+—

Some living, no one time for giving, I ain't got a dime,
Winds are blowing, wheat fields are growing, bit none of it's mine,
Gets so I just watch people go by, looking away,
I tell you I'm almost through, I'd hate to see another day.

Easy lady, I know you're always ready, selling your time,
My last dollar, I pinched it 'til it hollered and bought me some wine.
I'm past caring, it's all I got for sharing, so if you're for free
I tell you, I'm almost through, I'm tired as a man can be.

CHORUS
I want to go home to the Maker, home to the Chief,
The holy word made me sure my worried mind would find relief;
I'm going through life like a pilgrim, lost in a storm;
With winds that blow to make me cold, but the Holy Body keeps me warm.

Some morning I'd like to see me warming my feet by a fire,
Eggs and bacon, coffee I'd be making, couldn't be finer!
A good living, extra bit forgiving someone like me,
I tell you I'm almost through. I'm tired as a man can be.

CHORUS

PHARISEE
From Coffee House to Concert Hall, 1974

Pastoral Stan, circa 1974. Very much a period piece, its quasi-hippy sentiments haven't aged that well. Living proof that Stan the songwriter benefited from the distance that history and an invented point-of-view provided.

There used to be, a Pharisee,
Cynical and wise, telling rich ungodly lies,
Of humanity . . .
But in the market place was seated,
a cripple with a lyre, I looked at him and said,
"I've been rich but so unhappy,
What set's your soul on fire?"

He said "Look upon me brother, I am a man with piece
      of mind,
I know I never was much good at nothing
But the words I wrought and rhyme,
But I've a good woman to feed me, and friends to share it too,
Evenings we sit around and sing together,
It can be the same for you" . . .

CHORUS
Just hold on, To young friends you made of old,
And please too, the one who keeps us whole,

Keep a warm fire for all your friends,
who come in from the cold,
Love them all as brothers,
you don't have to know their names,
For you it might be different,
but for us it always stays the same.

Tonight the smoke is rising, from around the room,
And judging from the warmth and smells from the kitchen,
There'll be supper ready soon.
And our table's set for twenty,
room for more if they should come,
And later on we'll pass around the wine for our pleasure,
and sing until the morning comes . . .

CHORUS

POCKETFUL OF GOLD
Unreleased, 1972

Stan was very anti-American at one point in his life and it particularly angered him that much of Nova Scotia was being bought up by American investors. This song has a powerful melody, but it's too long. Perhaps this is why Stan avoided "political" songs: naturally pedantic, he tended to get wrapped up in the argument and would lose sight of the song.

———+———

Well, the track of my beginnings
Has been buried 'neath the years
For a dozen generations,
We have toiled the land here
But now my patrimony, my inheritance is sold

To an old Rhode Island Yankee
For a pocketful of gold.

And when he comes tomorrow
I'll be giving up the land
The hills above the harbour
The rocky fields, the sand
And I'll leave my crying ocean
With shoulder to the cold
And walk out to the jingle
Of a pocketful of gold.

Inflationary Judas,
As I stare down at my hand,
For a pocketful of silver
He betrayed the Child Of Man
By me and many others, the story is retold.
How we squander our existence
For a pocketful of gold.

Now it seems like only yesterday
My heart was in the land
From ocean unto ocean
We were true northern men.
But the invaders' smiles beguile me
And we sell all that we own
For baubles, beads and mirrors and
A pocketful of gold.

In a dozen years a new flag will be
Flying near and far
And the State of Nova Scotia will be
Just another star
And the bones of all my ancestors
Will be safe in their graves
And the beer cans and the bottles

Will be lying on the waves
Will line the shores like epitaphs:
"Our work was all in vain,"

And the Disney world of Uncle Sam Is all that will remain.
I remember how Grandpa
Used to stare out to the sea
And raise his fist to the south
And turn and cry to me:
"Don't give up the land.
For a pocketful of gold."

Now the governments and the teachers tell of
Building up the land
Of how the mills and factories
Were getting out of hand
Now simple are these "Kanucks,"
How often I've been told,
To throwaway a nation
For a pocketful of gold.

On the pocketbooks of Wall Street
The old nation is a state
And of the northern mysteries
What memories remain?
I remember how Grandpa
Used to stare out to the sea
And raise his fist to the south
And turn and cry to me:
"Don't give up the land . . .
For a pocketful of gold."

Now the scenes of my childhood
Are misting in my tears
As if a veil was drawn across
The views no longer clear

My father's patrimony,
My inheritance is sold
To an old Rhode Island Yankee
For a pocketful of gold.

———

THE PUDDLER'S TALE
From Coffee House to Concert Hall, 1983

The greatest Stan Rogers song you've never heard? The answer is "yes," unless you own FROM COFFEE HOUSE TO CONCERT HALL." A homage to his father Al, who worked as a "puddler" (an iron-worker) in Hamilton's steel mills, the song is the perfect marriage of old and new, lyric and melody. Not just the best song on this posthumous album: one of the best work songs, ever.

———+———

They neither know of night or day,
They night and day pour out their thunder,
As every ingot rolls away,
A dozen more are split asunder.

There is a sign beside the gate,
"Eleven Days" since a man lay dying,
Now every shift brings fear and hate
And shaken men in terror crying.

The molten rivers boil away,
A fiery brew hell never equaled.
To their profits the bosses pray,
And Mammon sings in his grim cathedral.

His attendants join the choir,
And heaven help us if we're shirking,
Stoke the furnace-altar fire,
And just be thankful that we're working!

CHORUS
Do this, then, charge the hoppers high
Lest you endure the foreman's choler,
Do this, then, drain the tankards dry,
And let us toast the almighty dollar,

That keeps us chained here before the fire
Where heat and noise set the weak a-quaking.
At the siren's infernal cry,
The open hearth sets the ground to shaking.

2nd CHORUS
Do this, then, raise the babies high
And make them shriek with love and laughter!
Do this, then, kiss your woman's eyes
And raise a song unto the rafters!

Wash the steel mill from your hair,
Heap the table 'til it's breaking,
'Nor let terror enter there
And in the hearth set the glasses breaking.

———

RAWDON HILLS
Fogarty's Cove, 1974

There actually are Rawdon Hills, and they can be found north-west of Halifax. Stan based the song on a story he heard about how the Nova Scotia government had spread a false rumor about gold in 'them thar' Rawdon Hills to encourage settlement in the area. Stan took his inspiration for the song from a Ministry of Mines and Resources report on gold-mining in Nova Scotia, published by the federal government at the turn of the last century. For some reason, the lyrics to this song were left off of the FOGARTY'S COVE liner notes.

—|—

Worn down shacks of labour past, on a hill of broken stone
Once brought by men to the stamping mills to crush away
    the gold
But before it could pass to their sons, the glory left the hole
The Rawdon Hills once were touched by gold.

The grandsons of the mining men scratch the fields among
    the trees
When the gold played out, they were all turned out with granite
    dusted knees
But at night around the stoves, sometimes the stories still
    unfold
How the Rawdon Hills once were touched by gold.

CHORUS
Grandsons of the mining men, you'll see it in your dreams
Beneath your father's bones still lies the undiscovered seam
Of Quartzite, in a serpentine vein that marks the greatest yield
And along the Midland railway, it's still told
How the Rawdon Hills once were touched by gold

Eighty years has been and gone since there was colour in the hole
And the careworn shades of the hard-rock men surround the old
    Cope lode
And through the tiny hillside farms, the miner's tales grow old
The Rawdon Hills once were touched by gold.
The Rawdon Hills once were touched by gold.

SAILOR'S REST
Home in Halifax, 1982

The only previously unreleased song on HOME IN HALIFAX, *Sailor's Rest* is a splendid combination of wit and sentiment. Stan wrote the song with his grandfather Stanley Rogers in mind, who, at the time of the recording, was in a rest home. He died shortly after the song was recorded.

——+——

It's acrimony down in the card room
With winning hands thrown on the baize;
Forgotten cards wait on the end of debate
On the good old days.
Captains and mates getting testy
With memories not of the best
And tempers are flying
Down at the Sailor's Rest.

Blue eyes in wrinkled Morocco
Still search the horizon for squalls,
And Zeros in the sky and the watch keeper's eye
And the pawn shop balls.
The spice in the wind off Java
And the bars in Papeete were best,
But the deck is too steady
Down at the Sailor's Rest.

CHORUS
And oh . . . how they talk of the day they arrived;
When after the years, all the storms and the tears,
Still very much alive.
And oh . . . how their lives were spilled out on the floor
From the battered old sea bags, the journals and logs
And the keepsakes locked in the chests

That were stowed in the attic
Down at the Sailor's Rest.

No rail on the mess room table
And you're dead if you spit on the floor.
No grog allowed, no singing too loud,
And no locks on the doors.
But there's always a fire in the card room
And the tucker is always the best,
And they'll end it together
Down at the Sailor's Rest.

 So, it's acrimony down in the card room
With winning hands thrown on the baize;
Forgotten cards wait on the end of debate
On the good old days.
Captains and mates getting testy
With memories not of the best
And tempers are flying
Down at the Sailor's Rest.

SO BLUE
Turnaround, 1975

This song loses a lot of its mystery when you realize that Stan
wrote it on a train, the *Ocean Limited*, from Halifax to Montreal.
So Blue is Stan's tribute to one of his idols, Joni Mitchell, whose
album BLUE was released in 1971.

———|———

I saw her cold in the morning light as
We roared through the rain
Swaying softly to the ever pounding steel

Drunk upon a night of train . . . the club car's gonna take her again
And I'm glad to be on my own
The ocean's gonna take me home, so hungry, so alone and so blue.

Somewhere back behind the darkness lies the City on the Sea
Gone already with a sleep stuck in between
I left so much behind to grow.
So much, too soon, but even so.
She sways along the aisle again
Crazy woman, dancing on a train, so hungry, so alone and so blue.

Cranky people do their morning jerks and the coffee bar has only tea
And somewhere up ahead beyond the day, there's a lady keeping
    warm for me
She's a mighty hand inside a silken glove
I've know it awhile, and I can't get enough
I want to listen to Joni Mitchell on the radio and make love.

A crazy lady on a daylight train is dancing for free
But everybody here just watches trees go by
She knows a bit of what this train can feel.
Swaying spirit of the moving steel.
She reminds me what I'm going to.
And even with the thought of you
I'm still so hungry, so alone, and so blue.
So hungry, so alone, and so blue.

———

SONG OF THE CANDLE
Turnaround, 1972

An incurable romantic, Stan loved candles. At night, he'd often
read or write surrounded by a dozen of them. This song is based
on a typical subject for writers: writers' block. Stan's intelligent
uses of metaphor and a very powerful melody lift this song from

the abyss of adolescent self-indulgence to a level that is really quite remarkable. "*Song Of The Candle* I wrote in 1972 in London," Stan said in a 1978 interview for *Folk Life Quarterly*. "The result of a very hard night trying to write a song the night before. You know, when you sit down to write and nothing comes out and you spend a white night because of it, and watch the sun come up and realize that nothing has been done. That old burned-out, tired and wasted feeling. It's essentially that trip, but done in a soft ballad way."

———+———

I took up my pen tonight. I couldn't seem to write.
It's like I got religion and then I lost the light
An old woman once told me she'd always felt that way . . .
She said "Taken from the mould when it can still run
A candle might not keep you from the cold
But buy another candle, son, it's not too much to pay
For one more try." And I had to smile
Before I walked away.

Coffee houses bother me. I cannot tell you why.
But, it never seems "hello" sounds as sweet as "goodbye."
And the waitresses, in passing, remember all your names . . .
They say "Look around and try to meet a single eye.
And empty cups will mock me if I stay, but
Buy another coffee, Stan, it's not too much to pay.
And we will try to raise your smile
Before you walk away."

CHORUS
Tonight in a room full of candles another cup of ashes drains away
And, at times, it gets so hard to handle
Knowing one more song has swiftly taken wing
And I'm left alone to hear the song a lonely candle sings.

The priest, I found, was nervous. He cleared his throat a lot.
But, framed in stained glass windows, his eyes were lost in
   thought.
And I said "Father, can you tell me . . . is some happiness my
   right?"
He said "Rather seek you joy, the blessings of your God,
And happiness from worship in his sight.
And buy another candle son, before you start to pray
And don't forget to cross your breast
Before you walk away."

2nd CHORUS
Tonight, in a room full of candles, another cup of madness drains away.
And at times it gets so hard to handle
Knowing one more simple song has swiftly taken wing.
And I'm left alone to hear the song a lonely candle sings.

One too many cigarettes, slowly burning down
And the final cup of coffee was cold and full of grounds
And maybe one last pipeful might send the words around
Still, underneath my hand this night has slipped away
And it leaves me as empty as this page
One more candle flickers out, the night is turning grey
And I just can't watch the dying flame
I have to walk away.

3rd CHORUS
Tonight I have burned all my candles
Leaving only ashes in their wake. . .
And at times, I get so hard to handle
'Cause simple songs leave me behind, they all have taken wing
And I'm left alone to hear the song a lonely candle sings.

———

STRAIGHT AND TRUE
From Coffee House to Concert Hall, 1974

The song marked a turning point in Stan's professional life. He wrote it in New York, when he was still being courted by Vanguard records. A little down and out, all of a sudden Stan could smell salt water and clam flats. He took it as a sign that home was where his heart was. The song was recorded at Daniel Lanois' first studio — in the basement of his parents' home in Ancaster, Ontario.

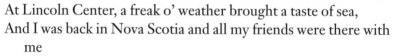

At Lincoln Center, a freak o' weather brought a taste of sea,
And I was back in Nova Scotia and all my friends were there with me
And they were drinkin' Diamond, singin' Carter and passin' them from mouth to mouth
It sounded like "goodbye" and I knew that I was headed South, the bitter South.
In my uncle's kitchen the songs are bitchin', or some Hank Williams' blues
And I can hear my cousin's voices singing, the very best that they can do,
And it doesn't matter what we're drinking, the ocean brings the flavour through,
And if none of this is fancy, the love is always straight and true.

CHORUS
Straight and true!
There's something about it,
I can't live without the coast,
The rhythmic ocean, the clean wholesome motion
Of most of my friends there,
Swaying by the trees, singing of the sea, now.

City streets, they can't hold me when I'm most alone
    I'm going on home.
I think I'm ready, my hands are steady,
'though that's something I've not always known,
And even if the west rejects me, there's some place I hold for my
    own,
And I soon will be there; do I love it? Yes, I guess that you could
    say I do,
'Cause I'll be picking with my people where the music's always
    straight and true,
Straight and true.

CHORUS

TAKE IT FROM DAY TO DAY
From Coffee House to Concert Hall, 1980

Another song from the CBC radio drama *Famous Inside*, produced in Halifax by Stan's friend Bill Howell. The play is the true
story of RCMP Captain Henry Larson, who took a tiny ice-
breaker, the *St. Roche*, through Canada's northern waters during
World War II. His purpose: to establish Canada's sovereignty
over our northern waters (before the Americans took them over).
One of the highlights from Stan's posthumous FROM COFFEE
HOUSE TO CONCERT HALL.

———+———

Well, it's not the hours of watch-on-watch,
And it's not the work that I mind so much,
Or the long cold miles from my lover's touch,
'Though for sure she's far away.

No stranger, I, to the touch of steel,
Or the honest fear any man can feel,
But I long for dust under my heels
And a pocket full of pay.
So I'll take it from day to day.

The pack-ice 'round us cracks and groans;
The old *St. Roche*, she creaks and moans.
The icy fog is in my bones,
And the ache won't go away.

Outside I bet it's warm and fair.
I could have her fingers in my hair,
But it's long, cold miles to her out there
So I guess I'll have to stay
And just take it from day to day!

We're as far North as I want to come,
But Larsen's got us under his thumb,
And I signed up for the whole damned run,
I can't get off half way.

But when I get back onto the shore,
I'm going South where it stays warm,
And there'll be someone on my arm
To help me spend my pay,
So I'll take it from day to day.

THREE PENNIES
RCA single, 1973

Another early flop single, this one leaning more to soft rock than novelty. It's not a bad song really, although not the kind you'd every associate with Stan Rogers. Let's thank God it flopped, or Stan might have found a niche writing '70s Can Pop schlop.

———+———

When day comes on this mountain,
To your well I will go,
Drink from you deep,
Watch you in sleep,
And down meadows green softly go.

Three pennies bright, thrown in the water,
Singing they fall from the light,
One's very bold; one glimpse of gold,
And one's for your thoughts in the night.

Then wild babies laugh,
Sprawled on the grass,
Dew from the moss your eyes gleam,
The sun draws the path,

The well draws a glass
I drink from your contents a dream..
White picket fence, built round your garden,
In strawberry rows a golden glow,
Winds from the east, day break brings peace,
And down meadows green softly goes,

And God bless the trees as they grow,
And God bring us peace as we grow,
And bless you and me as we grow.

TINY FISH FOR JAPAN
From Fresh Water, 1983

Government regulations and public tastes differ from country to country. The fishermen in this song catch smelt, which don't meet Canadian standards for taste and texture, and ship them to Japan, where they are considered a delicacy. This is another one of Stan's overlooked gems, and while hard-core folkies might object to the strings, it strikes me as a perfectly produced song. In 1998, in the course of writing *Consider the Fish*, my popular history of fish and fishing in Canada, I visited Port Dover and found the industry to be in even greater turmoil 15 years after Stan's death. "We used to eat fresh fish every day," one young ex-fisherman told me. "Now when we have fish, it's like Captain Highliner or Red Lobster. It's sort of pathetic, when you think about it." Note that a turtleback is a kind of fishing boat peculiar to the Great Lakes.

———+———

Where Patterson Creek's muddy waters run down
Past the penny arcades, by the harbour downtown,
All the old turtlebacks rust in the rain
Like they never will leave there again.

But leave there they will in the hours before dawn,
Slip out in the darkness without word or song;
For a few more years yet they will work while they can
To catch tiny fish for Japan.

No white fish or trout here, we leave them alone.
The inspectors raise hell if we take any home.
What kind of fisherman can't eat his catch
Or call what he's taken his own?

But the plant works three shifts now. There's plenty of pay.
We ship seventeen tons of this garbage each day.
If we want to eat fish, then we'll open a can,
And catch tiny fish for Japan.
In the Norfolk Hotel over far too much beer,
The old guys remember when the water ran clear.
No poisons with names that we can't understand
And no tiny fish for Japan.

So the days run together. Each one is the same.
And it's good that the smelt have no lovelier name.
It's all just a job now, we'll work while we can,
To catch tiny fish for Japan.
And we'll catch tiny fish for Japan.

TRY LIKE THE DEVIL
Turnaround, 1975

Written after one of Stan's few stints playing the Toronto bar
scene. The band had the hardest time playing this song for the
album TURNAROUND. They took numerous stabs at it, until
finally, late at night, they got a take they could use. The next
morning, they awoke to find the engineer had accidentally erased
the song. Fed up, the band went into the studio and did the song
in one take. Something must have gone right: it remains one of
Stan's most soulful recordings. Here's Stan's explanation of the
song, as revealed in 1978 interview with *Folk Life Quarterly*. "*Try
Like The Devil* is sort of a hard-edged blues, a white blues, almost
Ray Charles style — about being a folk musician playing in bars."

So it's come to the alley and playing in bars,
Coming on to the hustlers and the old burnt out stars

With the demons on my shoulders, smiling to show me the way.
Now there's one for ambition and another for greed
Here's a big one . . . he's a drunkard, and the easiest to feed
It takes a poor man to ignore them . . . A rich man to drive them
    away.

CHORUS
No more thinking! I don't care anyway,
I can't find an answer; I've looked for one everywhere.
I'll keep my head down, and smile when they sell me
I'll play where they tell me,
I'll try like the devil
To keep the demons away.

Now, it's so tantalizing, this little smell of success.
The monkey demon keeps me screaming, and he won't let me rest
Oh, someone, won't you listen, and help drive the demons away?

CHORUS

TURNAROUND
Turnaround, 1968

This song was a last-minute addition to the album, but made such
an impression that Stan decided to make it the title track. It was
written in a style Stan hoped to sell to folk singer Dee Higgins,
who lived in Toronto at the time.

———+———

Bits and pieces you offered of your life
I didn't think they meant a lot or said much for you
And all the chances to follow didn't make a lot of sense
When stacked up against the choices you made.

CHORUS
For yours was the open road
The bitter song
The heavy load that I couldn't share, though the offer was there
Every time you turned around.

Now, it's not like you made out to hang around
Although . . . you know, I made some sounds to show that I cared.
And when it looked like you heard the call,
I didn't say a lot although I could have said much more, had I
  dared.

And if I had followed a little ways
Because we're friends you would have made me welcome out there.
But we both know it's just as well, 'cause some can go
But some are meant to stay behind, and it's always that way.

2nd CHORUS
And yours is the open road.
The bitter song,
The heavy load that I'll never share,
though the offer was there
Every time you turned around.

WATCHING THE APPLES GROW
Fogarty's Cove, 1974

Written in June 1975 at Stan's rented farmhouse , just north of
Stratford, Ontario. This ode to Annapolis Valley may not be one
of Stan's best song, but it's certainly his best song about apples.

It's early up Ontario farm, chicken crow for day
I wish I grew Annapolis apples up above Fundy Bay
Oh it seems so far away

On the ridge above Acadia's town to the valley down below
The evening shadow falls upon the families listening to the radio
And watching the apples grow.

CHORUS
Down on the farm, back among the family, away from Ontario
Hear the ladies singing to the men, dancing it heel and toe
And watching the apples grow.

Ontario, y'know I've seen a place I'd rather be
Your scummy lakes and the City of Toronto don't do a damn
thing for me
I'd rather live by the sea.

I've watched the V's of geese go by, the foxfoot in the snow
I've climbed the ridge of Gaspereaux Mt., looking to the valley
below
And watching the apples grow.

CHORUS

WHITE SQUALL
From Fresh Water, 1982

Wiarton, a town near Owen sound, has provided the Great Lakes
with many of its mariners. This song may be one of Stan's finest
pieces of writing — and ranks with Lightfoot's *Wreck Of The
Edmund Fitzgerald* as the all-time greatest Great Lakes ballad —
but oddly enough, it's generally overlooked by his fans (and routinely butchered at folk festivals). A production note: this song

uses more guitar overlays, layers of guitar recorded over top one another, than any other Stan Rogers' song.

———+———

Now it's just my luck to have the watch, with nothing left to do
But watch the deadly waters glide as we roll north to the 'Soo',
And wonder when they'll turn again and pitch us to the rail
And whirl off one more youngster in the gale.

The kid was so damned eager. It was all so big and new.
You never had to tell him twice, or find him work to do.
And evenings on the mess deck he was always first to sing,
And show us pictures of the girl he'd wed in spring.

CHORUS
But I told that kid a hundred times "Don't take the lakes for granted.
They go from calm to a hundred knots so fast they seem enchanted."
But tonight some red-eyed Wiarton girl lies staring at the wall,
And her lover's gone into a white squall.

Now it's a thing that us old-timers know. In a sultry summer calm
There comes a blow from nowhere, and it goes off like a bomb.
And a fifteen-thousand tonner can be thrown upon her beam
While the gale takes all before it with a scream.

The kid was on the hatches, lying staring at the sky.
From where I stood I swear I could see tears fall from his eyes.
So I hadn't the heart to tell him that he should be on a line,
Even on a night so warm and fine.

CHORUS

When it struck, he sat up with a start; I roared to him, "Get down!"
But for all that he could hear, I could as well not made a sound.
So, I clung there to the stanchions, and I felt my face go pale,
As he crawled hand over hand along the rail.

I could feel her keeling over with the fury of the blow.
I watched the rail go under then, so terrible and slow.
Then, like some great dog she shook herself and roared upright
    again.
Far over side. I heard him call my name.

CHORUS

So it's just my luck to have the watch, with nothing left to do
But watch the deadly waters glide as we roll north to the 'Soo',
And wonder when they'll turn again and pitch us to the rail
And whirl off one more youngster in the gale.

But I tell these kids a hundred times "Don't take the Lakes for
    granted.
They go from calm to a hundred knots so fast they seem
    enchanted."
But tonight some red-eyed Wiarton girl lies staring at the wall,
And her lover's gone into a white squall.

———————

THE WRECK OF THE ATHENS QUEEN
Fogarty's Cove, 1974

Written in 10 minutes during a beak in the FOGARTY'S COVE session. Stan's economy of pen did not exactly translate into the studio: it took the band 11 takes to nail the song, an unusually high
number for the budget-conscious Rogers. Inspired by a story
Garnet had told Stan about some heroic Nova Scotians who
decided one stormy night to salvage a ship stuck on rocks of shore.
One lucky soul, fueled by liquid bravery, spent the night on the
sinking ship in order to retain salvage rights. Stan originally
kicked around the idea of writing a song based on Farley Mowat's
The Grey Seas Under, but quickly deferred. While not nearly his
best salvage song, it's important because it's the first.

We were drinking down to Reedy's house
When first we heard the blow
It seemed to come from Ripper Rock
So boldly forth to go.

And sure enough the rusty tub
Could just be barely seen
As her stern was high up in the air
We made out *Athens Queen*.
O, the lovely *Athens Queen*

Me boys I must remind you
There's a bottle left inside
So let us go and have a few
And wait until low tide.

And if the sea's not claimed her
When the glasses are licked clean
We will then set forth some dories lads
And see what may be seen

On the lovely *Athens Queen*

Some songs and old tall stories then
Came out to pass the time
Nor could a single bottle
Keep us all until low tide.

And so it was before we left
The house we were at sea
So we scarcely can remember
How we made the *Athens Queen*.

O, the lovely *Athens Queen*

O the waves inside me belly
Were as high as those outside

And though I'm never seasick
I lost dinner over side.

'Twas well there was no crew to save
For we'd have scared 'em green
We could scarcely keep ourselves
From falling off the *Athens Queen*.

O, the lovely *Athens Queen*

Well Reedy goes straight down below
And comes up with a cow
Hello I said now what would you
Be wantin' with that now.

You'll never take the cow home
In a dory on such sea
Well me friend he says I've always fancied
Fresh cream in me tea.

For the lovely *Athens Queen*

I headed for the galley then
Cause I was rather dry
And glad I was to get there quick
For what should I spy.

O what a shame it would have been
For to lose it all at sea
Forty cases of the best Napoleon
Brandy ever seen.

On the lovely *Athens Queen*

I loaded twenty cases boys
Then headed for the shore

Unloaded them as quick as that
And then pulled back for more.

Smith was pullin' for the shore
But he could scarce be seen
Under near two hundred chickens
And a leather couch of green.

From the lovely *Athens Queen*

So here's to all good salvagers
Likewise to Ripper Rock
And to Napoleon brandy of which
Now we have much stock.

We eat a lot of chicken
And sit on a couch of green
And we wait for Ripper Rock
To claim another *Athens Queen*.

O, the lovely *Athens Queen*

WORKING JOE
Northwest Passage, 1980

Stan wrote this song on a "mental health day." Even though he didn't have a regular nine-to-five, he needed a day off every once in a while. The song just sort of wrote itself, Ariel recalls. Baby Nathan was in the Swingomatic, its methodical click providing Stan with rhythmic inspiration, while Ariel was nearby cooking. "Knowlton" is Knowlton Nash, long-time anchor for CBC's evening TV news broadcasts.

I used to love these lazy winter afternoons;
Starting out too late giving up too soon;
Coming home to coffee and a trashy book;
Never paying any mind if things were never done on time.

Time was when a fella could just let time slip away;
No worries car or telephone just rent and food to pay;
And every night with single buddies boozing at the bar,
Living for the minute, taking every hour in it!

But now there's just too much to do in any given day;
The car phone the kiddies shoes too many bills to pay;
Running from the crack of dawn 'til Knowlton reads the news,
And falling into bed too wiped to even kiss the wife good night.
Oh, oh, oh . . . just another working Joe.

The baby's in the Swingomatic, singing Rock and Roll;
My Sweetie's in the kitchen, whipping up my favourite casserole.
I knocked off work at ten o'clock, the kids are still at school.
The coffee pot is perking . . . to hell with bloody working.
Oh, it sure is sweet to sit at home and let time slip away,
Through tomorrow I'll be scratching through another working
    day;
But when I start to come apart from all the things to do,
I know that I'll be taking soon another lazy winter afternoon.
Oh, oh, oh . . . just another working Joe!

———

YOU CAN'T STAY HERE
Northwest Passage, 1981

Stan Rogers airing his clean laundry. Some people love this song but
I have to say it's not one of my favorites: doesn't really go anywhere
and the lyrics approach a triteness not usually found in a Rogers'
mature work (an internal rhyme of "stranger" with "danger;" Stan

could do better than that!). The odd-song out on Stan's powerful third album, this one has nothing to do with the northwest, but falls into that unique sub-class of the Rogers' oeuvre, the groupie tune. Stan liked to introduce it as "an anti-seduction song, in case you ever feel like seducing your Auntie."

———+———

You can't stay here.
Your company's good, I know,
But I must wake up alone, and the party's over.
You can't stay here.
I'm moments away from sleep
And what you want to say can keep
Til I'm awake and I'm sober.

You can't stay here.
When everyone else has gone.
I've nothing for you, no song
To sing for you only.
You can't stay here.
And maybe you can't see why,
But I'm an old fashioned guy
And I'd rather be lonely.

Maybe you think I'm unkind when I tell you to go away;
I know what you offer, and I could be softer
And tell you to stay.
But to me, you're a stranger. To touch you is danger
I know it's true.
Cause what I've got at home is too dear.
You can't stay here.

I'll be alright alone,
And when I'm safe in her arms at home
I'll thank you for leaving.
You can't stay here.

YOUR LAKER'S BACK IN TOWN
From Coffee House to Concert Hall

A great cry-in-your-beer song about a bad love gone badder. One of the last songs Stan wrote, kept off FROM FRESH WATER because it didn't fit with the historical focus. Here Stan mixes traditional country and western thematic and musical elements with distinctly Canadian places and people. Was this Stan's first step toward a new hybrid, a kind of C&W (Canada and Western, that is)? Sadly, we can only speculate. A well-restored cassette demo is all we have left of the song.

———+———

I see it in your eyes,
Searching through the harbour,
And out across the bay.
His ring is on your hand;
He called you up from Cleveland yesterday.
Now who's he left behind?
The weather's fine, he'll soon be coming 'round,
I try to hold you closer,
But your laker's back in town.

Every forty days
He leaves you lying sleeping,
And clears for Thunder Bay.
You call me on the job,
And cry about how long he'll be away.
You need a country band,
A cheap hotel and me to run around,
But for now it's over,
Your laker's back in town.

CHORUS
A distant whistle moans across the bay,
Pulls us apart. . .
The singer says, "We're gonna slow things down."
Your cheating heart sounds like a clock run down,
Your laker's back in town.

He comes in looking like he owns the place
And he knows you're here.
The singer hollers, "It's the final round."
The final beer feels like a rock going down.
Your laker's back in town.
The band has gone away,
They're clearing off the tables,
And giving me the eye.
You took him out the door,
And never thought to turn to say goodbye,
And I'm the crying fool,
I know that you will call and I'll be 'round
To try to hold you closer,
'Til your laker's back in town.
And try to hold you closer,
'Til your laker's back in town.

———————

Writings

(Published and Unpublished)

Stan Rogers was doing a lot of freelancing writing near the end of his life. As well as doing some work for CBC radio, he was also contributing regular columns to the folk magazines *Come for to Sing* and *Canadian Folk Music Bulletin*. He was also experimenting with writing radio plays, though none were produced or published. Here we present some of his unpublished writings or bonus tracks — *The Boss Is Always Right*, a satire in his series of "Northern Carp" articles scheduled for publication in *Canadian Folk Music Bulletin*, and *The Greenway Curse*, a radio play.

___

BIBLIOGRAPHY

Songs from Fogarty's Cove, OFC Publications, Ottawa, 1982.

"The Principles of Performance," *Come for to Sing*, Volume 8, No. 2, 1982.

"Northern Carp: The Last of the Good Cheap Acts," *Canadian Folk Music Bulletin*, Volume 16, April 1982.

"Northern Carp: If This Is a Folk Festival, Why Aren't I Smiling," *Canadian Folk Music Bulletin*, Volume 16, October 1982.

"The Finest Kind," *Come for to Sing*, Volume 9, No.1, 1983.

"Those Elusive Festival Bookings," *Come for to Sing*, Volume 9, No. 2, 1983.

"Open Your Mouth and Close Your Eyes," *Canadian Folk Music Bulletin*, Volume 17, October 1983.

"Sell Your Song," *Come for to Sing*, Volume 9, No. 3, 1983.

THE BOSS IS ALWAYS RIGHT

When the plane went down in Cincinnati, Stan Rogers had one more article for his "Northern Carp" series in the *Canadian Folk Music Bulletin* almost completed. A hand-written copy of it survives, published here for the first time ever. While missing a proper ending, it's still an interesting piece, presenting an imaginary conversation between Stan and a sort of hayseed-savant folk club manager that offers a glimpse into Stan's vision of the life and role of a folk singer. It's sort of Stan Rogers' Performing Primer 101.

———+———

"Folksingers. Geez!"

"Why so?"

"Ya can't get 'em ta work."

"I'm a folksinger. I work."

"Nah. You're a professional. Like ya sent yer contracts on time. Right? And ya sent pictures an' all that bushwa about how good you are at the' same time. Right? An' ya got here on time to set up, right? An' ya been on time every show, every night. Right? See? That's professional."

"Geez, Rick, doesn't everybody do that?"

"You kidding me? Maybe one act in three."

"But surely that's not all there is to being a professional?"

"Nah. There's more. Like, I don't know from music, see. I only know that some acts do good in here, an some don't. What they play, I could care less, so long as the place is full and they sell beer. An' I know what kind of act brings people in. Professional."

"So, it's strictly business."

"Exactly. Business. Here, have another. The professionals, they're all business. Like, the best ones don't even drink. Ever. Right."

"Ah well, I, ah, wouldn't know about that I guess."

"Nah, nah. You drink, sure. But I never seen you drunk. Last month, we had this guy in here, and I had to pay him off Wednesday. He come in, he was so loaded he was an hour late getting on, and he was terrible. Couldn't remember words or nothing. And when he talked he sounded like some kinda idiot. And there was this band here, week before last, they was smoking up in the dressing room. Then when they come on stage, hardly nothing happened. Like, they'd all play a song, right, and then for like ten minutes, they just sorta stand around, not doing nothing. No jokes, no talking to the crowd. Nothing. They put the place to sleep."

"Okay. So no booze, no drugs. I agree with that. The way I see it. When people pay five dollar covers, they have a right to your best shot, and you can't do that when you're all screwed up."

"Yeah, but there's more. It's like repeat business, right? You can't make a living running a club or singin' songs unless ya get repeat business, and people won't come back to see ya unless they had a good time last time they was here. So, if they get lousy service, an' short drinks, or the toilet stinks, I lose customers. They don't come back an' I can't get no repeat business."

"Yeah. That makes sense."

"You betcha! Another thing, you do, like, a good show every night, no matter what. I mean, like, even if you're all pissed off when ya come in the door, ya do a good show. Smile. Tell jokes. Jump around. Whatever is eatin' ya, ya leave it offa the stage . . ."

"Yeah, but -"

"And you dress pretty good, too. Right? I mean, ya get some of these folksingers in here, if they was customers and dressed like that, I wouldn't let them into the place. I mean, I don't mind jeans, but when they're all dirty and ragged and like that, it just don't look good. They look like bums. I don't want bums in here. I run a nice joint. Like, if ya had a nice date, ya could bring her here. Classy. Right?"

"Well, I'm not exactly a fancy dresser, Rick."

"Nah. Yer not. Ya dress kinda square, really. But yer pants are pressed, and yer shoes shined, and ya got a tie. Makes you look like you mean it."

"Hey, what's with this square stuff? Look at you! White suite, black shirt and a big, gold Playboy medallion on your neck. Who are you, John Revolta?"

"C'mon. I paid three hundred bucks for this suit."

"They saw you coming."

"Look, don't get smart. Right?"

"Sorry."

"Forget it. You want another."

"Ah, sure. Thanks."

"Another thing I noticed about you. You kinda mix up your show. Like, it has different kinds of stuff in it. Lake, ya come out, and ya do two or three songs. Bang, bang, bang, like that. Right? Then ya tell a funny story, right? Then ya do maybe a sad song. Then maybe one o' them singa long things where ya don't play yer guitar. Then a fast, snappy one. Then more jokes. Then a sad one and a funny one with no talking in between. Say, ya oughta do more o' them sing-along. Singin' makes people thirsty, an' they drink more, right?"

"But you just said that I do all kinds of different things. If I do that, then . . ."

"Okay, okay. You know your job. I don't need to tell ya. But you know what I'm saying, right?"

"Sure."

"Geez. Some of these guys, they come in here an' they sit down an' sing one long slow sad song after another. Everybody just sits there. No smiles. NO nothing. And they don't drink. Puts the place to sleep."

"But Rick, some people like that kind of folk music."

"Bushwa! Maybe the say they do, but I never seen nobody didn't like some jokes and sing-along stuff and hand-clappin' stuff a helluva lot better. Maybe a nice sad song once in a while, 'cause people like to cry every now and then. Makes laughin' feel better. But not every damn song. Geez."

"Rick, you surprise me. You're something of a philosopher."

"Yeah. An' here's where it comes from. Want another?"

"Well, maybe one more."

"I noticed another thing, first night you was here. When you guys was settin' up, you took a lotta time getting' the sound set up so it was okay, an' then you didn't touch the mixer all night. I bet I know why you did that."

"I'd think it would be obvious."

"Ya don't want to be talking to the sound guy from on stage, right? People, they're sitting there, havin' a good time, enjoyin' the show, an' then the band starts bitchin' to the sound guy. It makes the crowd think they shouldn't be enjoyin' it, an' so they start getting all antsy about the speakers."

"Wha?"

"Really! It's like this, see. Yer on the stage. I'm sittin' here at my table. I'm enjoyin' myself. Sounds okay to me, an' I've maybe had a few beers anyway, so I ain't all that fussy. All of a sudden, you start talking to the sound guy. 'Hey burro-breath: I can't hear my guitar. Turn up the monitor, will ya.'"

"I'd never say that."

"Exactly. Only shut up a minute. So I'm listening ta this, and all of a sudden I'm not thinkin' any more how I'm having a good time. I'm trying to figure what's buggin' yer ass. I don't know from monitors. I just know maybe it don't really sound as good as I think. So I start listening real hard, and maybe for the rest of the set, I don't hear the songs. I just hear the sound system." . . .

[The article abruptly ends here]

THE GREENWAY CURSE
AN UNPRODUCED RADIO PLAY

Stan Rogers had a lifelong love of radio, and not just the music he heard. Radio drama had a certain fascination for Stan, and no doubt had impact on him as a songwriter. Some of his earliest recorded work was done at CBC Halifax, exploring musical and narrative forms with the poet Bill Howell, while songs like *Harris And The Mare* and *The Wreck of the Athen's Queen* have a curious documentary feel, which I think comes directly from Stan's exposure to Canada's public broadcaster. It's that CBC-ishness, in the nicest sense of the awkward term, that helps make Rogers a quintessentially Canadian artist.

Later in his short life, Stan's interest in radio — and in writing — became more explicit. Along with his work on radio plays like *Harris and the Mare* and *The Three Sisters,* he also began working on some original dramatic ideas of his own. *The Greenway Curse* is the only complete work from this period that we have. Written for the gothic series *Nightfall,* a kind of aural *Twilight Zone, The Greenway Curse* was never produced and has never been published before now. It's not a bad effort at all, and showed that Stan's talent for storytelling was only just beginning to expand to forms beyond songwriting. I wonder where maturing vision might have taken him and his music? He'd already tried his hand at "folk opera" with *So Hard To Be So Strong,* written for the 1976 Olympics. Perhaps one day he would have found a way to marry full-fledged dramatic forms with his songwriting to create a uniquely Canadian musical theater. In any case, here is *The Greenway Curse,* only lightly edited, from Stan's typewritten draft manuscript. (Note: SFX is the abbreviation for "Sound Effects.")

———+———

EXTERIOR — A forest and the Nova Scotia coast, late on an autumn night.

Two duck hunters, Jim and Clarence, approach an old cabin.

SOUND EFFECTS — Two sets of footsteps in sand and grave; wind and surf

                    CLARENCE
Lord old jumped-up, she's getting cold, Jim.

                    JIM
Hey. No kidding, eh? I'm freezing the old butt, here. How much farther anyways?

                    CLARENCE
Along here just a bit here just a bit more, then up over that hill there. The cabin's in back of that, and the path is just back of the cabin.

                    JIM
I sure hope that place of yours is warm. I 'm gonna turn blue any minute, now. You sure there's ducks out here?

                    CLARENCE
Never you fear, me son. My dad and me, we been comin' here for ducks every fall since I was a little feller, and grandpa useta bring dad here when he was a kid too.

                    JIM
Sounds good to me. just so's we can get warm, eh?

                    CLARENCE
We'll be fine. Here's the path, now you go on up ahead, and watch your step. This here ain't no more'n a sheep track, and there's lots of loose rocks.

SFX — Grunts, sliding footsteps, branches breaking, rolling rocks and gravel.

CLARENCE

Take it easy, there. That one nearly clobbered me. Like to stove me in the bloody head.

JIM

Sorry. Hey, it's getting some windy, eh?

CLARENCE

It is that. We're going to get us a little storm, tonight, cousin. But we'll be right keen, around a good little stove. Here we go. Up on top.

JIM

Hey, this is quite a view. Look, you can see the harbour from here. How far is that?

CLARENCE

About three, maybe four mile. Folks useta come: out here in the old days and watch for ships coming in. Grandpa useta tell stories about the big schooners, the saltbankers, coming around that head there, all tore up from the storms. As soon as they got in as far as that island over there, they'd be safe, and they'd run in and anchor just past the old light on Mossy Head just off from where the fish plant is now. C'mon, lets go. It's not much farther, and a cup of tea would feel so good right now.

JIM

You got that right. Hey, what's that?

CLARENCE

What?

JIM

That old building there.

CLARENCE

Just the ruins. There useta be a few old houses here, but nobody's lived in them since before the war, when the road got washed out by the storms. They're all tumbled down now, and nobody comes out here much except fellers like us, looking for deer or ducks.
(Pause.)
You coming?

JIM

Yeah, right now. Hey, Clarence!

CLARENCE

What now?

JIM

I thought you said nobody comes out here?

CLARENCE

So?

JIM

So who's that? Back there by the path?

CLARENCE

I don't see any — well, I'll be damned! Some fool woman. She'll catch her death out here.

JIM

Should go see if she's lost or something, eh?

CLARENCE

I suppose. She don't hardly look dressed for a night out here. It'll be dark soon.

ANN O'NEILL
(Outside, in the distance.)
Effie! Oh, Effie! Effie, you come home! Effie!

CLARENCE
Oh my god! Oh my god in heaven! Let's get out of here!

JIM
What the hell's wrong with you? Leggo my arm, eh!

CLARENCE
C'mon, I tell you! We gotta get out of this right now!

JIM
We'll, what about her?

CLARENCE
Never you mind about her, me son. I now who she is, and she won't pay us no mind as long as we leave her be. Now, come on! I'll tell you about it at the cabin. Come on!

JIM
I'm comin', I'm comin'. Clarence, this is really weird. Are you ok? I mean, do you feel sick or something?

FADE

INTERIOR — CABIN

Clarence and Jim enter.

SFX — Door closing.
CLARENCE
There's a lamp over there. Should be oil in it. See if you can get her going. I'll start a fire.

JIM
Check. You want the tea from the pack?

CLARENCE

Yes. and that bottle, too. Lord liftin', I could kill for a drink this minute.

SFX — Lamp being lit; woodstove lids rattling, matches being struck, fire starting.

JIM

Where do I go for water?

CLARENCE

Right under your feet. Lift that trap, and dip it up with that ladle on the wall there.

SFX — Trap door, water pouring into a kettle.

CLARENCE

Good enough. Pass me the kettle and the tea, and then pour us a drink, Jim. God, I wish me teeth wouldn't rattle so.

JIM

I sure wish you'd tell me what's got you worked up like this. Who is that woman out there, eh?

CLARENCE

For god's sake: pipe down won't you? I'll tell you in a minute. Now just give that drink will you?

SFX — Bottles rattling against tin mug, pouring whiskey.

CLARENCE
(Taking huge gulp. Coughing.)

Lord, sit down, Jim. I'm sorry to be carryin' on like this, but she scared hell outa me. That is the first time I seen her. Sit down. The tea is gonna take a while, and the stove's took fine, so we can sit.

> JIM

I thought you said you know her.

SFX — Chairs scraping on floor.

> CLARENCE

I don't know her, Jim. Oh, no sir, I don't know her, but I know who she is, all right. oh yes. I know who she is. I don't imagine there's anyone alive who knows her. it was all too long ago for that, I'd say. I mean, Grandpa got told about it by his dad, that's how long ago it was.

> JIM

Get serious, Clarence. she'd have to be over a hundred years old the way you're talkin'. She sure don't look like no –
> > (Pause.)

Wait a minute.
> > (Pause, then laughs.)

Hey, you really had me going there, eh? That's pretty good! That's funny!

> CLARENCE

Am I laughin'?

> JIM

Well, hell, you can't be serious. For her to be that old, she'd have to be . . . I mean, there's no way, eh? Nobody that great grandpa knew could be alive now. That'd be way over a hundred years ago. She'd have been1 dead for years.

> CLARENCE

Now you're getting it.

> ANN
> > (Distant screaming.)

Effie! Effie! Come to mama! Effie!

JIM

Good god! Clarence, this is scarin' me half to death, here.
(Panic stricken.)
I . . . you're serious? She's dead, and screaming like that? And she's
outside there. What the hell are we supposed to do? We gotta get
outa here!

CLARENCE

No way. It's nearly dark. W can't cross the marshes in the dark,
and to get down to the beach we have to go right past her.

JIM

You mean we're just gonna sit here and . . . and have a damn tea
party? You're off your nut, eh!

CLARENCE

Simmer down, Jim, sit down, now. There's nothin' we can do.
She's never bothered anyone out here. It's just scary 'cause it's so
hard to believe. But she won't come near us here. She's too busy,
looking for her daughter.

JIM

Clarence, I can't believe this. Is . . . is . . . she a . . . .

CLARENCE

Look here. It'll save a lot of time if I tell you the whole story, like
dad told it to me. Then you won't be so scared. This has been
going on a long time, and she ain't hurt nobody yet. Kettle's hot.
You want some tea?

JIM

Yeah. Yeah. And maybe I'll just have a damned big drink too, eh?

SFX — Cups, bottle rattling, kettle boiling

FADE.

INTERIOR — Cabin, a short time later.

CLARENCE

When great-grandpa was a kid, there was a couple of houses out here. One belonged to a fella named Ned O'Neill, who had a daughter named Ann. When she was about eighteen, her father died, and she was left all alone, out here by herself, with just one or two neighbours. Folks useta say she was a little strange, even then, cause she kept pretty much to herself, and didn't come into much. Say — you know McAllister's store, in town there?

JIM

Yeah. I saw the place when I got here the other day.

CLARENCE

That's right. The bus dropped you there. Well, McAllister's was Greenway's store back then, and O'Neill was seein' David Greenway, the son of the fella that owned the place. I guess she'd figured to marry him, and when he got her pregnant, she started buggin' him to set a date.

JIM

I guess she would.

CLARENCE

You bet. Getting knocked up was a big deal in them days, cause you just had to get married. Not like now. But old man Greenway found out about it, y'see, and sent the young feller off to Halifax for a year while he got things straightened out. He didn't want his boy marryin' a little nobody, y'see, so he fixed it so that David Greenway married some distant cousin of his in Halifax. By this time, Ann O'Neill, she's had the baby, a daughter, and everyone in town is lookin' on her like she's some kind of whore. Especially since she hadn't told anybody who the father was, not even the doctor.

JIM

How come?

CLARENCE

Well, it turned out the old man had bought her off by promising to look after her and the kid. And send the kid to school, if she wouldn't make trouble about the young feller marrying her. But as it happened, she was just biding her time, because the first Sunday morning after David Greenway and his wife got home, she met them on the steps of the Methodist church as they coming out from service.

FADE.

EXTERIOR — The town, 100 years earlier.

SFX — Badly played pump organ, soft voices, shuffling feet on wood floors.

REV. CLARK

Well David t good to see you. I had heard that you were coming home. Is this the new Mrs. Greenway?

GREENWAY

Hello, Reverend Clark. Yes, this is my wife. Mercy, this is Reverend Greenway. Mr. Clark, Mercy Greenway.

MERCY

Oh, doesn't it sound so wonderful: Mercy Greenway. I mean, I'm still so thrilled to hear it! How do you do Mr. Clark. I enjoyed your sermon.

REV. CLARK

Why, bless you Mrs. Greenway. I'm so glad to know you. I have know your husband all his life, and his father has been my friend these twenty-five years. I hope you will come to be my friend as well, and perhaps pay a call on Mrs. Clark. She is unwell, and cannot get about easily. But she would be pleased, I know, to make you acquaintance.

> MERCY

Why, I would be delighted. Perhaps tomorrow morning would not be too soon.

> REV. CLARK

I cannot see why it would be. I'll ask Mrs. Clark this afternoon, and tell you her reply this evening when I pay my usual visit to your father-in-law.

> ANN
> (From a distance.)

David! David Greenway! Come down here, David. I've got a thing to say to you.

> MERCY

David, who is that?

> GREENWAY

Ah . . . her name is Ann O'Neill. She . . . she was a friend of mine when I was younger.

> ANN

David, come down here or I'll come up.

> GREENWAY

I . . . I think I should speak to her. Please excuse me, my dear. Mr. Clark, would you stay with Mercy for a few moments?

> REV. CLARK

What? What? Why, certainly, David, but I hardly think you need speak to a wanton like that shameless Ann O'Neill.

ANN

I heard that, you old fool. We'll soon see who's the shameless one around here!

MERCY

Well, really! David, whatever does she want?

GREENWAY

Please wait here, Mercy. I'll soon discover what she means.

SFX — Footsteps on stirs, then gravel. The organ music slowly fades.

GREENWAY
(Hushed voice.)

Ann, for god's sake, what do you mean by this? What are you try-ing to do? And please, keep your voice low.

ANN

I just want you to tell me why it was that you left me to have your child, and went off to Halifax, without so much as a goodbye. Everyone in this town thinks I'm a . . . a trollop, thanks to you. And now you've married that fancy relative of yours, and don't want anything to do with me. Did I mean so little to you? Does your child mean nothing to you? Why David?

GREENWAY

Ann, I had no choice. My father would have cast me out. He would have cut me off without a cent to my name had I married you. But I made him promise to look after you and . . . and . . . the child. Has he not kept his word?

ANN

Oh yes. He's been very generous. I've got a little money, and Effie will go to school. But I'm still the town harlot to everybody now. But I want you to know that if I'm to live in shame for the rest of my days, you'll have no joy either, David. You see that fancy wife of yours.

GREENWAY

Ann! Leave Mercy alone! She's a good woman.

ANN

Meaning I'm not?

(Voice rising.)

Well, I tell you this, my false lover: You'll never have the joy of your marriage, nor issue either. Your line will die out. I prayed and prayed to God, and I know. No child of yours will carry your name. No child of yours will live! I call down a curse on you and yours, David. You are the last Greenway! The last!

Ann turns and runs off.

SFX — Running footsteps.

Mercy enters.

MERCY

David, I believe I understood her. Please take me home.

GREENWAY

Mercy, I . . .

MERCY

Take me home, David. I think your private affairs have seen enough public air for one day. We'll discuss this privately.

FADE

Back in the cabin, Jim listens intently to Clarence's story.

SFX — Fire crackling in woodstove, as the wind blows through the trees outside.

ANN
(From Outside)
Effie! Effie! Where are you? Oh God, no!

JIM
There she goes again! Clarence. I swear, that'll drive me crazy.

CLARENCE
Take her easy, my son. It's giving me the willies too.
(Pause.)
You see, the curse took. Seemed like every year, Mercy Greenway'd get pregnant, and she'd either miscarry or the kid would be born dead, or it would die before it was a week old. And of course the whole town knew about the curse, and they began to believe it.

JIM
And Ann O'Neill, she was still around the whole time?

CLARENCE
Oh, yes. And she saw to it that David Greenway kept his promise too, When Effie was ten, Ann had Greenway sent the kid to a boarding school in Halifax. And every time she saw him, she'd remind him about the curse, and tell him how God was punishing him. Folks in town got so they was afraid of her. They thought she was some kind of witch, and crazy to boot. But she was just living for two things: revenge on David Greenway, and her daughter. She was crazy about the girl, and was always after Greenway for more and better things for her. And he was pretty good about it, too. When he saw that Mercy might not ever give him a living child, he tried to make for it by being a father to Effie. By all accounts, she grew up to be a nice young lady.

JIM
So, what happened?

CLARENCE
Well, I guess it was a terrible thing. In December, when Effie was seventeen or eighteen, Greenway sent one of his schooners to Halifax to pick her up and bring her home fore Christmas. But there's been bad weather, and the schooner was way overdue. Now remember I told you a little while ago that folks useta come out here when they was expecting a ship and watch for it?

JIM
Ah, yeah. Just before we saw . . . her.

CLARENCE
Well, Greenway come out here with a couple o' fellers, and they was standin' on the cliff there, where we come up. They was watching for the schooner, and worrying. 'cause there was a hell of a storm brewing. Now Ann O'Neill, she was in her house, and she saw him out there, and got real mad. She decided she was going out there and tear a couple o' strips off of him . . .

FADE.

INTERIOR — Ann O'Neill's house, 100 years earlier.

SFX — Clock ticking, slowly, a storm rages outside.

ANN
What's *he* doing out there? I don't want to see him here, around my place. I'll soon tell him.

SFX — Quick footsteps across the floor. The door opens, and the storm sounds increase.

ANN
David Greenway, you get away from here! I've told you more than once not to come out here again!

GREENWAY

Ann, I'm watching for *The Reliance*. I sent her to Halifax last week to fetch Effie home to you for Christmas, and she should have left Halifax three days ago. She's overdue, and this storm is becoming worse by the hour.

ANN

Well, you can just go back and watch from the harbour, with that barren wife of yours. I'll not have you here. I can do all the watching from here that needs doing.

GREENWAY

Ann, you leave Mercy out of this. She's not well.

ANN

Yes, I know. With child again, not that it will do her any good. God's curse is still upon you, David Greenway, and there's no escape for you or yours. This one will die like all the others.

GREENWAY

Hold your tongue, woman. I will only stand for so much!

ANN

Your threats mean nothing to me. How could you do worse to me than you've already done?

GREENWAY'S FRIEND
(Distant)

David! David! *The Reliance* is in sight!

GREENWAY

Thank God for that.
(Shouting.)

Where is she?

GREENWAY'S FRIEND
(Moving closer.)

Just weathering the head. She's had a rough passage. She's lost her foretop and stays, and there's some kind of wreckage around the forepeak that's fouling the jib. She'll have a hard job of it to go about on the other tack for the harbour. Liable to wind up in irons, and tear the sticks out of her.

GREENWAY

I see her! What are they doing? She's . . . she's falling off the wind! They're . . . Oh, I see. They're going to wear her right around, and not risk coming across the wind.

ANN

Is Effie safe? Is my Effie safe?
                    (Pause)
Answer me, David!

GREENWAY

Yes. She'll be safe enough, now. The ship will run in very close by here, and Effie will likely come on deck. You can wave to her.

ANN

And you can leave. Take yourself off. Go down to the dock and meet Effie, and send her home to me. And keep your hands off her. I'll not have her touched by an accursed man.

GREENWAY

Woman, there is no end to your cruelty.

ANN

Or to God's punishment for you! All of your line will die, David Greenway. Go home and tell that to your precious Mercy. All of your line will die, including this latest one!

SFX — Tremendous peel of thunder.

GREENWAY'S FRIEND

My God! She's been struck! She's afire! Look, look her sails have

caught! David, she's going before the wind! She'll go on the rocks! George! Get some ropes! George!
(His voice fades off as he runs to help.)

ANN
Oh . . . oh . . . I see Effie! My God! She's on fire! Effie! Effie!

GREENWAY
Ann, don't go down there. You'll be carried away, or fall to your death. Look, Effie has jumped! Can she swim? Answer me! Can she swim?

ANN
I don't know! O, I can see her! Effie! Effie! Come to mama! Effie! Oh God, No! I . . .
(She screams in panic.)
My God! I can't see her! I can't see her! Effie! Where are you? Effie! No!

FADE.

INTERIOR — Cabin. Clarence and Jim are still sitting by the woodstove.

SFX — Woodstove crackling, bottle pouring whiskey into a tin cup. The wind is still blowing outside.

CLARENCE
Y'see, it was the curse. Ann always thought of Effie as just being hers. But Effie was Greenway's daughter too, and the curse was being evoked right there with Effie in sight. Greenway's curse. You know, there ain't a single Greenway alive today? Now, it seems, every once in a long while, Ann O'Neill has to stand out there and watch that schooner burn again, and Effie with it. And that's when folks see her. But I've never heard of her paying any mid to anything or anyone else.

                              JIM
So now she's a ghost?

                         CLARENCE
A ghost, or maybe just . . . undead.

                              ANN
                    (Close outside, screaming)
Effie! Effie! Where are you? Come to mama!

SFX — Bottle crashes to the floor. Chairs overturned.

                         CLARENCE
What! She's right outside!

                              JIM
What do we do now?
                          (Terrified.)
Oh God help me!

SFX — Tremendous hammering on the door.

                              ANN
Effie! Effie!

SFX — Door splinters, and crashes to the floor. The storm sweeps
into the cabin.

                              ANN
Effie! Effie!

Clarence and Jim scream.

SFX — The storm rises to a crescendo, then suddenly:

SILENCE.

                            END.

PS

Dozens of songs, stories and poems have been written in Stan's memory. This poem is my favorite. It was written by Stan's long-time friend and frequent collaborator, Bill Howell, in June 1990.

———+———

LAMENT FOR ANOTHER DEAD FRIEND

I long to feel more; everything about this
adds up to less.
                    This is nothing but
the death of another disremembered dream.
My best memories search for what
I used to believe was compassion.
                              Abstraction,
that boat I built to navigate the numbness, sails on
without us.
            God I miss you.

And who finally cares?
The rest of the old stories pale, turn in on
themselves.
            Nothing changes them, not even
boredom or bad memory.
                        Why change anything when
it's all I can do to remember you as you were?
                                            All
that heedless giving is over; some of my best friends
are becoming myths.

The hard part was learning to stop talking about
    You behind your back.
Even to myself I started sounding as if I was
    Bragging about how well I knew you.
Praising you became a contest with your other
    friends; the prize became the bolder noise of
    strangers.

From piracy to privacy, nobody knew you the way
    I did; but everybody knows you differently
    Now.
Including me.
Meanwhile even the weather has changed.
My address book is full of dead names, including
Yours.
We always wondered
    What would happen, but I haven't heard from
    You for quite a while.

I wonder what it's like when you haven't had a
    Beer for seven years.
I have a beer for you, then one for me;
    And then another for both of us.
This changes absolutely nothing that matters.
Generous to the end, our time preserves itself.
Let's drink a silent beer to that . . . .

Stan's Country

THE STAN ROGERS MAP OF CANADA

Gwen Foss
Chris Conway & Melissa Edwards

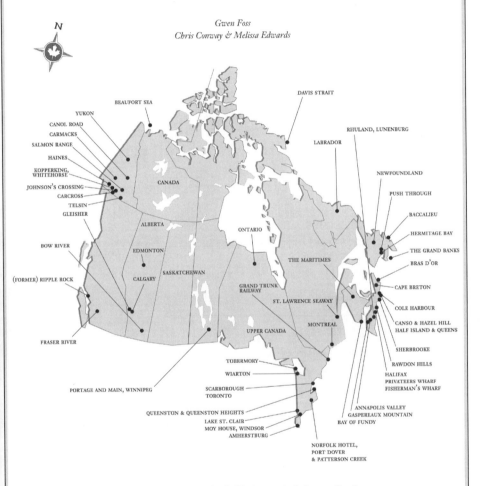

The place names on this map are named in the following songs by the late great Stan Rogers:
Barrett's Privateers, Bluenose, Canol Road, Cliffs of Baccalieu, Field Behind the Plow, Fisherman's Wharf,
Fogarty's Cove, Forty-Five Years, Free In The Harbour, Giant, House of Orange, Last Watch, Lazy Head,
Lock-Keeper, Macdonnell on the Heights, Make or Break Harbour, Man with a Blue Dolphin, Northwest
Passage, Oh No, Not I, Rawdon Hills, Ripper Rock, Scarborough Settler's Lament, So Blue, Strings and
Dory Plug, Two-Bit Cayuse, The Nancy, Tiny Fish for Japan, Watching the Apples Grow, White Squall,
Wild Rose. First published in Geist and reproduced by permission of the publisher.